READER PRAISE FOR
GEORGE BYRON WRIGHT'S NOVELS

Driving to Vernonia

"Leaving you panting to know how this is a page-turner. Your eyes will fly through this book.
— Maggi White, Book Review, Portland, Oregon

"[This novel took] me careening down the road of life full of plot twists and turns and even pot-holes I never expected. Vivid characters and a fast paced unfolding of events kept me reading right to the last page. *Driving to Vernonia* was a great read, and worth every penny I paid for the book."
— Douglas A. Pfeiffer, Portland, Oregon

Baker City 1948

"I just read *Baker City 1948*. I was absolutely knocked out! It is one of the best-told tales and interesting books that I have read in years."
— Jim Helliwell, Roseburg, Oregon

"Beautifully written with great attention given to plotting and pace. *Baker City 1948* had me absorbed to the very end."
—Hunter Gregg, Portland, Oregon

Tillamook 1952

"[Wright] dealt well with the mystery of the plot and the setting while developing a character who is able to grow and change with his experiences. I liked that; a man's story that is able to explore the ability or inability for people to relate to each other. Thanks for a good story!"
— Janice Nichols McLemore, Silverdale, Washington

[In *Tillamook 1952*] "Anger and guilt and love rise like the heat of the fire and are just as difficult to control. Wright's skillful use of narrative takes the unrelenting curiosity of a man who has been shielded from a dark secret and carries it like a burning torch to a terrible conclusion."

— Bob Olds, Reviewer, Colonygram, Oregon Writers Colony, Portland, Oregon

Roseburg 1959

"What a skillful and engrossing read. I thought the resurrection of Roseburg and Ross Bagby were a necessary commentary on small-town society and the state of marriage today. I too was surprised at the end...it was a masterful touch to the intrigue of the characters."

— Max Penner, Kansas City, Missouri

"[*Roseburg 1959*] was a great story, with interesting, likeable (and some unlikeable) characters, good villains, a few surprises, a satisfying ending, a sense of 'place', and a hint of a love story. I enjoyed every minute I spent reading it."

— Teresa Edwards, Vancouver, Washington

Newport
Blues

A Salesman's Lament

A NOVEL

To Ula, Great work!

Newport Blues

A Salesman's Lament

A NOVEL

GEORGE BYRON WRIGHT

C3 Publications
Portland, Oregon
www.c3publications.com

C3 Publications
3495 NW Thurman Street
Portland, OR 97210-1283
www.c3publications.com

First Edition

Library of Congress Control Number: 2011906688
ISBN10: 0-9632655-6-3
ISBN13: 978-0-9632655-6-2

Cataloging References: Newport Blues, A Salesman's Lament
1. Salesmen-Fiction 2.Oregon Coast-Fiction 3. Import business-Fiction
4. Predator-Fiction 5. Lost love-Fiction 6. Oregon-Fiction I. Title

Book and cover designs by Dennis Stovall, Red Sunsets, Inc.
Cover photo and art copyright 2011 by Dennis Stovall.
Map of the Oregon coast is a western slice of an Oregon Department of
    Transportation road map with the addition of Pacific City.
Author photo by Sergio Ortiz: www.sergiophotography.net.

Printed in the United States of America.

Novels by George Byron Wright

Baker City 1948
Tillamook 1952
Roseburg 1959
Driving to Vernonia
Newport Blues, A Salesman's Lament

"Every one is a moon, and has a dark side which he never shows to anybody."

—Mark Twain

Dedication:

In memory of
Austin Love Wright
for his life of trial and
error but never quitting.

Acknowledgement

After the creative juices start their flow, I very soon run up against the need for technical help. That's when I seek out those willing to lend their counsel to a storyteller. I thank attorney Bronson James, with JDL Attorneys, Portland, Oregon. Mr. James specializes in criminal law and generously gave me valuable insights into the law as it applied to my novel. Thanks also go to Sergeant Paul Weatheroy, in charge of the Cold Case Homicide Unit for the Portland Police Bureau, for his willingness to handle my questions on police procedure. Assistant Chief Hank Walling of the Depoe Bay Fire District was a great help in explaining emergency responses as would relate to an accident in Devil's Punch Bowl State Park on the Oregon Coast; likewise, James K. Woodle, Commander, U.S. Coast Guard, Retired, advised me on Coast Guard response procedures, as well as confirming the ocean tides at the time of the story. Any inaccuracies that may exist in this work are the fault of the author alone and not of the superb input of those mentioned above.

As always, my wife, Betsy, was my first reader—again with great calm and support. Thanks go to fellow authors Greg Nokes and Matt Love, who agreed to read the novel before it had been cleansed by my editor, and then willingly gave me generous testimonials. Professional photographer Harvey Thomas gave me the specifications for the Mamiya camera that makes an appearance.

Thanks again to my wonderful editor, Karen Brattain, who delved into my work with her usual mastery and gently guided me to refine and refine until I reached the better side of the story. Book design is a special art, and I thank Dennis Stovall, Director of Ooligan Press and Coordinator of the Publishing Program at Portland State University, for once again applying his creativity to the look and feel of this novel.

George Byron Wright
Portland, Oregon
August 2011

-1-

Sidney Lister had always enjoyed looking at Mary Ellen Conway when she wore no clothes. In fact, from the first time he had seen her naked there had been no going back. And right then, as he sat up in her bed and leaned against two pillows with his arms folded, he was as aroused from seeing her body as he had ever been. The amber cast from the bedside lamp seeped out and crept up her thighs, fleshier now but still something to see, and shone on the breasts she had been proud to exhibit back then—and still was.

She stood at the foot of the bed, shamelessly patting the moisture from her arms and her belly with a fluffy white towel, and smiled at him. That always made Sidney feel the fool because he knew that she knew he couldn't not watch her. It had been like that from the beginning when they were but kids. And because it was what it was—an addiction to her sensuality—he had taken Mary Ellen "Ellie" Conway to wed and bed two years out of high school, June 1977.

Of course the bed part had one inexorable rule, a tenet set by Mary Ellen from the very first time they'd touched each other; she had been adamant about not becoming pregnant. Sidney had never forgotten the time she had taken his manhood in her hand and held on until his eyes watered and he agreed to no sex unless she was protected. Having kids right out of high school wasn't her idea of a fun time. Ever, really. No children to this day by

Sidney or, later, the other man. So, no kids for Mary Ellen, no college for Sidney—he was off and running.

Mister Most Likely to Succeed assumed he could make hay any old way. Didn't he have his winning smile and his wily native intelligence? And didn't he have Mary Ellen Conway? Look out, world.

She blotted her face dry and padded off to the bathroom. He listened to the sounds she made: the medicine cabinet opening, water running, gentle humming—and watched the door like a dog for its master. She reappeared wearing an aqua-colored silky thing open at the front; it floated out as she walked back into the bedroom. Sidney did not take his eyes off her white skin, short black hair, and the triangular wedge beneath her navel; he pretended to ignore the smile on her mouth and the tease in her eyes.

———•———

But of course he hadn't succeeded, not as projected by the Grant High School yearbook staff, anyway, and not as Ellie felt she had every right to expect. The high point that first year was setting up housekeeping in a cute little apartment in northeast Portland and then admiring it—playing house. The wedding booty, all new and shiny, and the furniture the Conways had sprung for, made it seem almost real—their make-believe life. Claiming the success Sidney was due by proclamation proved more difficult. The routine of life bore down; meeting the same responsibilities over and over was a severe lesson. And a twenty-year-old still rubbing Clearasil on his pimples wasn't about to become a member of the Realtors Million Dollar Club even though he had decided that the road to his financial success lay in selling property. Sidney had to hand it to Ellie; she hung on for ten long ones waiting and watching Mister Ought-to-Be turn out naught-to-be. That was the way she saw it, anyway.

She sat on the edge of the bed up against his hip, curled her fingers back on first one hand then the other, and examined her nails. He watched her indifference, recognized it for what it was, then raised his arms over her head and stretched.

"You bored?" she asked over the growl of his yawn. "Done looking?"

"Never done looking," he said and reached out to swat her on the hip.

"We've got that, anyway. Don't we?"

Sidney pulled the sheet up on his cooling chest and clasped his hands behind his head. "What was he like?" he asked.

She turned her head, tipped it, and looked at him; her eyelids lowered slightly. "In bed?"

"No. Come on, Ellie. That all you think about?"

"With you it is. What else is there?"

"Yeah, well we've been over that ground."

She leaned across his legs and propped her head on an elbow, chin in a cupped hand. "So Ralphy—what was he like? Well, let's see." She clawed the sheet down and rubbed his stomach circling, the reddish blond hair into swirls. "You really want to do this? The other guy?"

Sidney lowered his arms and took her hand up. He kissed her fingertips and saw the liquidity come into her eyes. He could always do that; she had always been responsive to the sensual but never the domestic. The day-after-day waiting for Sidney to succeed had dragged her down. For Ellie, those years were an uphill grade riding on a downhill frame of mind.

"Thought we'd made a deal," she said. "To not go poking around back there."

"Forever and ever? Sacred?"

"It was the millennium, pretty sacred."

Seventeen years. Seventeen years without as much as a phone call or a *How the heck are you?* Not a Christmas card or even an accidental encounter on the street. Their separation came in the spring; it had been exactly one month short of what would have been their tenth anniversary. The new season of green, the crocus, the daffodils, it all spoke to Mary Ellen Lister, and it said *time to go.* Time to find a new avenue of promise. In the beginning she had risen to the lure of Sidney's next big break-through. First there was Earl Sidway's Used Cars. *Just until I get my real estate license,* Sidney had pledged; it was the one promise Mary Ellen could point to in ten years that had actually been fulfilled. Sidney studied, sold seasoned Dodges and veteran Fords and back-broken Buicks, and got his real estate license. But he was still a kid. No prospective buyers would have looked at the lanky boy with the tousled roan hair and seriously put the purchase of a lifetime in his hands.

Carl Draper didn't care if Sidney looked fifteen; Sidney had a license and was innocent to deception. Draper had purchased a chunk of land in east Multnomah County, built a fancy brick entrance and put a sign up: *Carlton Estates.* Then the boxes went up: cheesy construction, two-bedroom, one-bath houses with one-car garages squeezed in row after row on Vista Lane, Ponderosa Way, and Horizon Boulevard. Forget that there were no vistas, or horizons, or trees. Draper was the developer, architect, builder; and Sidney was the real estate agent. He convinced Sidney and Ellie to move into one of the houses, rent free, so Sidney could be his on-site agent and sell the boxes to other young couples. It was just like selling used cars: play up the image, downplay the product. Sidney barely eked out a living on Draper's salary and commission plan. Then, with three houses left, including the one Sidney and Ellie were living in, Draper fired him and gave them two weeks to move out because he had buyers for every remaining house. He didn't need Sidney and his pimples anymore. After following along as Sidney sold ranchettes in Idaho, beach cabins on the Oregon coast, then moved them back to Portland where the bright promise lay in pedaling wholesale janitorial supplies, Mary Ellen told Mister Most Likely to Succeed that she couldn't watch his frantic pursuit any longer. And the money was bad.

———•———

"Why'd you show up anyhow?" Sidney asked now. "At the reunion?"

She pulled gently at the hair around his navel. "Who knows? Curiosity. What would we all look like after twenty-five years? And be like. Geez, there was always so much BS when we went to those first ones. Five years was the worst, and after a decade people were still swaggering around about what they were doing or mostly were going to do." She slapped his stomach and sat up. "By twenty-five there had to be less phoniness. Why'd you go?"

"Not to swagger, tell you that."

She pulled her mouth down into a sympathetic pout. "Must be hard when you were labeled to go places."

"Let's not go there, okay?"

"What?"

"Ellie, come on."

"You still blaming me for your…for how things turned out for you?"

Sidney grinned and rubbed his hands over his face. "Jesus, it's that day all over again. We agreed, remember? The night of the reunion when we made the deal. No going back, not about us, ever."

She stood and drew the robe around her. "But it's okay to ask about Ralph?"

"Okay." He raised his arms. "You're right, forget it." He started to say how sorry he was that Ralph McCall had died on her—but he'd done that. Her man of means, drowning in a deep sea fishing accident, had left her alone but well fixed. That night at the reunion, her response to his regrets that she had lost Ralph McCall had been a wide-eyed blink. Sidney had recognized the expression. He'd been on the receiving end of one just like it moments before she'd walked out of his life.

She looked down at him. "What about you?"

"You mean other women?"

"Must have been some."

He blinked at her and tried to visualize the two who could have been serious—hell, *were* serious. Like photos in his wallet, their images had faded but not who they'd been to him: Clair compared him to a bearded mathematician, did the math, subtracted Sidney, and added the teacher. Kendra, like Ellie, just got tired of his attempts, no matter how determined he had been, and left. She got up one bright May morning and said, *I can do better than this. Good-bye, Sidney.* The faceless others, the ones who'd just been available, like he had been for them—each merely sympathizers over their mutual disappointments—they were gone from his memory.

"I think it was a good thing," he said, "the deal we made. It's been what, four years now? Four years of no digging, no regrets. It's been good. Hasn't it?"

Ellie looked at him.

"I mean, it's been a very civilized arrangement. Right? Ellie? It was your idea, your rules. No living together. Wouldn't work. Getting together like this whenever we feel like it." He laughed. "Which seems to work out to about every fourteen days as I make it."

She smiled and swatted at what remained of the hair on his head. "Yes, and it ought to be more often. Don't you think?"

"No, I don't think. Hell, it's tough when you care about someone but you can't live with her. When you lust after that person but neither of you wants to cook and wash with the other one, you know, live the day-to-day the way I do...or you do."

"God, your bathroom habits."

"Your cooking."

She raised an arm, palm up like a traffic cop. "No more tit-for-tat, okay?"

"I like your tits just not your tats."

"Cute."

"Come here." Sidney reached up and pulled her down onto him and tasted her mouth again. She relaxed and slid in beside him. "Yummy," he said. She hummed her agreement. "But Mister Yummy has to go to work tomorrow and can't let Miss

Yummy get him going again."

He washed his face and swabbed his body in the bathroom and dressed. She was in the kitchen heating water for tea when he came out.

"Anything you need?" he asked. "Any fixit stuff?"

"Toilet keeps trickling."

"Noticed. I'll bring a new flusher unit by in a day or two."

"So cosmopolitan we are."

"Only way it'll work until you find another Mister Wonderful."

"Not holding my breath."

"I'm just stop gap. Hate to leave your bed, but I will if this new guy works out."

"Stewart?"

"Serious?"

"Not a chance. Have to be someone incredible to give this up."

He nodded and saw the elsewhere look fill her eyes; it was over for now. Unless they parted right then the anchor of the known would begin its drag. They both knew it wasn't about toothpaste tubes or bland casseroles; it was over contrasting expectations. He let himself out and immediately ran into a guy from the next condo over with his arms wrapped around a bag of groceries. The man always smiled when he saw Sidney and said, "Hi there, Mr. McCall". He did it again. Sidney squinted, smiled, and raised a hand in passing then drove the two miles to his apartment. He dropped his keys on the kitchen counter, breathed in some of the stale block of air he was used to, got out of his clothes, and showered away the residue of his conjugal appointment.

He watched *60 Minutes*, found out what was currently rotten in the world, scrambled some eggs, ate them with toast and coffee, and went to bed early. He read a few more pages from the crime novel by his bed until sleep came.

Another day at Beeman's International awaited him.

19

-2-

Sidney had taken his first sip of Nina Beeman's weak-kneed coffee when her old man came waddling up to Sidney's office cubicle red-faced and cursing.

"Damn him! Damn him to hell." Ned Beeman looked around for a chair. Finding none, he turned completely around, stopping to mop his face with a meaty hand. "Jesus H." He was gasping.

"Who?" Sidney took his eyes off the screen of an aged computer monitor and reared back in his chair. The springs protested; he latched onto the arms.

Ned Beeman edged around and leaned stiff-armed on the edge of Sidney's desk. "Jonesy, the bastard."

Sidney pushed his chair away from the hot closeness of the man, craned his neck out, and waited. He had never heard his employer say anything derogatory about his top salesman, his only salesman of late. Ned Beeman was hyper and breathing hard.

"He died. Bastard's dead," he said, turning to face Sidney. Spittle came off his lips.

Some of it ended up on Sidney's left cheek. He didn't wipe it off. "Died? No. You're kidding."

"I am not—the pecker head." Ned Beeman raised his stubby body to a standing position, put his hands on his hips, and sighed. "Early this morning." His voice calmed. "Mildred called."

"How?"

"Who cares? Dead is dead." He looked into Sidney's startled face. "In his sleep, I guess. Hadda be his heart. Like I oughta know with my two bypass-aroos." Ned Beeman inhaled and waved a forefinger at Sidney. "I told him...I told him. Damn him. Told him to get his ass into the doctor and go under the knife like I did. We have group health, I told him. *I'm gonna, I'm gonna,* he always said. Gonna." Ned Beeman balled up his right hand and smashed it into the four-drawer file cabinet next to Sidney's desk. The sound boomed out like hitting a fifty-five gallon metal drum with mallet. "Health premiums on him would choke a rhino—and for what?"

"That's too bad," Sidney.

"Too bad? It's a goddamned crisis that's what it is. A major fuckup, that's what it is. Why did Oscar Jonesy Jones have to kickoff now? Why not next January? But no—the son of a bitch hadda quit breathing before we could get the summer orders booked on the coast."

"I seriously doubt that Jonesy passed away to get out of going back on the road," Sidney said with a touch of sarcasm.

"Wouldn't put it past him." Ned Beeman turned around again. "Well...he's gone, that's it. All she wrote."

"There'll be a service, I suppose."

"Suppose."

"His wife, she tell you when it would be?"

Ned Beeman was staring at Sidney. "Look you, forget about that. We'll send flowers, but that's not what's up here."

Sidney raised his eyebrows.

"You're gonna be making Jonesy's run down the coast. Decided."

"Me?" Sidney rocked forward, his chair squawking, and rose upright. "No I—"

Ned Beeman drew his mouth in and pointed a finger at Sidney. "Look, mister," he cut in; he rarely used Sidney's name, just

21

you or *hey there.* "This isn't no debating society. The man's dead, and we're in a shit-pot jam. You're the only stand-in I got, so by this time tomorrow you're on the road. Got it? Back on the road like you've done before."

Sidney inhaled and nodded and bemoaned how long it had been since he'd sold face to face, grinning and pushing cleansers and waxes and germ-fighting agents. Would extolling a line of curios be all that different? Tee shirts and beach towels and coffee mugs stenciled with ocean scenes, along with hand-produced Mexican pottery and Chinese-made epoxy figurines of dragons and gargoyles—could he do that?

"Okay then," Ned Beeman said, "I'll get the Caddy from Mildred. Belongs to the company. Leased him a new one every other year."

"That's okay, I can take my car. Don't want to leave the woman without a car."

"No, no. I've seen that beater of yours. Nah, we gotta look successful. You'll take the Caddy. Want my rep looking sharp."

Ned Beeman stood breathing like he'd just strained himself on the john, stared at the floor, nodded one more time, and was gone. Sidney heard him grumble something to his wife, Nina. She said something back that Sidney couldn't make out, and then it was quiet.

———•———

A few minutes later Ned Beeman was back, hands in his pockets; he stared at Sidney and ran his lips in and out. Sidney swiveled his chair and raised his eyebrows.

"I can't do it."

"Can't do what?" asked Sidney.

"Go in there. Jonesy's office."

Sidney studied the man's red face. "That right?"

"That's what I said." He paused. "Want you to go in there with me."

"Now?"

22

Need Beeman took in a big breath. "Yeah—now." He snapped it out. "We gotta go through his…desk and look for stuff."

"Stuff?"

"Geez. His records, the info you're going to need for this sales trip. You get it?"

Sidney nodded. "I get it."

"All right then, come on."

They stood peering into Jonesy's office as if they weren't authorized to enter the sanctum. The paper clutter and the smell of spent cigars were familiar signatures that made it seem like the man had just stepped away for a moment. The corner office was the only space worth coveting in the cinder block building, a runty, flat-roofed box built in the fifties. The environs of Beeman's International consisted of three claustrophobic offices, a toilet, and one stifling room where a microwave, a refrigerator, and a coffee maker were squeezed in with Sidney's cubicle—being the width of a desk and one file cabinet defined by a four-foot-high office partition that teetered on chrome feet; this one was covered in orange burlap. There was a small, drafty warehouse out back where Sidney saw to the unloading and loading: where he sorted, packed, grunted, heaved, and shipped and stayed to himself.

Ned Beeman stood in the doorway, his stance almost apologetic, and motioned for Sidney to go ahead. He watched while Sidney walked in, lowered himself cautiously into Jonesy's chair, and looked at the disarray on the desk.

"What am I looking for?" Sidney asked.

Ned Beeman raised an arm and waved his hand. "You know… oh hell," he said stomping over. "Get up, get up, I'll do it. But stay right here—don't leave the room."

He took Sidney's place at the desk, inhaled, rubbed his hands together then reached out to a day-at-a-time calendar and thumbed two pages over until coming to Monday, March 15, 2004. There were four words scratched large in blue ink, COAST RUN, START TODAY. Ned Beeman sagged back in the leather chair

23

and leaned his head against the spot darkened by the oil from Jonesy's hair. A family photo sat in a tilted frame on one corner of the desk: wife, grown kids, grandkids—one of those. Ned Beeman knuckled his eyes and pulled on his nose and blinked dampness away.

He looked up at Sidney. "I've been sloppy, derelict in keeping up on what Jonesy did and how he did it—even when he did it." He sighed. "Now I'm going to pay the price for turning too much over to him." He raised his voice. "And for giving him all those bonuses, and...and leasing a new Cadillac every two years. Hell, I don't even know my own customers anymore. I handed the soul of the business over to a fat, cigar-smoking pitchman, and he's died on me."

Sidney stood calmly as his employer sorted through the papers and file folders on the desk; Ned's rhythm became grasping when he didn't find what he sought. Then he turned to the file drawer in the desk and began thumbing past the tabs. His face turned pink, and his forehead moistened. At one point he leaned on his elbows, saw the ashtray full of cigar stubs, threw the putrid mess, ashtray and all, into the wastebasket, and shouted, "Fuck!" His wife called out "What?" "Nothing!" he yelled back. When he dug into the letter tray on the credenza, he found all he was going to find: a coffee-stained computer printout customer list and a yellow legal pad with notes scrawled on it. He tossed it onto the desk and reached back to pick up the figurine sitting next to the letter tray. *An Iggy.*

Sidney watched Ned Beeman fondle the bug-eyed iguana. He'd heard the story ad nauseam, how the artistic rendition of a smiling iguana had made Ned Beeman wealthy—for while, anyway. Ned had discovered the glazed-pottery lizard with the humanized eyes in 1972 in Mexico on an after-college year of rambling and drinking with some fraternity brothers. In this state he stumbled onto one Carlito Quezada, an artisan who lived in the small town of Tonala. Ned became fascinated with some pieces gathering dust on a back shelf in Quezada's shop: cups, bowls, plates, and small planters all using the unique image of an iguana. The caricature intrigued him: the scaly skin and notched spine topped off with luminous eyes and a smile. Carlito Quezada had humanized the reptile.

But they never sold very well, so Quezada had abandoned them. On a lark, Ned made an offer for all the iguana art and paid Carlito Quezada to ship them to Portland for him. Months later, when he at last gave up on his wanderlust, Ned returned home to find boxes and boxes of iguanas in his parents' garage. He had forgotten his quixotic act. When his favorite aunt saw the big-eyed reptile, she had to have a set, and soon her friends all wanted an iguana piece. After this enthusiastic response, Ned Beeman showed his iguanas to an acquaintance who owned a gift shop. Iggy was born. Iggy, the smiling, big-eyed iguana was almost as big as the Pet Rock. For nearly a decade, Iggy was a cash cow, making Carlito Quezada and Ned Beeman very well off. It seemed Iggy would go on forever. He didn't.

———•———

When Ned Beeman seemed to calm down, Sidney suggested that he go back to his desk. Ned Beeman merely nodded and kept shuffling through papers. Nina Beeman was pouring herself a cup of coffee when Sidney returned to his cubical and sat staring at the wall above his computer monitor. She poured a second cup and walked over. Sidney turned in his chair to face her. She continued chewing her Doublemint gum, scrunched a smile at him, and held a coffee mug out. He took it, nodding, and set it on his desk.

Nina Beeman pinched the wad of gum off her tongue and dropped it in the wastebasket near Sidney's feet. "Poor Jonesy," she said on an exhaled breath that ended in a hum. "Can't believe it."

Sidney looked up, blinked, and hesitated. "Yeah," he responded.

"He was something."

Sidney sipped more coffee. "If you say so."

"Well he was."

"That right? Never was my flavor of the month."

Nina Beeman squinted. "You may not know it, but Jonesy's the one been keeping this place afloat. Hadn't been for him…" She looked over her shoulder and lowered her voice. "Hadn't been for Jonesy out there making the sales, we'd be history."

Sidney swiveled and set the cup down on his desk. "That's something, then."

"What's that supposed to mean?"

"Nothing. Forget it. Bad day all around."

"You got something to say, mister, just say it."

Sidney looked up. Her eyes were pinched in accusation; heavy eyeliner made her dim blue eyes almost disappear. "Look," he said, "he's dead. Nothing we can do for him now."

She looked away; when she looked back her eyes were shiny with tears. "So what, just erase him? That's what you and Ned would like—just write him off and move on. Right?"

Sidney folded his arms. "You were close then? You and Jonesy."

She ran a red-nailed forefinger beneath one eye to cut off a tear on its way down her cheek. "What are you suggesting?"

Sidney shrugged. "Nothing. There something to suggest?"

Nina Beeman looked over her shoulder again. "Look, you." She leaned forward. "You keep your disgusting thoughts to yourself. Jonesy was a good man. That's all I meant."

"Yeah, that's what I meant."

She sniffed. "Yeah, well then. Better be."

Sidney nodded and she nodded and they fell silent, looking this way and that.

Nina Chapman had been a real beauty, and Ned Beeman had been at the height of his Iggy success when they met. They each had something the other wanted, so they married in 1980 and rode the wave on high right onto the beach. In twenty-four years Ned Beeman had grown fat and desperate, and Nina had gotten harshly skinny and sour.

"Hear you're going to be getting the Cadillac."

Her voice brought Sidney out of his thoughts about the state of things. "Huh? Oh. Yeah, guess so. Not my idea."

Her smile was not kind. "Last thing you expected on another sluggish Monday morning, right? Filling in for Jonesy."

Sidney tightened his mouth and shrugged.

"Well, you're in deep doo-doo now," she said.

He stared at her, opened his mouth to speak then closed it; he had nothing to say.

"This is make or break time," she went on then waved a hand. "Hell, even with Jonesy it was dreadful. As soon as Jonesy went on the road, Ned would start with the Rolaids. Jonesy, he'd call in every couple of days and feed Ned the good news–bad news. God awful 'round here. My old man." She shook her head. "He'd pound on that desk if sales were good or if they were bad. He'd drink to celebrate and drink to bury despair. You saw it."

Sidney shook his head once, right to left. "Never took note."

"Come on. You saying you never heard the fussing and ranting?"

"Been hearing things right along—just never took note of the details. Got my job. Do that."

"I don't believe you for a minute," she said. "I can see it in your eyes. You hear everything that goes on, Sidney. You're lying to me."

"Think what you want, Nina. I do my job. The rest of it goes on by."

"Well." She took a swallow of cooling coffee. "Not this time. Put on your selling shoes."

"Why me? Why not do it himself?"

Nina snickered. "My Nedder? On the road? Piss his pants. He'd swell up and die."

"Can't believe that. What about the Iggy days we hear about all the time?"

"Iggy sold himself. Back then the world was beating the door down. Was a flaming phenomenon. You don't have to sell a phenomenon. But you sure as hell have to sell a has-been phenomenon. Bless his soul, my Ned couldn't sell a virgin to Ted Bundy."

"Jesus, Nina."

"It's true."

"Ought to be on the Internet," he countered. "With an interactive website we could do most of the sales online." He stabbed a finger at the computer on his desk. "This is from the dark ages. Barely keeps inventory."

Nina chewed on her lower lip and looked away. "Maybe you're right," she said, turning back. "Probably are. Maybe one day we'll get there, but Ned is a Luddite when it comes to technology. Besides, we can't afford all that right now."

"Well, that's crazy."

"Look, Sidney, that's just the way it is!" she snapped.

Their eyes locked. Nothing was said for a few moments.

"You ready to be our savior, then?"

"Savior? Hell no," he answered.

"Well, the man's desperate. Desperate men grasp at anything to keep afloat. Wouldn't you say?"

Sidney stood and pulled up on his pants and sat back down. "Well, I'm not gonna do it."

Nina smiled. "Course you are. You've been out there, selling face to face. It says so on your résumé. Ned dug it out. I saw it on his desk. So you'll do this—otherwise why would we need you?"

Sidney didn't have an answer for her.

-3-

The interior of the silver Seville had been impregnated with the fuming of a thousand cigars. The black leather power seat was butt-shined and tracked as far back as it could go. Country and western CDs were loaded in the changer. Sidney was discovering that you could determine a lot about a man if you could go through his car right after he died, before the interesting stuff was gotten rid of.

Tuesday morning Ned Beeman repossessed the Caddy from Jonesy's widow, threw the keys at Sidney, and told him to dung it out. Sidney began by emptying the ashtray of cigar butts and ashes, shaking Jonesy's DNA into a plastic bag. Then he picked through the mélange of catalogs and snack food leavings and paper coffee cups and golf balls and tees. The glove box was a jumble of road maps, peppermint Life Savers, ballpoint pens, matchbooks, unopened packs of Roi Tan shorts cigars, and an address book. In the trunk he found a collection of porno magazines beneath the sample cases and golf shoes clotted with dried grass, a bag of scarred clubs, and jumper cables still in the cardboard sleeve with a price sticker on it.

"Okay, so Jonesy was a slob." Ned was studying Sidney when he spoke across his own cluttered desk.

Sidney smiled, massaged his just-disinfected hands, and kept his mouth shut.

"Well, maybe he was." Ned looked away, out the window then back. "But he was one son of a bitch of a salesman. Man was an artist. A blooming artist. Watching him work was…well, it was something."

"Never had the pleasure," Sidney said.

"Yeah, well, he was something. Gonna have our hands full without him, let me tell you."

Sidney looked into the florid face of his employer and felt his stomach roll.

"It'll be on you now. Up to it?"

"Why you putting this on me?" Sidney asked. "I'm not Jonesy. I was hired on to keep things moving out the back."

"Well, mister, won't be anything going out the back if we don't sell some merchandise." Ned picked up a sheet of paper. "Anyways, you've been on the road before—says so right here in your résumé. Would you look at that? Hell, if you can sell encyclopedias, this here'll be a piece a cake."

"Long time ago," Sidney said, his face reddening. *And not that many sales,* he might have added.

"Real estate, industrial cleaning supplies, used cars, hell." Ned was running a finger down the page. "Lookie here, traveling baby photographer even. You been around."

The phone emitted an electronic warble. Ned snatched the receiver from its cradle and grunted into the mouthpiece. His eyes locked onto Sidney; then they drifted upward.

"Yeah, I know." Ned swiveled his chair until he was facing away from Sidney, his voice low. "Like I told you…I know, I know. Okay, something by Friday. Yeah." He turned back and hung up the phone. After a moment he said, "Don't ever own your own business."

Sidney stayed silent and nodded. He had been there, knew the day-in, day-out gut cramps of nursing a lost cause.

Ned inhaled and let it out slowly then picked up a thin sheaf of papers. "So here's the background stuff: list of customers—Astoria to Brookings—printout of what they've ordered over the last... looks like last three years. These here still owe us something. Getting their order and payment at the same time is tricky, but Jonesy...he had a way of doing that." He sighed. "Do the best you can, something on account anyway. This page is places we haven't done business with. Give 'em a go. This here's a list of all our products. Not much new except for this Mexican jewelry and them epoxy dragons—Chinese junk. Jonesy's been selling them, though—no accounting for taste. Oh, and the new Iggy plush toy, push that. Should be some sales there, especially for the die-hard Iggy lovers. Anything checked in red is product we're trying to dump—push that stuff. You can give up to thirty percent off, hell, even fifty if you need to. You've seen our full-color catalog, right? They cost a bundle, but they're getting outa date...hell, take what we got left and hand 'em out. Might as well."

Ned shoved the pages across to Sidney and slumped back. "That's about it, I guess. Oh wait—here's his cell phone. Just use it for reporting in, business, not for personal calls. It's just a basic phone, no frills." He rubbed his face with both hands. "Damn it to hell," he said. His eyes were watering again. "No more Jonesy."

"It's a shock all right," Sidney said.

"Shock, hell. It's a damned catastrophe—that's what it is." Ned picked up a ballpoint pen and tapped it on the desktop. "You up for this?"

Sidney shuffled the papers and looked at the printing until it blurred. "Yeah, I think so."

"Hey. There's no *think* so. 'Cause if you're not up to it, I sure don't need you out back. Either suck it up and put on your sales-man's face or—"

"Okay. Yeah, I can do it." Sidney felt a rush of anger, but he swallowed it. "Jonesy, he on a commission?"

Ned's head snapped up. "Never you mind."

"Just like to know what the going rate is."

31

"Look," Ned pointed a finger, "Jonesy was a star. You're a fill in." He paused and leaned back. "You do a decent job, we'll see. Got it?"

Sidney shrugged.

They sat in silence, Ned nodding and Sidney sorting through the papers, top to bottom, bottom to top. They were still sitting that way when Nina Beeman walked into the office.

"You boys bonding, or is this a séance?"

Ned looked up at his wife. She was chewing more Doublemint. "What do you want, Nina?"

"Don't use that tone with me." She popped her gum and squinted.

"Pardon me all to hell. What do you want, dear?"

"Here, Sidney, you'll need these. This one's a gas card, Arco. And here's a MasterCard for meals and lodging."

"Wait." Ned looked anxious. "Those got room?"

"Enough," she said. "What he means, Sidney, is that you need to be prudent."

"Prudent?" Ned broke it. "Nuts to that. You need to eat cheap and sleep cheap and drive with an egg under your foot else you might end up walking, looking foolish when that there card won't pay for your dinner or you end up sleeping in the Caddy some night."

———•———

Ned Beeman's face was the shade of a rare rib-eye, and his eyes wide and uneasy when he handed Sidney the car keys and urged him to "Sell large". Sidney slid into the silver Cadillac, with its Iggy vanity plates, buckled up, and nosed the big car out of the parking lot. As he drove away, he saw Ned Beeman in the rearview mirror, staring after him like a beleaguered father who was seeing a son off to war.

Sidney drove the Caddy through a car wash, vacuumed it out, and bought one of those little pine tree deodorizers from a vending machine and hung it from the mirror. Doing all that gave the misadventure he was on a few moments of lucidity and even a sense of purpose—that was until he thought of the dead man, the shaky credit cards, and the desperation. It didn't take long to pack: four pair of chinos, couple of slacks, sport shirts, blue blazer and tasseled loafers, no need for dress shirts and ties.

The only person he had to let know that he'd be out of town for a spell was Ellie, and then only because she might call needing something fixed or expecting the other thing. She said that worked out to be longer than two weeks and tried to lure him by for the other thing before he left town. Sidney listened to her purring invite and felt himself rise to the bait, but managed to engender great restraint because he knew that Ned Beeman intended to call him later at the Beach Nugget Motel in Astoria. He put a hold on the paper, decided to let the mail pile up—didn't get that much anyway—and checked his message machine. There were two messages: one was a wrong number reminding Charlie to bring the beer; the other was from John Marr.

John Marr. Damn.

-4-

Sidney mulled over John Marr's message while he made a smoked turkey sandwich and brewed some coffee and filled his travel mug for the road. *Some things just never back off,* he thought. Least ways not the bad things like John Marr. He dropped an apple and a over-ripened banana in a brown sack with the sandwich, gathered up his wardrobe and duffel bag, and carried it all out to the car, the mug dangling off one finger. The Cadillac still smelled of cigar, but now with a hint of pine.

Sidney readjusted the power seat, refining its many positions to his particular dimensions, and drove out of the city on Highway 30. Soon enough he couldn't keep John Marr's phone message from invading the silent running of the big car.

Sidney. John Marr. We have an agreement.

The assured baritone voice was always that of someone who might be asking a favor or extending an invitation—that is, if you didn't know what was behind the voice. To Sidney it was a voice of persecution, a grinding down he could not escape.

Got your hundred. Late. Besides, deal's three bills. Every month. See now, you're forcing me to up the rate from 10 to 15. Why'd you want to go and do that?

———•———

In early August 1998, Sidney took his last photos for DuPree Baby Shots at the Valley River Mall in Eugene, turned to the twenty-something woman he was working with, and said, *Helena, picture me gone.* He yanked off the red and white polka-dot clip-on bow tie he'd had to wear (*babies love it*, he'd been told), threw it in the trash, loosened his collar, helped Helena pack up, and walked away. After three years on the road, going from town to town photographing cherubs—spit-up, drool, poop, squalling babes, and snarling mothers—he'd had enough. He took his meager savings and final pay from DuPree and his Mamiya RB67 Pro-SD portrait camera and opened Portraits by Lister in a small strip center on the outskirts of Eugene where rent was cheaper.

He managed to get posted in the new businesses listing in the newspaper, offered free portraits to some business owners nearby if they'd let him display them, passed out business cards and flyers about the city, and waited. The Asian couple that owned the cleaners two doors down hired him for their daughter's wedding as long as he would take a third of the bill out in trade. He made a cut-rate deal to photograph the students of a karate school in various threatening poses. And one of the students came by to have a picture taken of him astride his ninja motorcycle.

And that was it for three months until the day John Marr walked in and hired Sidney to photograph his new granddaughter. Daughter, hubby, grandmother, and grandfather were all giggly over Sidney's photos of their cherub. Soon thereafter, John Marr, who owned Marr-Tech, a computer furniture manufacturing company, retained Portraits by Lister to photograph all his employees and take pictures of the plant for an annual report. So when invited by John Marr to join an exclusive marketing association, Sidney blanched at the $500 dues but accepted and ate ramen noodles for a couple of months.

The Ventures Business Council was limited to 150 members of non-competing businesses; its sole purpose was to generate new business for its members. John Marr was president of the council, so when he vouched for and sponsored Sidney Lister, acceptance was immediate. And in a short time Sidney was getting some business from members of the council.

That's when things turned sour. When the subject of a new membership directory came up, John Marr coerced Sidney into taking on the job and promised his fellow members that Sidney would produce a flashy publication that would be the envy of every other business in town. Sidney would do the photography, write the copy, and contract for the design, printing, and binding. Every member was assessed a fee to cover the cost of printing ten thousand directories. The Ventures Business Council board advanced the funds to cover the project and Sidney got under way.

Three months later the directory was completed to great acclaim, but by that time everything was swimming in red ink. Sidney had been compelled by John Marr to sharpen his pencil and come up with a quote for the directories that would make Marr a hero to his colleagues. But with the budget too sparse to begin with and a bevy of cost overruns, the outcome cut Sidney's piece of the pie to pocket change and left him thousands short on bills owed to vendors and unable to clear his own debts. John Marr denied Sidney any additional funds and accused him of mismanagement of the money advanced to him; he was told to suck it up and make good on his contract. Three weeks later, Portraits by Lister was vacant. Sidney had disappeared, taking just enough money on which to survive for the short term but owing nearly ten thousand dollars to a combination of his landlord, local printers, binders, photo processors, and a woman who had designed the directory; Sidney felt the worst about leaving her holding the bag. By the time overdue bills began showing up John Marr's desk, Sidney was once again trying to reinvent his life in another place.

Don't forget. I know where you work, Sidney.

John Marr was a bitter man. His reputation had been tarnished when Sidney skipped town; he had been embarrassed and made sport of. His ego was too large for humiliation. After John Marr tracked him to Portland, Sidney could not convince him of the justification of his actions: of the project being underfunded, of his own his pressing debts and the fact that he didn't make a dime. *Too late, he'd said to Sidney. We advanced you fifty grand. Every member ponied up a chunk of change. You are a sneak and I despise sneaks. I paid your debt. Now you will pay me, plus interest.*

In his phone message, Marr ratcheted up his threat: *Don't make me go to this Ned Beeman and garnishee your wages. I will. Embezzlement is a serious offense, so I've got you by the short hairs. Never forget that.*

Sidney smiled to think of Ned Beeman, a man at debtor's door, taking that call from John Marr. *Who knows,* he thought, *maybe Ned and I would have bonded; maybe he'd call me by my name instead of mister.*

Sidney, John Marr had chided. *Come on. Make up the two hundred your down, plus forty-three seventy-five for being tardy.*

Life is a bitch, Sidney was thinking as he drove through St. Helens, the county seat of Columbia County. *Here I am cruising along in this fine automobile. People looking as I pass, if they notice at all, could assume that there goes a person of worth—not there goes that weasel Sidney Lister who's a cheat, the same Sidney Lister named most likely to succeed. Nor would they know that this fine Cadillac belongs to a man whose credit cards are at the high-water mark and the driver is only filling in for a dead guy.*

———•———

It was raining hard when Sidney hit Astoria. He throttled back the 275-horsepower V8 and coasted into town looking for the Beach Nugget Motel. The big wipers swept the water away as if the car couldn't be bothered—arrogant tub. He found the place in the south part of town on Marine Drive across from a row of corrugated metal warehouses. The motel was tired but hopeful. Indeed it was blue, pale blue, one of those two-floor motels, square, flat on top, all the doors and windows facing the parking lot. The parking stripes were barely visible anymore, and here and there tufts of weeds were shoving up through cracks in the asphalt.

Sidney pulled beneath the canopy by the office and went inside. It was raining harder, thudding on the metal roof of the drive-through; the tangy aroma of sea life met his nostrils when he stepped out of the car. A woman he would describe as hefty came wandering in from the manager's apartment. She'd done something blonde to her hair that hadn't worked. She looked past him at the car and shoved a registration card at him; it was attached to a little clipboard.

"Where's Jonesy?" she asked after reading his registration.

When Sidney looked up with question in his eyes, the woman blinked through smudged glasses and said, "Beeman's. Saw that and the big car with them Iggy plates. Been expecting him 'bout now."

"Well." Sidney turned to look at the Cadillac. "Jonesy died Sunday."

The woman's eyes popped open. "You don't say." She studied the registration card again then shouted over her shoulder. "Stan, fella here says Jonesy died." A voice hollered back about that being something. The woman yelled "yeah" back and shook her head and asked Sidney how he was going to pay. He shoved the company credit card across the counter.

"Want Jonesy's regular?"

"Guess not."

She nodded her blanched hair. "Gotcha," she said and handed him a key. "Downstairs. Number one-o-eight. Halfway down."

Sidney was going out the door when she said, "You know, we had some good times with Jonesy. My old man and me. Tell ya, he could brighten up a day. Took us to dinner couple of times. What was it?"

"Heart."

"Figures. Not surprised, really. So, you the one now…Sidney?" she said, checking the registration card again.

"Who knows? Just second string for now."

"Well hey, anything we can do for you…"

Sidney raised an arm at her and let the door close on her heartfelt pitch. So much for Jonesy. One-o-eight smelled of cigarettes and disinfectant spray. He decided that he preferred cigar and pseudo pine. He hung his wardrobe bag in the accordion-door closet, tossed his duffel on the bed, and stashed the toiletry kit in the bathroom. He emptied his bladder then went to the window and stood staring out into the parking lot. Still raining. What the hell, March on the Oregon coast. He was mulling over being in yet another motel room, in solitary, when the room phone rang. It was Ned Beeman.

"You made good time."

Sidney sat on the edge of the bed and looked at his shoes. "Guess so. No traffic. Just got in, actually."

"Remember, egg under the gas pedal. That bitch likes her octane."

"I'll watch it." Sidney shook his head and pinched his nose at the place between his eyes.

"Good. What time is it there?"

"Same time zone, Ned."

"Oh shit, I knew that. Knew that. Anyway, so it's three-twenty. Still time for you to make a call."

Sidney bit down and breathed in. "On the list, looked like there's only a couple of live accounts here. In Astoria."

"Okay, I know that. Point is, you got time to get your butt out there and—"

"Hey," Sidney said, his voice low but clipped. "This the way it's gonna be?"

"What's that? I don't much like your tone, mister."

"Yeah, well, it's like you think I need training wheels for this. Thing is, are you gonna be coaching me every step? If so, let me write it all down."

Ned was breathing hard into the mouthpiece. "Now you listen up, mister. I'm not about to take that kinda lip. I'm the one calling the shots, and you—"

"Sidney."

"Huh?"

"My name is Sidney."

"So what?"

"Never mind. Listen, Ned, tell you what—I can be back in Portland in an hour and a half, drop the Cadillac off, and be out of your hair. How's that?"

Ned's short breaths hissed into Sidney's ear. "You son of a bitch. Okay, fine."

"Fine then."

"Yeah, fine. Get your ass back here. And you take care with that car."

"Pedal to the metal. Forget the egg. Let's see what all that horsepower can do."

"Bastard."

"Jerk."

Sidney slammed the receiver down and dropped back onto the concave mattress. *What the hell,* he thought. *Won't be sleeping on it anyway.* He jumped up, yanked a pillow out from under the butt ugly brown and orange bedspread and beat the bed with it, whopping the flaccid pillow until bits of latex foam skittered out like frightened bugs. The solitude of the room closed in, and the old feeling was there, the one that told him he was alone and no one was going to call or drop by or invite him over for dinner.

So now what, Sidney? You dinkus.

He moved again to the window. Moisture had eased onto his brow from the exertion of his one-man pillow fight. The Seville stared back at him. Rivulets of rain coursed down the windshield. An elderly couple was checking into a room next to his; when the man passed the window and looked in at him, Sidney drew the balky drapes and turned on the television and stared at it with the sound muted. The little refrigerator in the room clicked on and hummed. *I'll leave in a little while,* he thought. When the cooking program went to commercial he went to the bathroom again.

He was washing his face, bracing himself for the drive back, when the house phone started ringing. He came out and stood over it. On the fourth ring he picked up; he didn't speak. Someone was breathing on the line. He knew who.

"I know you're there," Ned said.

"Yeah. So?"

"Figured you'd be gone."

"Well I'm not. Getting good and drunk before I drive your big car back."

"Cute."

"What do you want? Me and my friend Jack are busy. You've met him, Mr. Daniels."

"I don't drink bourbon."

"Only assholes drink scotch."

"Watch your mouth, mister."

A woman spoke in the background; there was an edge to her voice. Sidney knew it was Nina Beeman.

Ned grumbled. "Okay, all right," he said to her not Sidney. "Okay, ah… look, Sidney, you still set on this?"

Sidney cleared his throat into the mouthpiece. "Me? You're the one who pooped his britches."

"God damn it!"

Nina hissed, and then the line became muffled; Ned had put his hand over the mouthpiece. All he heard was a rumble of voices like a marital squabble through a motel room wall. Sidney sat on the bed and waited and hoped.

"Sidney? You still there?"

"Yep."

"Look, fella, can't we just bury the hatchet? You know, get on

41

with the job at hand? Forget our little rumpus. Damn it all, anyway." Ned forced a chuckle and paused for a few heartbeats. "So, whatcha say? Deal?"

Sidney crossed the fingers of his left hand, held the phone with his right, and took a chance. "I don't know."

"You don't know? What the...Nina, damn it, leave me be." The line was quiet; Ned was gathering himself. "All right. Now, Sidney? I...I need you to stay with me, stay out there. Really do." His voice dropped. "Okay? And I'll give you a free hand. How's that?"

A door clunked shut in a room next door. Sidney counted to ten. Waited.

"Sidney? Look, I'm sorry as hell for...you know. It's just, well, we're up against it and—"

"What the hell," Sidney said, breaking in on Ned's painful confession. "Guess I'd better sober up and get on over to Beulah's Sand and Sea. Who knows, she may even be a bourbon drinker."

Ned Beeman laughed like he meant it, but it was probably more relief. "Okay, back on track then."

"For today anyway."

"Come on, be good now. All right then, that does it. Right?"

"Guess it does."

"Oh say, I forgot to give you a heads-up on one customer. Our biggest, Lamont Courter."

"Courter's Curios?"

"The same. Has eight or nine shops on the coast."

"I know. What about him?"

"Kid gloves, friend. He's our bread and butter, but he can be one nasty piece of work. Used to manhandle Jonesy at first. Then it all smoothed out. Don't know what old Jonesy did. Wished I did. All I can say is watch yourself in the clinches."

"Just what I need—a bad ass who's got us by the balls."

"Yeah, well, you know what Ricky Nelson sang—I didn't

promise you a rose garden. By the way, some guy called here looking for you. Said to tell you he'll try another time. Wrote his name down. Here it is. Marr, John Marr."

Speaking of rose gardens.

-5-

Beulah Strong was that. Lanky woman—loose jointed and big boned. She was tall, had a pleasant face and a set of buckteeth that she followed around. Beulah's Sand and Sea Gifts was empty of customers at three minutes ahead of 4 p.m. The place smelled of scented candles and soaps, blending fragrances like sandalwood, vanilla, and bayberry. The bell above the door tinkled when Sidney entered, and the woman rose from the desk behind the sales counter and dropped the half-glasses from her nose where they hung on a cord below her clavicle. Some new age music hummed out from a couple of wall-mounted speakers.

Sidney wiped his wet feet on the doormat and took out one of the generic business cards Ned Beeman had given him, cupped it in the palm of his hand, and squeezed out his salesman's smile. Been awhile. It was like using muscles you'd let atrophy, kind of tight and reluctant. The woman smiled back, her big teeth taking over her face. Beulah Strong reached over the counter and took the card Sidney was holding out, looked at it, then turned her confused eyes on Sidney.

"I know," said Sidney, "I'm not Jonesy." Even at six feet he had to look up to meet her eyes.

She smiled just a bit and looked at the card again. "Yes," she said. Her voice was low for a woman's. "Well, I mean," she laughed like she didn't want to, "I'm just surprised is all. You know, you get used to seeing a certain person."

"I understand. By the way, it doesn't say so on the card, but I'm Sidney Lister."

"Mr. Lister." She laughed and held out a carpenter's hand. "Has a ring to it, doesn't it? Mister Lister. Bet you've heard that one."

"I have," Sidney nodded.

"I'm Beulah Strong."

"Nice to meet you," he said, his fingers lost in her grip.

"Yes. So…has Jonesy left the company?"

Sidney ran a hand over his damp thin hair. "Ah—I'm sorry, is it Mrs. Strong?"

"Yes. Missus." Her face was full of question.

"There's bad news, Mrs. Strong." Her eyes widened. "Jonesy, he passed on."

Sidney was maybe expecting the woman to give comment, how sad she was or the like. He wasn't prepared for her virtual collapse. Beulah Strong actually sagged to the floor and lost consciousness. Sidney knelt on the thick carpeting and took up one of her hands and patted it like he thought you were supposed to. He called her name calmly, and then he raised his voice and said her name a second time. In a few moments her eyelids moved then fluttered opened, and she looked up into Sidney's face. She tugged her hand from his grasp and sat up and began to cry.

She sat like that for several minutes, sobbing into her hands, regaining herself only to cry more. Sidney found a box of tissues on her desk and brought her several sheets. She nodded her thanks and dabbed at her eyes. When her spasms of grief had ebbed, she rolled to her knees, rose, and stood twisting the spent tissues in her hands.

"I'm sorry," Sidney said, "I should have been more sensitive. Are you all right?"

She nodded and wiped at her nose.

"How about a cup of coffee? I saw a little shop not far from here. Can you close up? I'll take you there."

45

"No." She shook her head and inhaled. "I need something stiffer than coffee."

———•———

Beulah Strong refused to ride in the Cadillac. Not in that car. Not now. She waved Sidney into a vintage red Datsun pickup with the name of her shop painted on the doors and prodded the little truck down the road for a mile or so before jouncing into the parking lot of a place called The Lagoon. The engine rattled twice before quitting, and the windshield wipers jerked to a stop mid-swipe. Beulah Strong leaned forward on the steering wheel for a moment then grimaced at Sidney before swinging her long body out of the small cab.

When she shoved through the door to The Lagoon, a big-gutted guy behind the bar called out her name like she was a regular. Beulah Strong waved a hand but didn't respond; the guy shrugged and picked up a cigarette burning in an ashtray, sucked on it, and squinted the smoke away. She legged out three or four long strides, slid into a booth against the wall, folded her hands on the table, and stared down. There were no windows in the place, and it smelled like it should, smoky, musty, closed in—all the comforts. Sidney looked around. It was quiet, just two guys sharing some nachos and having a beer at the bar and talking low.

"What'll you have?" Sidney asked Beulah Strong.

She looked up into his face as if he had just materialized in front of her. "Did you know him?"

"Jonesy?"

"Uh-huh. Did you?"

"Beulah, how you doing?" It was the bartender. When she didn't look at him, he turned his eyes on Sidney and said, "So what can I getcha?"

Sidney sat back. "I don't know, couple a beers maybe. Beulah, beer okay?"

"Bourbon. On the rocks."

"Okay," Sidney said slowly. "Make it two, I guess." The bartender bobbed his head and tromped off.

She was staring at Sidney. "Yes, I knew Jonesy," he finally answered. "We weren't close, what with him being on the road most of the time. But, yeah, I knew him."

"But you didn't like him." She raised a hand. "You don't have to say anything. I can tell. Guy like Jonesy, way he lived life—you know, at the top of his voice—figures some people wouldn't like that. But I did. First time he hit my shop it was like I'd known the man since grade school. Funny." She tried to smile, but the tears came again; she wiped her eyes with a bar napkin.

The drinks came, and they sat swirling ice cubes with red plastic straws.

"Just thinking about riding in that car again…well, you could see—I couldn't," she said. "I mean, he used to take me for a drink, like this, or we'd go to dinner. You know, the salesman bit. And I can remember the smell of him in the car. His cigars mostly. Even imagining him at the wheel. I know it sounds crazy, but…"

"No, I understand," Sidney said. "Can imagine that, really. I cleaned the car and, you know, tried to get the smell out, those blasted cigars." She smiled; he laughed. "Even hung one of those little pine tree things, deodorizer, from the mirror. All I got was pine stogie."

She put a hand to her mouth and tried to not laugh then sipped more bourbon.

A man and woman came through the door barking good-naturedly at the bartender, asking if it was still happy hour. He boomed that they knew dang well it was and supposed they'd want their usual cheap booze and nachos. Beulah Strong shook her head and smiled and mumbled something about small towns.

Sidney leaned on his elbows and decided to not make idle talk. He would wait, let her take the lead. It seemed dishonest to keep in mind that he was making a sales call and needed to come away from this with an order. But he did. It was dawning on him that at every stop along the way he would be the grim reaper's messenger. *Hi, I'm Sidney Lister, Jonesy's dead, let's make a deal.* Smelling salts might become an essential part of his sales kit. Being understudy to a dead man, the kind who never met a stranger, would make for a very long trip.

Beulah Strong had finished her drink and held her glass aloft for a refill. Neither of them had spoken for several minutes. Sidney sipped and waited, intrigued by the woman's grief over a rep's death, a guy who happened by once, twice a year selling smiling reptiles and other trifles. The bartender brought another bourbon; Sidney signaled that he was still working on his first. Beulah Strong raised her glass in salute and took a long drink then set the glass down hard and blinked at more tears.

"Was his heart, wasn't it? Yeah. You see…darn it anyway. Last time he came through he bragged that he was going to lose fifty pounds. We even drank to it." She chuckled. "Isn't that something? Last thing he needed was more booze."

"How long did you know him?"

"Oh, ever since Beeman's hired him. What's that? I don't know, maybe six or seven years. Something like that."

"So he'd been by here a dozen times or so?"

Beulah Strong's eyes opened up and Sidney saw her expression change, like an old movie was running in her head. She sat like that, quiet with her eyes focused on something other than him and The Lagoon.

"No," she said, coming out of her thoughts. "Oscar, I mean Jonesy, visited more often than that."

"That right? I figured at most twice a year—early spring, like now, and late summer."

"Not true," she said and swallowed more bourbon. The glass clinked against her front teeth; two drinks on an empty stomach had reached judgment tissue. "Mr. Lifter," she said slurring, "I'm married. But I'm not married. Understand?"

"Not sure."

She smiled, her eyelids drooping. "Come now. Figure it out. I can tell you're getting the drift here. About Oscar and me. Never called him Jonesy, leastwise not after we got to know one another. Know what I mean?"

"I'm getting it, yeah."

She sobbed again, quietly, closing her eyes and sucking in a breath that gurgled. Sidney shifted his buttocks on the Naugahyde-covered bench and looked over his shoulder. No one was paying any attention to the crying woman slowly getting drunk over the death of a fat, cigar-smoking curio salesman. She snuffed and wiped at her nose again. Sidney reached back to pull out his handkerchief and handed it to her; she took it, dabbed her eyes, and handed it back blotched with eye shadow. He left it lying.

"I'm alone again," she said.

Sidney took another sip from his glass and thought that he knew the feeling—being alone with people all around.

"You married, Mister, what's your name?"

"Lister."

"No, your first name."

"Sidney."

"Sidney. Had an uncle named Sidney," she said. "He was a bastard, too. No, no, not you. I mean like my husband, Skitch. Like the bandleader? Skitch Henderson? Except my Skitch isn't music to my ears."

Sidney smiled.

"So you married, Sidney?"

"Was once."

"Was. What a nice sound. I know, can see the question on your face. Answer is there's no answer. Except …well, you know what they say? The hell you know is maybe better'n the one you don't."

She emptied what was left of the bourbon, the ice cubes sliding down against her teeth.

"But then there was Jonesy. Oscar."

"Yeah." She looked into the glass.

"He was married, too."

She nodded. "Margaret. He talked about her. He loved her, just not like he used to. He wasn't in love anymore. I felt guilty about her, about being with her man because my man is such a nothing."

"Guilty."

"Darn right." Her voice rose. "But she had Oscar all the rest of the time."

"Did she?"

She knocked the glass against the table and waved to the bartender. They sat without speaking until her third drank came. Sidney put a hand on hers when she went to raise the glass. There was a moment of hesitation before she pushed his hand away and took a drink.

"Bet you can't imagine someone like Oscar being attracted to a gangly old broad like me, can you? Well, I can look pretty good when the sun goes down and there's been some serious drinking going on."

"I doubt that that's what happened," Sidney soft-soaped.

"It didn't matter. It was being held by a man who told me nice things and made love to me like I was more than a sack of meal."

Sidney waved a menu at the bartender and ordered two steak sandwiches, something to sop up some of the sour mash fogging Beulah Strong's head. The rain had muted to mist by the time they left The Lagoon. Sidney talked her out of her keys, coaxed the pickup back downtown, and parked in front of her store on Commercial, where they stood shivering in the dampness. After a couple of minutes looking at his shoes, Sidney told her he enjoyed meeting her and told her again that he was sorry about Jonesy.

At the mention of her dead lover, she fell against Sidney and cried some more, hung on him with her long arms and tried to kiss him. He let her push her mouth against his, felt her teeth against his lips, smelled the vapors of whiskey, then gently patted her and pushed away, looking sheepishly about. No one else was there to see them; the street was nearly vacant, its wetness shining under the streetlights.

"Why'nt you come in?" she said. "Got a bed in back. Stay the night." She wiped at her nose and looked down at him. Her eyes were hazy; she tried to focus them but couldn't.

There beneath the cold glow of vapor lamps, Beulah Strong's face did not stir him. He had been in this same place with other women on other nights when the pain of being alone overrode the degradation either of them felt by their pathetic circumstance. But Sidney knew that it had to be mutual humiliation for it not to be predatory.

He patted Beulah Strong on the back, whispered assurances to her, and guided her into the store, one hand under an elbow, the other on her back. And darned if there wasn't a bed in a back storage room. Her body folded down, heavy and lifeless, onto a brightly stitched quilt. When her head fell back on the pillow she burped, mumbled she was sorry, and passed out. Sidney pulled the quilt up from the side, rolled Beulah Strong's long body on edge, and covered her as much as he could. Then he studied her for a moment, tried not to think of her as a sack of meal, and left the store.

The day was finally over, but not the damnable trip.

-6-

The red message light was blinking on the beige house phone on the nightstand when Sidney returned to his room at the Beach Nugget. He watched the light flutter and wondered if he could stand one more go around with Ned Beeman. He breathed several deep sighs and called the front desk. But it wasn't a call from Ned—it was from John Marr. How the hell?

Sidney paced, turned on the television, put CNN on mute, and propped himself up on the bed. *Give him a call,* that was the message. Larry King was interviewing some celebrity lawyers about some rich psycho who supposedly killed his wife.

John Marr had set up shop in Sidney's head; first it was just a little corner, but his presence had expanded and was becoming maddening. How'd he find him? Sidney looked at the number again. It was Marr's office number; he knew that from past experience. He looked at his watch and relaxed a bit. It was after hours, so if he called right then he could leave a voice mail and not have to talk directly with the guy. He decided to call on the house phone and pay for it when he checked out. He squeezed the receiver handle for a long moment before he dialed. The line clicked.

"John Marr," the voice said

He was there. Sidney froze.

"Who is this?"

Sidney licked his lips but didn't speak.

"Sidney, that you?"

"I was going to leave you a message."

"Surprise, surprise. Lucky you. Got me in person. I'm working late. That's how you get ahead, if you're interested." When there was no response to his tip for success, John Marr said, "Well, Sidney, can't say that I've been expecting your return call. Usually you don't—call back. Got my message, did you? One I left on your home machine?"

"Yeah, got it. How'd you find me?"

"Ah, my little secret."

"Nina Beeman."

"Nice gal. And so helpful. With a good friend trying to locate his buddy, she couldn't have been nicer."

"Why you doing this? Tormenting me isn't going to get you your money any faster. I'm only making so much."

"Torment? That's a serious word. That what you're feeling, tormented? Hope so, Sidney, surely do." John Marr's voice lowered. "Because you owe me more than money. You owe me a piece of my reputation, a chunk of humiliation. I endured disgrace because of you—"

"I've heard all that." Sidney raised his voice. "Get off it. I owe you, and I'm paying. Give me some slack, and you'll get it all and then some. Just quit this harassment. I mean it."

After a moment John Marr cleared his throat and said, "You threatening me, Sidney? I sure hope you are. Gets my juices going thinking of old Sidney fighting back. Man needs a psyched-up adversary, someone worthy of the contest. And frankly, Sid old boy, you've been pathetic so far."

"What you mean, so far? This some kind of game to you?"

"Oh yeah. And we're still in the first quarter."

"You son of a bitch."

"Now, now," John Marr chuckled, and Sidney could hear ice against glass and the tinge of a slur in the man's voice. "Why be so riled, Sidney? After all, you scored first, ran the ball back. I never laid a hand on you. Rocked me."

"Why you doing this?" Sidney asked again. "Why keep poking at me?"

"Because," John Marr's voice went down several octaves, "and listen to this now, you little piss-ant—it's because I can and it amuses me. And it's payback."

Sidney was sitting on the edge of the bed, leaning forward, elbows on his thighs, one hand pressing the receiver to his ear. He stood up slowly and turned in a circle. "Be careful the games you play," he said, swallowing against the quiver in his throat.

"Ah, the prey is fighting back," said John Marr. "I like it. I'm even getting aroused. Go, Sidney."

"Get off it. Leave me alone." Sidney slammed the receiver down just as John Marr was beginning a mocking comeback.

Seconds later his cell phone chirped. Sidney hesitated before thumbing the connect button. He didn't speak.

"Yep," said John Marr, "got your cell number now, too. I'm on you like smell on goat cheese, Sidney. Get used to it."

"I can turn it off."

"Yeah, but I'll still be there when you get curious. You know, when you're dying to see if I left you a message. Me and all my happy little messages. Now don't you worry—I can find you wherever you are. Sleep tight."

Then the connection was dead. Sidney held the phone in his hand and swore.

It was impossible to sleep, what with John Marr in his head and the cheap little refrigerator thrumming. At about two, he scooted up in bed, used the remote to turn on the television, and found an old Gregory Peck movie, a thing called Mirage. A man suffering amnesia can't figure out why people are out to get him. Sidney knew the feeling. He made coffee with the miniature Mr. Coffee knockoff in the room and sat up until light began to seep in around the drapes. He had dozed on and off but never really slept. John Marr and what to do about him had set up house-keeping in his head, and he couldn't give it a rest.

———•———

Around six Sidney showered, shaved over a mottled ugly brown epoxy sink, reassessed his lean face pockmarked from teenage acne, palmed his thinning hair, dressed, and packed. It was still dark outside, and misty; but, standing in the parking lot, Sidney could look up in the gloom and make out the huge skeletal outline of the Astoria-Megler Bridge in the distance. Its Erector Set image rose high above the highway and connected Oregon to the state of Washington; it spanned the mouth of the Columbia River—the longest continuous truss bridge in North America. As Sidney loaded the Caddy, he toyed with a fleeting temptation to take the bridge and leave his demons behind. But he slammed the trunk lid closed, went to turn in his room key and pay for the one long-distance call he'd made to John Marr. He found the Astoria Coffee House open early, nibbled on a cinnamon and walnut scone, washed it down with two cups of black coffee, and read nearly every word in the Portland paper. It was still only eight o'clock after all that. When he drove back down Commercial Street, the red Datsun pickup was parked right where he'd left it in front of Beulah's Sand and Sea; the shop was locked up tight. He held a hand up to the front door window and peered in, rattled the door handle, and rapped a knuckle on the glass. Nothing came of it. He was knocking again when an old man walking his dog paused against a straining leash to note the obvious: that the place wouldn't open until ten—said so on the door.

Sidney nodded a silent agreement, strolled away down the block, and wandered the streets. He approached the river, looked across its broadness as the wind skipped off the water and stirred his hair; he patted the strands back down. With every step he stewed over the things currently aligned to test his resolve: tracking through a dead salesman's territory, trying to drum up business over his ashes while being hounded by a sadist. As he

55

stood at the waterfront gazing out across the Columbia River, he wondered if there was a way he could put an end to John Marr's persecution.

Since he had all of one hundred and twenty-three dollars in a non-interest-bearing savings account, paying Marr off in one lump was not an option. He had thought before of borrowing the money from Ellie but decided against it. She had enough money, and he knew she would do it—thought she would any-way—but the humiliation would be too much. But enduring John Marr's bullying was becoming too sickening. Was he low enough, disgusting enough, that he could grovel before his ex-wife's smugness and not feel the mortification? He thought he could, but then he wouldn't.

————•————

On his way back to the car, Sidney paused in front of Beulah Strong's shop, scribbled a *Nice to have met you* note on the back of a business card, and slid it under the door to the shop along with an order form. Right on nine o'clock, he made a call on Seafarer's Treasure Chest down on the pier and found the shop open. The owner, a handsome woman who appeared to be of Middle Eastern decent, didn't ask about Jonesy, so he didn't offer the grim news and instead managed to squeeze out a descent order before heading south on 101. Time to start hitting his stride because he could visualize Ned Beeman behind his desk chewing Rolaids and drinking scotch.

His first stop after Astoria netted a measly order of a dozen Oregon Coast coffee mugs in Gearhart. The woman who owned a tiny gift shop there, one that specialized in aromatics and hand-woven goods, tsked dryly about Jonesy dying; she said she'd pray for him. When Sidney offered her a red-hot special from Ned Beeman's dump-it list, bright orange epoxy starfish and some scented votive candles, she frowned her answer. So much for the bereavement edge. Maybe Beulah Strong had been the anguish peak of the Jonesy funeral tour; one could only hope.

That gave Sidney solace until he'd wheeled up Broadway in Seaside, a promenade of tee shirt vendors, bumper cars, eateries, and trinket shops. In spite of a fine cool mist the street was fairly busy for a Wednesday, with young males and females parading, looking and being looked upon amid a smattering of young parents wrestling strollers and hyper energy.

Courter's Curios was wedged into a spot between a kite shop and a taffy puller. It was crammed with ticky-tacky; on this day, St. Patrick's Day, smiling leprechauns were taped to the windows, and green crepe paper streamers were draped about. The woman he assumed was the manager, a trim brunette with short hair and a delicate mouth, was waiting on a large woman. Sidney stood back and sorted through a rack of little license plates with first names on them—no Sidneys. He watched until the customer waddled out with three sand buckets and miniature shovels then approached and introduced himself, went through the *Jonesy has passed ain't it awful bit,* and waited for the woman's reaction. At first, tiny wrinkles formed between her eyebrows, then her chin dropped and sadness crept into her eyes. Sidney suggested that he buy her a cup of coffee. Her amber eyes assessed his face for a moment before she told a too-smiley assistant that she would be back in a little bit. The young woman said *sure* three times and grinned at actually being left in charge.

Paige Peterson was her name. She led the way to an espresso shop off the main drag next to a bookshop; they sat outside on the sidewalk in the mist under an awning so that she could smoke. Sidney went inside and ordered two lattes. Paige Peterson had already smoked her first cigarette down to the filter by the time he came back out. He put the paper cups down and sat on a tiny metal chair with a mesh seat; his rump needed more seat and less ventilation.

She snubbed out the smoldering filter and sat looking out into the street. "So Jonesy's dead," she said. "You know what I think at times like this? I think of how there goes another one. One more person I didn't get around to saying how I felt about them. One more person I won't see again—ever." She looked at Sidney for the first time since they'd left the shop. "You know?"

"Don't you suppose he knew?" When she looked at him blankly, he added, "What you thought of him, I mean?"

A smile edged onto her delicate mouth. "That's a guy's way of looking at it. Like saying, *You know I love you,* without ever really saying it out loud. Haven't you ever had someone confirm their feelings for you, I mean really *say* it?"

"Not often. Not like that, anyway. Had a bunch tell me off." He grinned while considering that Ellie had never really reciprocated when he'd told her that he loved her—not her style.

Paige Peterson looked at him without blinking then shook her head and pulled out another cigarette. "Well that says something...I guess."

"So," Sidney said, "what would you tell Jonesy if you had the chance?"

She dropped her lighter back in her purse, took the cigarette out of her mouth, tipped her head back and blew smoke away from them. "Never mind," she said, "too late."

"Really, I'd like to know."

She shook her head and sipped her latte.

"It's been interesting," he said. "You know, coming along behind someone who's just died. People's responses, I mean."

She squinted at him. "How'd it happen?"

"Heart, I guess."

She nodded and sucked. "Figures." Smoke came out of her mouth when she spoke.

"Did you know him long?"

"Couple of years." She inhaled. "Couple of bitch years."

Sidney licked milk foam off his lips and watched Paige Peterson decide if she was going to say more to this perfect stranger. That was when his cell phone rang. He said sorry and stepped away from the table.

"Sidney my man, how you doing?"

It was John Marr.

"I'm with a customer," he breathed into the phone.

"So?"

"Are you a mental case, John? Don't call me."

"You'll think mental case, asshole. I can call you whenever I like. I own your pathetic little soul."

"We'll see about that. I'm about to come up with the whole amount," Sidney fabricated. "Then you'll have to go play with yourself for sadistic entertainment." With that he held the end button down until the phone died.

The store manager was on her third cigarette when Sidney sat back down. "Sorry," he said.

"He deserved to know that he got me through it," she went right on.

"It?"

She came out of her thoughts and stared at Sidney.

"Never mind. So what are you pushing this trip? Bet you got some junk Beeman's trying to dump." She smiled. "Jonesy and I used to laugh over Beeman's line...then I'd order a bunch of it anyway."

"How's this work with you? At Courter's, I mean. Does each Courter's store order its own merchandise or what?"

Paige Peterson looked at him and raised her eyebrows. "Just sent you off, did they? No manual, no directions or anything?"

"All in Jonesy's head. I'm winging it. Last time I was on the road I was selling toilet bowl cleaner. And that's been awhile."

She laughed and jammed the half-smoked cigarette into the ashtray. "Here," she said holding out a hand, "you have your order form? I'll fill it in. Got anything new that isn't crap?"

"You said bitch years. Something to do with the store?"

She took the order form from him and laid it on the table. "No, real life."

"Oh. That."

59

"Yeah. That." She hesitated. " A divorce."

Sidney watched Paige Peterson scan down the order form and every so often write in a number. *Jonesy the therapist,* he thought. If this kept up, he wagered he would have a support group by the time he finished the trip. Hell, maybe Jonesy had already formed one.

"There," she said and slid the order form over to him.

"Thanks. Order any Iggys?"

She smiled. "Always keep a few Iggys in stock. Orders from the boss man. Nostalgia, I guess. Mugs, I sell a few Iggy mugs and occasional platter."

Sidney looked at the order form. "Did you see the new Iggy plush toy?"

She smiled again. "Uh-huh. Ordered a couple. If they sell I'll get more."

"How about some Mexican jewelry, have a few nice items. You want to look at those?" He pulled a plastic bag with samples out of his case.

She fingered them, held a necklace strand up and draped it over her hand. "Okay, give me a dozen each of the necklaces and six each of the bracelets."

Sidney wrote in the numbers and drained the last of his latte. "I've been down that road." When she wrinkled her forehead, he said, "Divorce."

"Yeah? Well, who hasn't?"

"I gather that Jonesy was a sympathetic ear?"

She started to paw in her purse for another cigarette. "More than that."

"Really?"

She thumbed her Bic lighter and looked at him over the flame. "Yeah, really. But not what you're thinking."

"What? No wait—I didn't mean anything. Honestly," he added.

She lit up and shook her head. "Whatever."

"Another latte?" he asked.

She shook a watch from under the sleeve of her burgundy blazer and checked the time. "Okay, why not? Quiet day, doing business here. Sure. Make it a mocha this time."

When Sidney came back with her mocha and a black coffee for him, Paige Peterson was snubbing out her cigarette seemingly lost in thought. He set her drink down, settled slowly onto the little chair again, and sipped from his cup.

"He reminded me that I was a person of value." She spoke without looking at Sidney. "That's what he did for me. And he listened."

Sidney remembered, when Ellie had walked out, just how much he had needed someone to listen to his side of things, how he was suffering like no one ever had in the history of the world. Thing was, the only ones who would listen were women needing to unload their own misery right back—and usually needing another drink.

"Yeah," Sidney said, "listening. It's a real art."

She turned her head. "I was ready to kill myself. Knew how I was going to do it, had it planned out. In my mind it was a done deal. Then this overweight, cigar-smoking salesman takes me to dinner and listens to my tale of woe." She chuckled. "I got drunk and told him I didn't want to live. Know what he said? Would I please give him an order first?" They laughed.

"Kind of took the edge off doing yourself in, I gather."

"Yeah. Even seemed silly after that." She blew her nose on a paper napkin. "Good old Jonesy."

"So you're okay now? Life's good?"

She shrugged and swallowed some mocha. "Getting there. But yeah, mostly."

"Probably already have a new person in your life."

"You mean like a woman isn't whole unless she has a man?"

"No, not at all. It's just that you're an attractive woman, good personality, and—"

"And I suppose you'd like to be nice to me."

"What?" Sidney sat up quickly, tipped over his coffee, and jumped up as it dribbled through the metal mesh tabletop and pooled raggedly on the sidewalk.

Paige Peterson stood up and stepped back and watched as Sidney daubed at the table with a napkin. "I've been hit on by some real charmers," she said, "creeps with smiles. And let me tell you—there was only one Jonesy, and that isn't you."

She smiled a patronizing smile and left Sidney with puddle of coffee at his feet.

-7-

When Sidney drove into Cannon Beach, Paige Peterson's rejection over his supposed come-on was still pecking at him. He'd never figured out how to process a perceived insult never delivered; mostly they were hit-and-run encounters with no fair way to offer a refutation. After chewing on the matter for the short drive from Seaside, he shook it off with a grumble, parked the Cadillac in a public parking lot, and walked into the upscale beach town, noting that even mid week in March a healthy number of visitors from the city were wandering about on the main street. They came to walk the beach, take a peek at Haystack Rock when hospitable, shop and eat—mostly to shop and eat. In a loamy-smelling garden shop, a lanky woman with whipcord hands and forearms and a sour disposition groaned about the economy then ordered a selection of Mexican planter pots anyway, but scoffed at the bargains. Sidney didn't bother to say anything about Jonesy; she hadn't asked about him anyway.

At José's Imports, a Mexican-themed gift shop, a reddish-faced man who looked more Irish than Hispanic gave Sidney a big order of everything Mexican, plus a few of Iggy items.

Out on the street, a stiff breeze met him; people he met going the other way had zipped up their jackets, put on baseball caps, pulled up hoods, and kept right on going—intrepid in their shopping. Sidney hustled on to the next block and the Cannon Beach edition of Courter's Curios. The manager, an egg-shaped woman half a foot shorter than Sidney, stood close to him and tipped her head back.

"You asked to see me?" Her voice came from somewhere south of alto.

Sidney stepped back. "If you're Molly Maguire."

"I am," she answered. "And don't say it. I've heard every coal-mining gag about the Molly Maguires that there is."

"Okay." He smiled in defense. "I'm Sidney Lister. Beeman's International?"

"You don't say." Molly Maguire rested her hands in the scoop pockets of a maroon apron that rode high on her oversized breasts.

He watched the woman's eyes narrow in question. "*Where's Jonesy,* you're wondering." He counted to three, inhaled, and said, "Sorry, but he's passed."

The woman grunted and did a complete turn. "I knew you were going to say that," she said. "Drat."

"I'm the grim reaper's messenger of bad tidings on this trip."

She nodded. "Gad, could've sent out a notice or something. Sorry-ass way to do it, if you ask me."

"Just happened day before yesterday. Hasn't been much time to—you know—get the word out."

"Such a thing as email," she chided then waved it off. "Musta been his old ticker that got him, right?"

Sidney nodded. "Seems so."

She shook her head. "And so business is business, and here you are."

"Gave me the keys to Jonesy's company Caddy. Told me to hit the road."

Molly Maguire looked at the floor. "Geez Laweez. Well, he was quite a guy. Real character. I'll miss him." She raised a hand to her mouth.

"I hardly knew him myself. Him being on the road most of the time. You customers knew him better than me."

Molly Maguire bobbed her head and pulled a wadded tissue out of her apron pocket and dabbed first one eye then the next. She smiled meekly and said, "Weddings and funerals, you know. You start remembering stuff." She blew into the tight wad and swabbed at her nose. "Come on," she said and led him into a small storage room at the back of the store where she offered him the only chair and she sat on a stack of unopened cartons that teetered under her weight.

She sat quiet for a long moment then laughed. "He could be a rascal. Liked the ladies and liked to drink. Nearly broke up a couple of marriages around here." When Sidney raised his eyebrows she said, "Hard to imagine huh? Fat old guy. I know, hard to figure—but he had his way, I tell you. Yeah, hard to figure. Good listener, for one thing."

"That right?"

She nodded hard. "Yep, that and feeling the vibes, you know. Sensing how a person was doing, how they were feeling." She stared off again. "Take me, for instance. My Harv, he up and died on me going on a year and a half ago. Seventeen months and two weeks it's been." She sniffed and inhaled and looked at the ceiling. "Geez Laweez, thought I'd got over this part. Sorry."

Sidney smiled and looked away.

"Specially since Harvey was a sometimes bastard." She snorted a laugh. "But like they say, he was my bastard. Anyways, we never got around to making up a will. Call that intestate. You learn stuff like that when you screw up. Makes a mess of things when you don't have a will, let me tell you. Jonesy saved my ass." She pointed a finger. "Don't laugh. Talking figuratively here, not about this real ass." She reached back and slapped her rump.

Sidney chuckled and held his hands up in surrender.

The woman looked up in thought. "Jonesy came to town a week after the funeral. I was back at work but a mental wreck.

65

Took me for a drink, listened to me blubber, then called a lawyer friend of his in Portland who made me up a *get out of jail* card. Even paid for it."

"The lawyer's fee, paid for that?" said Sidney. "Really?"

"Yep," said Molly Maguire. "Joked that he'd put it on his expense account. *Customer service,* he said. It came outa his own pocket, I'm sure."

Sidney nodded but he'd bet it hadn't. "Well," he said, "I don't smoke cigars, but I can buy you a drink. Game?"

Molly Maguire looked at her watch. "Not even noon."

Sidney grinned. "How about coffee, then? 'Course I'm speaking of Spanish coffee. Strictly business, just like Jonesy."

Molly Maguire liked Spanish coffee just fine and liked to order merchandise as well. Except for Beulah Strong, Jonesy's dying had so far been good for business. Sidney was rehearsing his death and dying routine when he entered the small Courter's Curios in Manzanita. But Esther Watson wasn't about to tumble for a salesman's silly-ass smile. She was sipping a cup of herbal tea at the counter when Sidney stood back to let a customer pass him at the door then ambled in all loose and obvious. Esther Watson wore her hair long and braided in a strand that hung over one shoulder down over a hand-knitted gray sweater and narrow chest. She looked at Sidney as if he was about to pass gas.

"May I help you?" Her voice was disinterested and her eyes even more so.

"Yes, I'm Sidney Lister with Beeman's International?" His offered hand hung in the air.

"Are you?" She sipped from her flowery mug, the steam rising past her face.

"Yes." He lowered his hand and brought out one of his hand-lettered cards. She looked at it, turned it over, and set it aside for later disposal. "You've been dealing with Jonesy Jones?" he said.

"Mr. Jones has called on the shop," she answered. "Are you replacing him?"

"I am." Sidney did his count before saying, "You see, he's passed on."

Esther Watson set her cup down and stared at Sidney, her expression painfully neutral. "I see," she said. Nothing else.

"It was quite sudden—a shock, actually."

"I'm sure."

"Yeah, a shock." Sidney cleared his throat and placed the ordering form on the counter. "Anyway, I've been pressed into duty to cover his territory."

She sipped again from her mug but said nothing.

"Would you have a few minutes to go over an order and maybe consider some of our specials?"

"We always order from your company, don't we? Just like we always carry those Iggy things."

Sidney squinted. "Is there a problem? I'm sorry—is it Ms. or Mrs. Watson?"

"Esther will be fine. Problem? No. Now is as good a time as any. Is it the usual order form? I assume so. If so, I can tell you exactly what I'll order."

Sidney fingered the form. "I guess it's the same one. We do have some specials and a few new items. Jonesy, he would've had all this down cold, but—"

She raised a hand. "I don't want to hear about the man's demise. Please don't."

"Sure. Sorry. I know death is a hard matter."

She offered no response.

"So, would you like to tell me what you usually order, then, or shall we go over each item? How do you—?"

"Oscar," she said, cutting him off again.

"Pardon?"

"His real name was Oscar."

"That's right. But most everybody called him Jonesy."

"I disliked that silly nickname. When we did business I called him Oscar."

"I see," he said. *You and Beulah Strong have dibs on that,* he thought.

"Yes, well, that's the way it was."

Sidney closed the order form and felt it coming on, the Jonesy thing taking form.

Esther Watson plucked a loose piece of fuzz from her sweater and rolled it between her fingers and looked at it. She hummed a small laugh, the kind one emits when considering something not quite funny.

"He was an abuser," she said and looked up at Sidney. "Oscar. He was an abuser."

"I'm sorry, I don't understand. Abuser?"

"Oh, not like that. He was an abuser of life. He abused his body. The environment. His brain. Time, even. He didn't think there were consequences." She cupped her hands around the mug of tea. "Now he knows that there are, or *perhaps* he knows."

"Who knows?" Sidney said and smiled.

The woman didn't smile at his rejoinder. "He was so obvious—abusers are, anyway. Waddles into this shop like the poster child for gluttony, steaming away on one of his smelly cigars. And that, that boat of a car. Was all I could do to keep from running him out of the place, that and laughing my head off, like maybe somebody put him up to it." She paused. "But they hadn't—he was the real McCoy."

"Hadn't thought of him that way," Sidney said. "It's been odd, but most folks I've called on liked him. Some even adored the guy. Hard to believe, I guess. But you're right, probably abused himself to death."

Esther Watson drew herself up. "Disrespect hangs well on no one, Mister..." she picked up his card, "Mister Lister. Sullying someone's memory is shameful."

"What? Wait a second—I'm not sullying anybody's memory. I was only agreeing with your observation. Actually, I hardly knew they guy. Besides, sounded to me like you weren't too respectful of him yourself."

"I would like you to leave, sir. If you please."

"What?"

"I'll fill out the order."

Sidney stepped back and studied the woman. Her face was flushed now, and her eyes were clouded. He started nodding his head. "Okay," he said. "Okay, I get it."

"You get what?" Her voice had thickened.

"I get it that you cared for the guy." She stared back at him, her face frozen but blooming red at her cheeks and in the whites of her eyes. "I'm sorry," he said.

"You know nothing." She raised a forefinger and wiped the corner of one eye. "Just leave. I'll put the completed order form under the mat at the front door. Don't come back in the shop, not today."

He tried to say again that he was sorry, but she only waved an arm for him to be on his way.

Jonesy's trail of tears. How'd that happen?

-8-

He waited on Esther Watson in the Sand Dollar Café up the street, loitered over the remains of his turkey and Swiss sandwich, the dill pickle he hadn't eaten, the ice tea with melted ice cubes, and shuffled and reshuffled his thin sheaf of orders. It had begun to rain, one of those fine straight-down rains that look benign but soak you through in the time it takes to walk across the street. He wasn't really reading the print on the order forms. They were merely a blurred distraction as he ruminated over the vapor trail of Jonesy's exit. He didn't have it in him to tolerate more elucidations of either the heroics or the affairs of the dead man; he was only a stand in. Then again, what choice did he have?

He switched to black coffee and sat sipping and stared out into the penetrating mist and waited until he thought enough time had elapsed before driving back to the gift shop. The order was there, peeking out from beneath a large cocoa mat on the porch of the shop. Sidney plucked it up and left without looking through the window, but when he was backing away he saw Esther Watson standing behind the glass door watching. He didn't wave.

In Rockaway Beach, he parked off 101 next to the town's information center, housed in a bright red caboose. He checked to see that his cell phone had a signal before calling the office. Nina Beeman answered on the first ring and ripped into him for not

70

calling earlier; then Ned Beeman was on the line barking about where the hell he was. Sidney listened and watched a man and woman walk by arm in arm under an umbrella and wondered if there was a single person he knew who'd be glad to hear from him. Anyone who would simply say, *Hey Sid, how the hell are you?* Anyone.

"I'm in Rockaway," he answered, when Ned finally took a breath.

"That's it? At this rate I'll be on Medicare by the time you get this done."

"Nice talking to you too, Ned. You want to run on down and take over from here all the way to Brookings? Been fun so far. Telling everybody that Jonesy's expired. Want to do it—take over?"

Ned exhaled into the mouthpiece. "Take it easy. Just wondering how we're doing out there is all."

"All right, we're doing all right. You gotta know, Ned, that not only am I trying to get orders, I'm on a grieving run here, too. Have to look every one of these people in the eye and tell them Jonesy's dead. Then I have to hang my face and wait out each person's reaction to the news before I can flip out an order form."

Ned hummed. "Yeah, okay. Hadn't thought of that. So how're people taking it…the news of him dying and all?"

A seagull landed on the hood of the Seville. Sidney tapped the horn, and it rose up and flapped away. "You wouldn't believe it."

"Suppose. Well, forget the bereavement report for now—you can tell me later. How's business?"

"I did zippo with that shop in Astoria, the Sand and Sea. Other than that we're doing okay. Jonesy croaking has actually been good for orders. Maybe next trip I'll die. Give me a bonus for that?"

"Geez, don't talk like that. Gives me the creeps."

"Fact is Jonesy left a trail of sadness and broken hearts behind him. You believe that? There was something different about the old goat. I can't figure."

"Hell, every salesman's got his gimmicks. It's simple—the good times and the yaks sell more stuff. By the way, that woman in Astoria? What's her name?"

"Strong? Yeah, Beulah Strong."

"That's the one. She called in an order."

"You kidding me?"

"Nope. Even said to say hello to you. Ordered more than usual, too. What'd you do, sleep with her?"

Sidney scoffed but thought of sad Beulah and her big teeth. He sparred with Ned for a bit longer, promised to fax the orders next chance he got, and ended the call with a sigh. His cell was letting him know that he had messages—messages he had no interest in listening to, but he did anyway.

When John Marr's voice filled Sidney's ear, he shuddered and, after hearing more of the same fiendish invectives, punched delete. Sidney leaned his head against the headrest and closed his eyes and calmed himself before listening to the next message.

It wasn't John Marr. It was a woman's voice he didn't recognize. He sat up when she began to speak. There was reason to. He saved the message and restarted it.

"Mr. Lister, my name is Ginny Snyder." At first she spoke like a schoolteacher, no nonsense. "I've been John Marr's executive secretary for the last eleven years. Or I was, I should say." Then her voice became shaky. "Last week I was fired. Would you please call me? There is something you need to know." She recited her number.

Before leaving Rockaway Beach, Sidney made a couple of cold calls to shops not on the list and came up empty on one. He opened a new account with the other, a bead shop; the owner mostly wanted Mexican jewelry. With his head still churning over the cryptic message from the Snyder woman, he made a quick call on Hal's Shells and Rocks before heading south. Hal was a huge man in a wheelchair who was crestfallen to hear of Jonesy's death. Hal and Jonesy had spent many an afternoon sipping beer, chewing over the issues of life, and playing check-ers. *I swear to heaven,* Sidney thought, *I'm going to write a book and call it* The Jonesy Factor. Hal bit on the orange epoxy star-fish special and assorted other ticky-tack, and Sidney left him swallowing hard over losing his once-in-a-while drinking and checker buddy.

The tone of Ginny Snyder's voice stuck in his head like an *Urgent you call home* message, the kind that lies like a cold snake in the gut. It was only mid-afternoon, but after a moderately successful call at the Tillamook Creamery gift shop, he checked into a low-budget motel on 101 and considered returning Ginny Snyder's call. What if it was a trick? Something John Marr had contrived to pull Sidney's chain even more?

Sidney paced his motel room and stared through a sweating window out onto the highway. He stepped off the room in mea-sured strides twice more, took a leak, and entered in the numbers on his cell phone. After four rings a woman answered.

"This Mrs. Snyder?" Sidney asked.

"Yes." Her voice was hesitant. "Who is this?"

Sidney inhaled and sat on the edge of the bed. "I'm returning your call. I'm Sidney Lister."

"Oh." She didn't say more, just *Oh.*

"I got your message." Sidney could hear her breathing. "How'd you get this number, by the way?"

"A woman at your company," she almost whispered. "I told her it was a family emergency. I lied."

"I see." When she didn't go on, he said, "Sorry about your job."

"Yes…well."

"Must have been a shock."

"It was." Her tone became firm.

He decided to wait her out, but the dead air was too much. "You said there's something I should know," he said.

She coughed then said, "No, I was wrong. I'm sorry to have

73

inconvenienced you, Mr. Lister. It…it was nothing. I shouldn't have troubled you."

"Wait. Mrs. Snyder, why did you call me? Who do you think I am? I mean, I'm not a customer of John Marr's company."

There was a pause. "Oh, I know who you are, Mr. Lister. And I am sorry for you."

"Sorry? Why ever would you be sorry for me?" Sidney laughed.

"For years I was closer to John Marr than his wife. I choreographed his life, you might say. He counted on me." Her voice trailed off; then she came back stronger. "I knew everything, Mr. Lister. When you are good at the job I had, you are often invisible. And I was good at my job, you see. I heard everything. I knew everything, really. So yes, I know all about John's vendetta against you, sir. About the sick sport he is having, playing with your life."

"I see. And now he's fired you."

"Yes." The hiss in her voice chilled Sidney. "Culled out like an old cow. I turned sixty this year. John wants to think he's still thirty-five. Dyes his hair. Even thinking about plastic surgery for his sagging jowl. Right after the office party for my sixtieth, he started in. *Morning Granny.* Holding my elbow in front of folks like I was doddering. It was a campaign of treachery…just like yours, Mr. Lister."

"Sidney."

"Yes." She paused. "He's a cold-hearted bastard, Sidney."

"It must have been distasteful working for a man like that."

"The money was good," she replied. "I went along, I'm sorry to say, looked past the man's cheating and cruelness. At least I did until last Friday."

"But age discrimination, he can't do that."

"Oh there's nothing in writing. Nothing discriminatory. No, in writing it's all about a new direction for the company. No pension, but I was given a good severance package."

"But that's not it, is it?"

"Thrown away, Sidney. You know what it feels like to be thrown away?"

Fact is, he did. "I can imagine."

"No…I doubt you can."

For a long moment, nothing was said.

"I'm sorry, of course," Sidney broke the silence, "but why did you call me?"

"I don't know. My husband says I oughtn't to do this. Maybe he's right."

Sidney stood and stared wide-eyed at the floor. "Do what, Mrs. Snyder? What is it?"

"I don't know, I don't know, maybe—"

"What? Say it…it's okay." He waited for her to hang up on him, but she didn't. "Ginny, I figure this is about getting back at the guy. Right? That's okay. I mean…it's okay…to tell me."

"He gets what he wants," she said in a voice of resignation. "Always has. Pushed, shoved, ran over people—but he got it, whatever it was. But you, Sidney, you *got* him." She laughed softly. "Stung him good, you did."

"I'm not a thief—it's just that I was broke. I…"

"Oh I know that. I know it all, remember. I sensed you were an honorable person caught in a bind. But that didn't matter—John wanted revenge. You became a sick pastime for him. An obsession, really. How he would cackle over his scheme of torment and tell me every detail.

"But there is something else," she said. "Something disreputable way beyond his toying with you. It is your chance, Sidney. Your chance to rid yourself of John Marr."

———•———

Sidney listened to Ginny Snyder. She first made him promise that he never let on where he heard what she was about to tell him. *Never, ever,* she insisted. He promised. Then he listened, and he heard his release from bondage.

Ginny Snyder had enacted her revenge.

-9-

The next morning, Sidney woke with a beating headache, downed four Excedrin, toyed with a short-stack of buckwheats at a local pancake house, and left them behind only half-eaten. He had no appetite. His mind was still in turmoil over what Ginny Snyder had revealed to him about John Marr. He bought coffee to go, wandered into Flora's Paper & Gifts, and stood mute before the willowy woman who owned the store. After blinking back the ache in his head, he swallowed the last of his coffee, and finally admitted who he was and why he was there, for which he received the predictable *Oh my* and turned-down mouth. However, after two heavy sighs, the woman set aside her moment of grief, ordered a nice selection of hand-tooled leather-bound blank pages notebooks, and gave Sidney a sympathetic pat on the hand. He left Tillamook like he'd entered it, sick to his stomach, head throbbing but somehow feeling a sense of relief; in a way, Ginny Snyder had given him a gift.

Just south of the town known for its yellow cheddar, brilliant green pastures rolled out. And rising up behind them, like a gargantuan Quonset hut, stood a World War II blimp hangar, covering seven acres, standing fifteen stories high, with huge black letters painted on its sides shouting AIR MUSEUM. There were patches of blue in the sky, peering out from among enormous white clouds. Sidney opened the side window and took in the brisk air as he passed pasture after pasture of grazing dairy cows amid falling-down barns, spiffed-up barns, and working barns.

In Pacific City, he cajoled a decent order for Mexican vases out of an art gallery that sold gifts to pay the rent then found a real estate office that had a fax machine. The woman on duty, who was spending her days trying to sell time-shares to beach bunnies from the city, agreed to let him fax his orders to Ned Beeman at a dollar a page.

Somewhere north of Lincoln City, his phone came to life and warbled its tune. Sidney swung the Cadillac off onto a view-point turnout and answered the phone—his skin crawling. But it wasn't John Marr. It was Ellie.

"My toilet's still trickling," she said. "When will you be back?"

Sidney sighed into the phone. "Geez, Ellie, you got nothing better to do than call me about your stupid john? Call a plumb-er—you can afford it. I'll be gone a while yet. Miles to go and sales to make, so call a plumber. I'll see you in a couple of weeks or whatever. Gotta go now."

"Wait, wait. Almost forgot. A guy called me, strange. Got it written down...Marr. You know a guy name of John Marr?"

"You're kidding me. He called you?"

"Yeah. Who is he?"

"He's a boil on my ass, that's what. What'd he say to you?"

"Nothing. Just to call him when you can. Nice voice."

"Yeah, well, if he calls again just hang up on him. He's de-praved."

"What's going on, Sidney? Who is that guy, anyway?"

"Never mind. Really, I've got to keep going here."

"Sidney?"

"Bye, Ellie." He pressed the phone dead and nosed the car back onto the highway.

———•———

A soft rain had begun; it picked up some wind off the Pacific Ocean and turned peevish. So much for the sun breaks. Sidney tweaked the wipers up a notch and rolled into Lincoln City around noon. He went to a little cafe he remembered, Dale's Eats; it had a counter and six booths and made a great Ruben sandwich. Or used to—not anymore. There were new owners who now specialized in teriyaki and so-called American. Sidney had a soggy burger with fries, bolted back into the rain, and slid into the Seville just in time for his cell phone to ring.

He yanked the phone out of his coat pocket and wiped at his wet face. "Yeah?"

"Sidney."

"That you, John?"

"Certainly is."

John Marr's voice smiled over the phone. His smugness was the same, but this time the sound of his voice roused new reactions in Sidney. He watched the rain sheeting down the windshield and shuddered when a chill coursed through his arms and torso. He didn't know what to say. Should he even let on about what he knew?

"Sidney, you still there?"

"I'm here."

"You sound a bit down. Am I ruining your day? Hope so."

Sidney hesitated then spoke before thinking. "I'd like to ruin your day."

"Woo, strong comeback, Sid old boy. So what is it? You got my money, that it?"When Sidney didn't respond, John Marr said, "Don't tell me. You're gonna kill yourself." His laugh was coarse.

"No. But I considered putting out a contract on your life. Couple of people offered to do it for free."

"Okay, sport, have your fun and games. But don't get too cute, or I may call in some chips and have you up on charges. Me and 150 of my closest friends. "

"You low-life bastard." Sidney scooted up in the seat, nervous and tingling.

"Hey, I'm losing my finely tuned sense of humor here. Playing with your life is a lot of fun, best I've ever had, but I'll only take so much crap outa you."

"Let me ask you something," Sidney cut in.

"Oh yeah, what's that?"

Sidney took in a deep breath and gripped the steering wheel. "How long has it been since you've seen Heather Cole?"

The hesitation made Sidney hold his breath.

"Don't know anyone by that name," Marr said after a moment.

"That right? Played softball—a pitcher. All league, right?"

"Wouldn't know." Marr's voice had become the kind a person uses when the IRS is on the line and it's not a courtesy call.

Sidney shifted his bottom on the leather seat. He licked his lips and said, "I don't believe you." When Marr didn't respond, Sidney began to feel some slight control over the situation. "You've been a bad boy, John. Very bad. Haven't you?"

"So what is this? You all of a sudden sassing me, Sidney? I wouldn't push my good side too far. I haven't got time for this nonsense."

"Hey *you* called me, John. All set to put the screws to my gonads again, weren't you? So you have time to listen to me and answer some more questions about Heather."

"Don't know what you think you're doing here, Sidney. Don't have a clue."

Sidney turned on the ignition so he could lower the driver-side window a crack; the car was fogging up. He clenched his teeth and decided to lay it all out. "You're a sicko—you know that? A rock-bottom slime ball. Tormenting me was low, but diddling a fifteen-year-old girl—damn. Why'd you do that, coach?"

"Coach? What you talking about?"

"John, John, John, I know. I *know*, John—get it? I know you coached the Argonauts. I know you had relations with that poor girl. John, you listening?"

"I'm here," he said with a leaden voice.

"And…John, I know the rest of it."

A low hum drifted into Sidney's ear.

"You know, I've never amounted to a whole lot," Sidney said, "not like I had planned on. Not a big tycoon like you, John-Boy, not even close. Big plans, I had big plans, but I've always been a day short on execution. So yeah, I'm a weenie. But I never fucked little girls!"

Sidney sat up and pounded a fist on the steering wheel causing the horn to burp. A man and woman passing jumped and frowned. Sidney waved and tried to smile.

"Look, Sidney," Marr said, his voice beseeching, "you're right. It was wrong. But, hey, it was just one of those things, came and went, over. No harm, no foul. Lost my head for sure, but it's over."

Sidney swallowed sour saliva and thought about not saying it but couldn't keep from it. "She's dead," he squawked. "Think I don't know that? The girl's dead, the fetus is dead, you bastard." Sidney reared up again and shouted into the phone. "She killed herself because of your dick!"

After a moment's silence, Marr said, "How you know all this?"

"That's all you can say?"

"Must have been Ginny."

"Who's that?" Sidney felt a chill; he didn't want the woman endangered.

"Yeah, Ginny Snyder."

"Don't know anyone by that name," Sidney lied. "You think I was gonna just be log-rolled by you the rest of my life, John? No way. I've been digging and scrounging, except I wasn't rooting deep enough or foul enough. Then I found it."

"Nobody knows about this." Marr's voice rose.

"You mean nobody you haven't paid off. You even paid for her funeral and the cremation, right, John?"

Marr didn't respond to Sidney blundered on.

"*Why cremation?* I wondered. She took pills, as I understand it. That right?" Again, no response. "Not like she'd disfigured herself with a gun or by jumping off a tall building. But then cremation removed the paternal DNA, didn't it? For god's sake—how'd you get her parents to go along with this sordid mess?"

"Had to be Ginny," Marr mumbled.

"Does your wife know about it, John? This *no harm, no foul* defilement of a child? This rape? She know? Your wife?"

"Stop this. You have to listen to me, Sidney, it wasn't like that. She was—"

"Heather, John, her name was Heather. Can't you use it? And she was what, coming on to you?"

"Yes, she was. That's right. You gotta believe me—she was a seductress."

"Poor, John. This child forced a big guy like you to get naked with her and put your prick into her. She bullied you into it."

"No, listen! It was…she was…oh," he groaned.

"John," Sidney said in a quiet voice, "I hear you've been nominated as Eugene's Citizen of the Year. That right? Sounds like you may even have a lock on it. Guess you've been angling for such an honor for a while now. Don't suppose the folks deciding on who's been naughty and nice would pick the one that's been the naughtiest. What do you think?"

"Sidney," Marr said, "don't do this." His voice had chilled.

Sidney put his thumb on the end-call button of his cell while Marr was still talking. He hummed out a sigh, leaned back.

He felt sick to his stomach about what he had just risked.

-10-

Lincoln City, an amalgamation of several small Oregon coastal towns that were merged into one strung-out municipality around 1965, was someone's idea of a visionary marketing strategy way back then. But many older locals still pined for the lost hamlets of Delake, Oceanlake, Taft, Cutler City, and Nelscott. The resulting phalanx of storefronts, motels, fast food restaurants, and gas stations pressed up tightly against the sidewalks on opposing sides of Pacific Coast Highway 101 stretched out for several miles. Sidney drove the length of it and back, rewinding his confrontation with John Marr. The initial feelings of justification had mostly dissolved, and he could only think of Marr's last words. *Don't do this,* he'd said, his voice tinged with a new tone of desperation. Sidney felt a small chill across his shoulders.

———•———

On a gray Thursday, the few people who were out on the Lincoln City strip were leapfrogging from store to store, trying to avoid the rain that ranged from drizzle to downpour. Sidney parked on a side street and walked to the next Courter's Curios, stuck in between an antique store and a coffee house. He walked by a window of questionable collectibles and pushed his way into a cookie-cutter replica of the other Courter's shops: same merchandise, same smells. A tall, slender woman with crinkly gray-black hair, half-glasses resting on her nose, was the manager; it turned out Selma Knight had been expecting him.

Sidney had barely gotten his name out when she said, "I know who you are." Her voice was matter of fact; she stood at attention behind the counter and seemed to be daring Sidney to disagree with her.

Sidney tilted his head. "Oh," he smiled, "is that right?"

"And I know about Jonesy," she sniffed, raised her chin, and smoothed her hand over the countertop before saying, "about him dying."

"Really? How—"

"Esther Watson. She called me." When Sidney looked confused, Selma Knight said, "She manages our store in Manzanita?"

"Ah, sure, sure, Manzanita," he said. "Saw her yesterday."

"So she said."

Sidney chuckled and reached out to finger strands of cheap necklaces hanging on a counter spinner rack. "Afraid I didn't hit it off with Esther," he said.

Selma Knight continued to stare.

"I tried." Sidney pled his case. "It's…well, it's been difficult telling people about Jonesy's passing. It happened so suddenly, and then they put me right on the road to pop in on people, tell them he's passed on, and then want to make sales—you know, all at once." He raised his arms and let them drop. "I'm sorry if—"

"Esther's just that way," Selma Knight said. "Excuse me." She took a pair of earrings from a teenage girl and rang up the sale. When they were alone again, Selma Knight said, "Esther has her own way of thinking. Mostly it's her way or the wrong way."

"Seemed that she didn't think much of Jonesy's lifestyle," Sidney offered. "But when I agreed, she practically threw me out. Hard to figure."

Selma Knight smiled for the first time. "Origami," she said.

Sidney blinked. "Excuse me?"

"You know, the Japanese art of paper folding? Origami. Flowers. Animals. Shapes. Jonesy was an expert at it. You didn't know that?"

Sidney shook his head and smiled resignedly. "An expert—at paper folding?"

"Well, he was," she said. "That's what connected him with Esther."

"Origami?" Sidney repeated. "I can barely fold a towel."

"You must be good at something."

"Nothing I'd brag about," he said. "Certainly nothing that would impress Esther Watson. But I'm beginning to collect Jonesy stories, so, please, tell me about origami."

Selma Knight smiled and nodded. "Okay. Esther, she's hard to please. Jonesy did it the hard way—by one-upping her. Esther had no use for him, until," She raised a forefinger. "Origami. Esther prides herself on being skilled at several art forms: painting, weaving, pottery, and…origami. One day Jonesy waddled in, found her practicing her paper folding, complimented her, and asked if he could try it. Esther admitted that she scoffed but gave him some paper and…well, he simply wowed her."

"And that changed everything," Sidney said.

"Absolutely," she laughed. "It was like the man had dropped 100 pounds, quit smoking, and become a vegetarian."

"So they became friends," Sidney offered.

"One of her few friends. Now she's lost him. Here, give me an order form," she said with the bit of an edge.

Sidney reached into his briefcase and handed Selma Knight the order blank and a catalog. He stood aside to let a woman buy a plastic statue of a white unicorn. After the sale, Selma Knight went back to the order form. "You know old man Courter?" she asked as she scratched out an order.

"I've not had the pleasure," Sidney answered. "Guess I'll be seeing him soon."

"Well, likely won't be a pleasure. He runs these shops hard, takes no prisoners, and treats all of us managers like we owe him our souls. Hires mostly women who need every dime and keeps us cowering in fear of his next phone call." She paused. "That descriptive enough for you?"

Sidney smiled crookedly. "Sounds like a real charmer"

"Snake charmer." The woman's face went slack for a moment. "I have my own Jonesy story for you. A few years back, my old man, Clyde? He's a long-haul trucker. Anyway, he was clear down in San Diego. Plowed his truck into a bridge abutment and was in the hospital pretty beat up. I had to get on down there. But I had nothing but high school kids working here part time—and I knew I wouldn't get any sympathy from Courter. Right then Jonesy comes calling." She smiled. "The short of it is, he ran the store for five days until I got Clyde home."

Sidney started to laugh. Selma Knight raised her eyebrows. "Sorry," he said, "it's just that I keep hearing stories about Saint Jonesy," he said. "Didn't the man ever piss on his shoes?"

"You mean like the time he groped one of my high school girls in the storeroom? That took some cleaning up, I tell you."

"That makes me feel a whole lot better."

Selma Knight tipped her head. "Glad to help."

———•———

Sidney lugged his sales case down the sidewalk and wondered if he could continue to stomach Jonesy's aftertaste. He was still mulling that over when he entered Seabird Gifts; it was on the "Has never bought" list, but what the hell? The owner, a man who appeared to be in his fifties, vaguely remembered Jonesy but offered words of condolence and gave Sidney an order, anyway. Sidney chalked it up as another bereavement sale.

At the Gleneden Beach Marketplace a few miles south, the owner of an upscale gift shop merely smiled at Sidney and proffered that she didn't carry trinkets and such things; her clientele were into style and décor. Sidney smiled, excused himself, his ears burning, and drove on to Depoe Bay. There he found two shops that did carry trinkets and such and one where the owner, a wild-haired woman, literally ran him out of the store shouting "No! No! No!" No reason was given. Sidney fell into the car laughing himself breathless; for once Jonesy hadn't been favored. He then drove on to Newport, checked into a Best Budget Lodge, ate a Kentucky Fried Chicken meal, drank the Bud Light he had bought en route, and watched television as another day on the road faded away.

He was dozing on the bed with his clothes still on when his cell phone rang; he awoke with a start, heart pounding, and reared up, knocking the box of chicken remnants onto the floor. He blinked, shook his head, and grabbed the phone before being seized with the fear that it might be John Marr. He'd been jittery after jousting with Marr earlier, nervous that he had done the wrong thing by confronting the man. What might he do? He pressed the talk button.

"Yeah?" he said and looked at his wristwatch. It was shortly after nine o'clock.

Someone coughed into his ear. "Sidney?" The voice was slurred.

"Uh-huh. What do you want, Ned?"

Ned Beeman coughed again. "Ah...where are you?" he asked.

"Newport."

"Oh," he moaned, "you there already? Doggone it."

"Why?" Sidney asked, "I miss somebody?"

Ned inhaled a ragged breath that gurgled at the end. Sidney pulled the phone away from his ear, counted to three then gingerly brought it back. Ned was mumbling something.

"What's that?" Sidney said. "I didn't get it."

"Courter. I didn't tell him."

"Tell him what?"

"About Jonesy. Didn't tell him about Jonesy dying on us."

"Hell," Sidney laughed, "you didn't tell anybody. I've been

running bare the whole way. I'm a bloody death and dying coun-selor."

Ned breathed into the mouthpiece for a long moment before spitting out, "Yeah, but it's different with Lamont. He'll...he'll take it personal. He will, I tell ya."

Sidney pinched his nose and chuckled. "So what's the worst he can do? Hold me down and tickle me?"

"Listen, asshole, this is way over your head. Hear me?" Ned snarled out of his drunken thought process.

"So, Ned, what do you want from me? Just tell me, will you?" Sidney raised his voice at the end. "Is Nina there?"

"Nina?" Ned said. "Yeah, she's right here."

"Put her on, Ned. Ned, just put Nina on the line."

There was some mumbling and fumbling and then Nina came on. "Sidney? Yes, it's me. Sorry, he's had too much...again."

Sidney took in a deep breath. "So what's this about Lamont Courter? He the angel of death or something? Ned sounds para-lyzed."

"Almost that bad," she answered then hesitated when Ned grumbled something in the background. "Ned, be still. We have no choice."

Sidney waited and listened and wondered what the hell he was doing in this melodrama. He had been in so many you'd think he'd have learned. But no, his life was a patchwork of psycho-dramas within festering little kingdoms; here he was again, this time waiting for the dark side of selling curios. He was shaking his head when Nina spoke again.

"Sidney?"

"I'm here."

"Okay," she breathed, "here's the thing. Lamont Courter he...he—"

"Nina, just say it."

"Okay," she said again. "Courter had Ned in a vise. He... Ned, he did some double billings and short shipments a while back—well a long time ago, really. Just to get us through a rough time was all. Ned had it all planned out, paying it back before Courter found out."

"Except it didn't work out that way?" Sidney said. "Right?"

Nina sighed. "No. Courter discovered everything before we could set it right and threatened to take legal action and spread the word to our other customers." She inhaled. "Would've ruined us." She paused and added, "And there was a kickback discount on every order, too."

Sidney lay back on the bed and held the phone to his ear. *Unbelievable,* he thought. *The whole world is a cesspool of one side screwing the other.* Ned Beeman had his own version of John Marr. Sidney started to laugh.

"You laughing, Sidney?" said Nina. "You think this is funny?"

Sidney sat up. "No, sorry Nina. So did Ned clean up the mess?"

"Oh yeah, way back," she answered. "It's old news, but Courter kept all the paperwork and kept threatening us with it. That was, until Jonesy took over sales."

"Then what happened?"

"We don't know. Jonesy came to Ned one day and said to forget about Courter's threats, that he had him where he wanted him and that it was over. Done deal, he said."

"So?"

There was more mumbling from Ned. "Too late for that, Ned," Nina said, her face obviously away from the phone.

"Nina?"

She took in another deep breath. "Okay, thing was Jonesy told Ned that he had Courter under his thumb because he knew something that would keep him there."

"Like what?"

"That's it," she said. "We don't know. He'd never tell Ned. Said it was his own insurance policy."

"Now it's nobody's," Sidney said. "Where's that leave us?"

"I don't know." Her voice was small. "It's been driving Ned insane. Between Jonesy dying and financial pressures, I'm afraid he's going to have a heart attack. I just don't know..." Her voice tapered off.

Sidney could hear her crying. "Nina?"

She sucked a breath in. "Yes?"

"You remember getting a phone call for me from a guy name of John Marr?"

It was a moment before Nina Beeman answered. "Yeah," she sniffed, "your friend. He ever get ahold of you?"

"Yeah," Sidney answered. "You know who he is?"

"No idea." She sounded less than patient.

"He's my Lamont Courter. He has been a threat to my sanity. John Marr has been my nightmare." Sidney forced a chuckle. "Seems like our worlds are made up of people having something on one or another of us, and the ones on top at the moment relish making their victims' lives hell."

"And I led him right to you, Sidney," she said. "I'm so sorry."

"Well, maybe this worm has turned, Nina. I'm not sure, but I think I'm about to walk away from my demon. Now we need to find out what Jonesy had on Lamont Courter."

"But how? Jonesy is..."

"He told someone," Sidney said, "probably his wife."

"Mildred?"

"Yeah, Mildred. You get on with her?"

"Yeah but she's...Ned didn't treat her very well after Jonesy died," Nina said. "You know, he was upset about the business and—"

"Did you two go to the funeral?"

She hesitated.

"Oh, that's great," Sidney said. "Well, you still have to go see her and make nice, Nina. Apologize, make up with her, and find out what Jonesy knew about Courter. She knows, Nina. Guy like Jonesy couldn't keep from bragging about something like that to

89

his wife. She knows, and you have to get it out of her somehow."

"I don't know."

"And do it tomorrow."

———•———

That's the way the conversation ended, with Nina saying Okay and Ned slurring something irrelevant in the background. Sidney stuffed the chicken box and its leavings in the wastebasket by the bed and took a quick shower; afterward he sat propped up on the bed with the television on with the sound muted. He considered. He considered that if he left right then he could be home in a few hours, turn in the Caddy, quit, and be with Ellie before morning. He also considered hanging in and taking on whatever this Lamont Courter threw at him—after all, it wasn't his company to lose.

He considered those things, but mostly his day ended with him wondering about John Marr. Marr had been shaken by Sidney's revelation that he knew of his monstrous act. If the man had felt no hesitancy about tormenting him over a mere debt, what would he do when something so heinous might threaten his status and freedom? Shortly before three, after tossing and rousing, Sidney finally fell asleep with the light and television still on.

Sidney realized that he had turned a light on the darkest corner of Marr's life.

-11-

It was at breakfast over black coffee and a maple bar. It was Friday morning. Sidney was sitting at the counter in Duke's Dune Donuts when he saw it. A fellow who had been seated next to him left the *Eugene Register-Guard* morning paper behind; Sidney held up the front page, and there it was below the fold: "COUPLE DIE IN LATE-NIGHT FIRE." A color photo showed a house engulfed in flames. Sidney fumbled his cup, and it tipped over; coffee pooled out across the counter. A waitress sauntered over and swabbed it up with a towel. Sidney leaned on his elbows, heart pounding, and read the account of Randolph Snyder, 63, and Virginia Snyder, 60, perishing when their house was totally destroyed in an intense late-night fire that was fully engaged before fire fighters arrived on the scene.

Sidney sat stupefied, finally telling the waitress no after being asked three times if he wanted a refill. He paid for the half a maple bar and spilled coffee and left the shop clutching the paper. Outside, a foggy mist met him. He walked blindly along the sidewalk, his mind whirling with shock and panic and dread. After wandering many blocks, he revived while staring into the window of a vacuum cleaner and sewing machine store. A row of vacuums stared out at him. After numbly reading the gaudy CLEARANCE price tags, Sidney stepped back, wiped a hand over his damp hair, and retraced his route back to the Cadillac still parked at the curb in front of the donut shop. The car's windshield was covered with a cataract of translucent mist. Sidney slid in behind the wheel and brooded over the deaths of Ginny Snyder and her husband and his suspicion that John Marr was responsible. He picked up the paper and read the story again; it ended predictably with: "The cause of the fire is unknown at this time". He was certain John Marr caused that fire; he knew it—at least, he felt it. He stared into the blur of the wet windshield and shuddered.

When he started the car, the windshield wipers swung up and in an instant cleared the fogginess. The clarity made Sidney blink; he hesitated then drove off. After about a quarter of a mile, he turned off the highway and drove down to Nye Beach and parked next to the Sylvia Beach Hotel, renowned for its restoration from a flop house into a charming inn with each room decorated and named for a famous author—a fact of little concern to Sidney at that moment. He looked out at the ocean, pulled out his cell phone, and dialed Ellie. Whom else did he have to call?

She was home. She listened without interrupting for once, sensing the tension in his voice. When he was finished, Ellie merely said she was sorry, and then she asked him if he feared for his own safety. He hesitated before saying yes. Her reaction was that he should drive straight back to Portland, right then, and they would find a way to keep him safe. It was tempting and made sense, so he rejected the idea.

———•———

By nine o'clock Sidney hadn't heard from either Nina or Ned Beeman. He decided that he wasn't going to call on Lamont Courter until he learned what Jonesy had known. Instead he checked his list of gift shops in Newport and began the slow process of driving around, from store to store. He traded barbs with the owner of Briny's Gift & Gallery, a woman in her sixties with sadly dyed blonde hair who had a road map of a face and was an obvious chain smoker. *Sure, she knew Jonesy. What about it?* When Sidney dropped *deceased* on her, she squinted away the smoke curling up from a cigarette clamped between thin lips and looked straight into Sidney's eyes. "Be damned" was her comment. She stabbed the cigarette out in an ashtray cluttered with butts, held up a coffee mug with the words NEWPORT OREGON on it above stylized ocean wave artwork. She ordered four dozen coffee mugs just like it and nothing else. As Sidney wrote up the order, she lit another cigarette and watched him in silence. When he tore off her copy of the order form and handed it over, she said, "I stiffed Jonesy last time he was through. Wished I hadn't." Nary a tear or a sad smile, but Jonesy's wiles had still played at Briny's.

After a couple more calls on the highway, both fruitless, Sidney drove down to the waterfront. The historic fishing harbor on Yaquina Bay, along with a couple of fish processing plants, was now mostly restaurants and gift shops with a picturesque fishing fleet at anchor as the backdrop. Most of the gift shops down there were primping for the coming weekend, ready to troll among the almost-spring but not quite end-of-winter weekenders who always came out in mid-March hoping for benevolent early beach weather. Sidney called on all of the small shops, racking up several respectable orders and some gasps and headshaking over Jonesy, before calling on Courter's Curios flagship store. He had held it until last and for some reason felt a twinge of apprehension when he pulled at the mock driftwood door handle and stepped inside.

It was twice as big as any of the other Courter's stores, wider and deeper, but it was filled with the same merchandise, had the same look and feel to it when he entered. The sameness made Sidney feel tired. He approached a middle-aged woman wearing the company maroon apron, smiled perfunctorily, and asked if the manager, a Janis Hill, was available.

He was staring out the front window and didn't hear her until she stepped into his line of sight and repeated herself. The first impression he had was of Dorothy Malone, the striking actress in her hey days of the forties and fifties: the cheekbones, blue eyes, shoulder-length ashen blonde hair, even the mouth of the movie star.

"May I help you?" she repeated.

Sidney's eyes widened. "Uh, yes. I'm sorry, daydreaming. Are you Janis Hill?"

She smiled tolerantly.

"I'm Sidney Lister. With Beeman's International?"

"Oh?" She looked quizzical.

"I'm here in place of Jonesy…Oscar Jones."

"Is that right?" she said, her eyes taking him in with more scrutiny. "I'm surprised. He seemed like such a permanent fixture with your company…Jonesy. Someone hire him away?"

Sidney readied himself. "No, Jonesy passed away last week."

"Oh my," Janis Hill said with a tilt of her head. "That is sad. How?"

"Heart attack."

"I see. Well, I'm sorry to hear it," she said.

"Uh-huh," Sidney responded.

"He'd been one of the regulars," she said. "Don't get as many over-the-road salespeople these days. What with the Internet and all." There was a pause; then she added, "Had a wicked sense of humor, Jonesy." Sidney wondered if that was it for the woman, or would she soon break down in a spasm of tears? All she did was continue to look at him.

"Lister," she said finally. "Not a common name. Sidney you said?"

"That's right."

"Sidney Lister." Her voice was even. "From Portland?"

He nodded.

"Grant High School?"

Sidney took a step back. "Janis Hill? Class of '75?"

"Yes."

"I'll be darned. What are the odds of running into our youth on a Friday in Newport?"

"Not long enough, I guess," she said.

Sidney laughed and swiveled his head toward the store window then back. "Yeah, who needs reminding, huh?"

"Something like that."

They stared at one another, each gracing the moment with a shallow smile.

At that moment two couples barged into the store, talking loudly. Janis Hill took Sidney by the arm and pulled him aside. "Have you had lunch yet?" Sidney shook his head. "Okay," she said, "I'll ask Anne to cover the store...if you want."

"Sure." He shrugged, and she walked off.

Janis Hill had always been stunning, a beautiful girl who could dance and sing as if she had been born for that purpose. Boys were mesmerized mouth-breathers whenever she performed, dancing on legs so spectacular she made every other girl seem prepubescent and stunted. She was a woman; the other class females were yet girls. At every talent show she and a kid named Danny Miller, a tap-dancer, took turns winning first place. Sidney remembered admiring her from a distance. Even as Mr. Most Likely to Succeed, Sidney had never cranked up enough courage to approach her. She became the class celebrity after high school, rising to a career as a showgirl in New York and later Las Vegas.

She reappeared, gestured to Sidney, and exited the store. He had to hustle down the sidewalk to keep up, his sales case banging against his leg. It had been nearly three decades since he'd last seen Janis Hill, and now here they both were selling geegaws to a gullible public. He was only too familiar with his own circuitous route of minimalist achievement, but he was dumbfounded to find this woman in his path. It wasn't right, coming up on a person in circumstances for which she had not been destined, catching her unaware and unable to draw the curtain before being discovered out of context.

She led the way to a place on the waterfront called the Rusty Anchor Fish House, where they settled into a booth and studied menus. After a self-conscious silence, Janis Hill raised her head and turned to the window but still said nothing. Sidney looked out at the harbor as a slow-moving fishing boat went by, leaving a bubbly wake in its passing.

"Nice view," he said.

"Yaquina Bay," she said. "The best oysters in the world."

"That right out of the Chamber of Commerce brochure?"

"Sort of," she said.

Sidney looked out the window again.

"I usually get the fish and chips," she offered.

Sidney followed her advice.

After another block of quiet, she said, "What's new?" When he looked confused, she said, "From Beeman's. You bring me anything with some zing to it?"

Sidney glanced down at his sales case. "Don't know about zingy, but there are a couple of new things. Have some real bargains too, maybe you'd—"

"You know," she interrupted, "I remember those years at Grant High as being miserable." When Sidney looked surprised, she added, "I never fit in, not really."

"Come on, you gotta be kidding," he said. "I mean, you were—"

"What?" she pressed. "I was what?"

He coughed a self-conscious laugh. "Amazing, that's what. You were amazing."

She was looking right at him.

"You *were*," Sidney assured. "I mean, every girl in school envied you. And every guy thought you were gorgeous and—"

"Oh please." She looked out the window again. "I was...I was in prison—that's what I was."

Sidney waited a beat. "But you were popular."

"Popular." She shook her head. "I was a freak because I could dance and belt out a song." Her smile was cheerless. "Those talent shows were twice a year. Ever think what I did the rest of the time?"

"No, guess not. But it always seemed that you were...I know the other girls envied you."

Janis Hill sat up and stared hard at Sidney. "No, they didn't envy me. They...well, they sure didn't envy me." She traced a finger along a seam on the wooden tabletop. "I almost wish I'd had buckteeth and couldn't carry a tune. Maybe then I would have had some friends."

"Well, I guess life's a charade a lot of the time." Sidney laughed softly. "Maybe you don't remember, but I was voted most likely to succeed my senior year."

"Didn't know that. And did you?"

"Oh sure. I'm a Nobel prize–winning psychologist on sabbatical studying the underlying factors inspiring people who sell crap to the U.S. consumer."

Her laugh was the first genuine sound of lightness to come from her. She paused and smiled, looking again out at the harbor. "Like Sinatra said, *That's Life*."

Their fish and chips arrived, giving them the moments of inspecting the food, shaking on malted vinegar, and arranging their napkins; time to adjust their thoughts around this unsuspected encounter and the cold reality of how life had played its will on each of them.

"So, Sidney," Janis Hill said finally, "it's been twenty-nine years. Can you believe it? Twenty-nine years. I just did the math."

"Yeah," he laughed. Even after all the years, he still felt self-conscious looking at Janis Hill.

"Who'd a thought, Sidney, right?"

He smiled some more, nodded again. "Right. Who'd a thought?"

Janis Hill laughed. "I can't even cheat on my age with you, now can I?

"I don't know. You still look great. If a person didn't know, they'd easily knock off ten years."

"Ha," she laughed. "Now there's the salesman's blarney coming out."

"Seriously, Janis. You look wonderful."

She took a bite of fish and looked up. "Thank you...I guess."

Sidney held a French fry in midair. "Did you really remember me?"

Her eyes met his; she started to say something but hesitated.

"Over at the store when you asked my name. Did you?"

"I recognized the name," she said. "But no, I didn't really recognize you. Sorry."

He dipped his French fry in a blob of catsup. He used the laugh he'd perfected over the years to cover moments of embarrassment. "Yeah, well, it was a big school."

"Yes," she agreed, "it was a big school."

When his cell phone rang, Sidney slipped out of the booth, waved his apologies at Janis Hill, and stepped away. It was Ned Beeman. He was breathing into the phone, almost panting.

"That you, Sidney?" More heavy breathing.

"Who else, Ned?"

"Huh? Oh yeah, it's a cell isn't it? Okay." A cough. "This is Ned."

"You been drinking?"

"Huh? Nah, got a lousy cold is all."

"So what's up? Nina find out anything from Jonesy's wife?"

"Uh, yeah."

"And?"

"Ah, Sidney?"

"Yeah."

"Thing is, you gotta...you're gonna have to go easy with this now. You know what I mean?"

"Not a clue, Ned." Sidney looked back toward the booth. Janis Hill was looking out the window again. "Can you get to this, Ned? I have someone waiting—a customer."

"Okay, but like I said, you gotta be careful now 'cause—"

There was a muffled disruption, and Nina was on the phone. "Sidney, I got what you asked for. Up to you how you use it—or if."

"That sounds cryptic. What did you find out?"

Nina heaved a big sigh. "Let me tell you, I had to pry this out of Margaret. Took me three hours and a good bottle of Merlot."

Sidney turned so he could keep looking toward Janis Hill. He saw her reach into his sales case and pull out an order form. "Okay, Nina," he said, "drop it on me. Will it give us any leverage?"

"Yeah, it will that." After a moment of empty air, she said, "If you want to use it."

Sidney looked toward Janis Hill; she was holding a ballpoint pen, going over an order form, checking boxes and writing. "Let me have it, Nina. I'll use it."

Nina inhaled before she unloaded the details. Sidney listened while he kept an eye on Janis Hill. The telling took several minutes. By the time Nina was done, Janis Hill had put her pen away and was looking at her watch; for the moment, Sidney had forgotten Janis Hill and was staring at the wall, at a photograph of the harbor. He wasn't really seeing the picture.

"Jesus, Nina," he said when she finished.

"Yeah." Neither one spoke for a long moment. "So what you gonna do with that?" Nina asked finally.

"Hell, I don't know. Shove it under his door, maybe." Sidney saw Janis Hill looking his way. He waved. "Yeah, well guess we have to use it, right?"

"Probably," Nina said. "Then again, maybe he won't remember his threat to Ned."

Sidney snorted a laugh. "Yeah, and maybe the tide won't come in. Look I gotta go. Have a customer waiting."

"Sidney?"

"Yeah?"

"Let us know."

"Don't worry, I'm not going to carry around any bad news by myself."

He ended the call and retraced his steps to the booth where Janis Hill waited. She rose and held out the order form.

"Here," she said and strode past. "I have to get back to the shop."

"Wait," he called after her. "Janis?"

She stopped and looked back at him unsmiling.

"I'm sorry. It was my boss."

"Uh-huh. Old Ned? Was he sober?" she smirked. "Well, back to work. Hail to the old Grant High blue and gray—I guess."

She wheeled and walked away. Sidney looked down at the order form. Clinging to it was the check; he was paying for lunch. Fair enough. He paid the bill, hoping the MasterCard would clear. It did. *Must be running on fumes though,* he thought. He looked for Janis Hill outside the restaurant, but she was nowhere on the street. So much for alum fun.

Lamont Courter, that was another matter.

-12-

Sidney went back to the car where it was parked on the water-front, scrunched down in the front seat, and mulled over how he was going to confront Courter with what he knew. Just casually walk in, say hello, and unload Jonesy's gotcha on the man? No. He wasn't up for that, not yet. He decided to head on south and complete business between Newport and Brookings. He could be back in two days. That would give him time to think on how to handle Lamont Courter—if there was a way.

He considered saying good-bye to Janis Hill but decided against it. She was miffed; let it go. Instead, he checked out of the motel, paid the manager to fax his orders to Nina, then pointed the Caddy down 101. He had just cleared South Beach State Park when a chill named John Marr hit his shoulder blades and the newspaper photo of a house burning returned to his head. He slowed the big car and plowed off the highway at the first wide spot, skidded to a stop in shoulder grit, and gripped the steering wheel as cars flew past, upbraiding him with a cacophony of horn blasts. He sat still for several minutes, staring straight ahead, feeling the car rock slightly whenever a big truck passed.

Where was John Marr? Right now, this moment. On his way to Newport to find him? If he was, then what? Sidney fumbled around, found the newspaper, and studied the picture and the headline again. *He's a cold-hearted bastard,* Sidney. That's what

Ginny Snyder had said, *a cold-hearted bastard.*

It took several minutes for the icy unease to abate. Sidney looked out at the wide flat beach in the distance and watched the frothy surf roll in and slide back out; he inhaled, waited for an opening, and plunged back onto the highway. As long as no one knew where he was, John Marr wouldn't know where he was, either. After a few miles he was able to get his mind back on track. He began hitting shops; he put his sales face back on and rewound his pitch. He made good time, even though a Friday can slow things down because shop owners are likely to have more customers and less time for salespeople—especially when he had to throw in his Jonesy act.

In Waldport Sidney faced another distraught woman who owned Felicia's, a small art gallery and gift shop. At the mention of Jonesy's demise, the very large woman, who was wearing an enormous yellow mu-mu, fell back in a dead faint, pulling a tapestry off the wall that covered her like a shroud. Sidney helped a woman who happened to be in the shop get Felicia into a chair, where she sat panting. She stared at Sidney glassy-eyed. He quickly suggested that he stop by another time. No argument was given. The vision of the woman disappearing under the cascade of fabric caused Sidney to erupt involuntarily in moments of laughter all the way to Yachats. Yachats, the town whose motto is La De Dah, the equivalent of no biggie. Pronounced Ya-hots, not Yack-its, a common mistake that isn't appreciated.

———•———

"Still owes me twenty bucks."

Sidney stared into the ruddy face of Stuart Firth, owner of Ocean Treasures and Souvenirs. "That so?" He looked around the scruffy little shop and wondered if it wasn't the other way around.

"You betcha." The man was short and unshaven.

"Well, Mr. Firth, the man's dead, isn't he?"

Firth lifted a paper cup and spit a stream of tobacco juice into it, all the while squinting at Sidney. "Yeah but…oh, hell, forget it. He's really dead, then?"

"Dead and buried."

"I'll be," Firth said. "Well hell, give me one of them dang order forms."

Sidney shoved one across the counter. "Those marked in red are the deals."

Firth studied the sheet of paper. "You know, Jonesy, he could be one sick son of a bitch."

"That right?"

Firth looked up. "Yeah, like when him and me got snockered one night. I was bombed, so he drove me home. Course he weren't much better off than me, but he could still see to drive somehow. Anyways," Firth giggled, "we got to my place, and he half-carries me to the house. And this old gal I was living with, she was standing in the doorway looking the two of us over. Mona, that was her name, Mona."

Firth looked puzzled then said, "The two of 'em musta dragged me into the bedroom—I ain't gotta clue 'cause the last thing I remember is looking into Mona's frowning face." He lifted the pen he was using and looked directly at Sidney. "You know what that sick bastard did?"

Sidney smiled. "Have an idea."

"I can see you do. And you'd be right." Firth spit into the cup again. "He banged Mona while I was passed out. I couldn't fault him, really. Mona had some miles on her, but she was still a fine-looking woman. But screwing another man's woman in his own place while he's unconscious in the next room—now that's just mean. Here." He handed Sidney the order form. "Best order Beeman's ever got outa me…honor of old Jonesy. He was pretty often a high spot on a dreary day."

"So I've heard."

"Yep, me and old Jonesy, he made many a dark night pass by with a few laughs and some stiff drinks. Sorry to see him pass."

"So what about the twenty bucks?"

Firth grinned, spit the clump of chewing tobacco into the paper cup, and tossed it all into a wastebasket. "Thinking on it, guess Jonesy paid me back last trip through." He raised a hand. "Wait a second." He pulled a black spiral-bound checkbook out from under the counter, scribbled in it, and tore the top check off. "Here," he said, holding it out. "Shock yer boss, something on account."

———•———

It came to Sidney just north of Florence. He drove down into the Old Town district, found Laughing Clam Gifts & Books, parked on Bay Street, and pulled out his cell phone. He retrieved the slip of paper he had put in the ashtray and eyed the numbers before thumbing the phone. After two rings a young female voice said "Thank you for calling Marr-Tech". Sidney hesitated until she had repeated herself before asking for John Marr. The voice was sorry but Mr. Marr was away on a business trip.

Sidney felt a buzz run up his back: *Away on a business trip.* He listened to the young woman say "Sir" several times, but he disconnected without comment and squeezed the steering wheel until his knuckles complained. He felt a surge of fear, the kind he had never before encountered: the fear of being prey. Where was John Marr?

He entered the Laughing Clam gift shop, inhaled the fusion of aromas amid the space brimming with merchandise, and faced the owner with a smile even as the whereabouts of his pursuer continued to circle in his head.

"Sidney Lister with Beeman's International."

"That right? So, did they finally fire Jonesy?"

Crystal Thompson was a full-bodied, red-haired woman, bespangled with a cluster of bracelets on each wrist, garish earrings that dangled from surprisingly petite earlobes, all accented by a wave of flowery perfume.

"Should they have?" he asked.

She looked past Sidney. "No, I just saw you drive up in that big Cadillac, the one he always drives." She raised a ringed finger and pointed. "Still have the Iggy license plates on it?"

"That it does."

Crystal Thompson drew herself up. "So Jonesy, he's either been fired, quit, or…is maybe sick or on vacation." When Sidney didn't respond, she said, "None of the above huh? So…when'd he die?"

"Almost a week ago," Sidney answered. "Be a week this Sunday."

She picked up a scented candle and sniffed it. "Bayberry," she said. "Must have been a heart attack, right?"

"Yes."

She smiled sympathetically. "And here you are…Mr. Lister, the bearer of bad tidings. Would you be up for a cup of chamomile tea? All I have."

"Chamomile is nice. I'd enjoy a cup of tea."

Sidney strolled about the shop until he heard his name and joined Crystal Thompson at a small table at the rear of the shop.

"He named this shop, you know," she said as she poured the tea.

Sidney leaned back, picked up his teacup, and readied himself for yet another Saint Jonesy tale.

"When we bought the place it was called Trina's Trinkets. I know, pretty awful. Jonesy happened by soon after we opened, and the first thing out of his mouth was that I needed to change that silly name. Said it needed to be clever, one that piqued people's interest. He scribbled *Laughing Clam* on the back of his business card and handed it to me. Told me if I used that name people would come in just to find out what a laughing clam was." She smiled. "They did and still do."

Sidney pulled an order form out of his case and laid it on the table. Crystal Thompson noticed, sipped her tea, and said, "Ah yes, business must go on. Sorry, Jonesy."

"So tell me," Sidney said, "how would he get around to the order? No, I'm really curious. Have to tell you I'm learning a lot about good old Jonesy as I make way down the coast."

"Must be fun." She smiled. "Well, he didn't...get around to the order. Least ways not with me. We spent most of the time talking about everything but business. Usually he wanted to know what was going on in my life. I know sounds suspicious, even thought so myself when we first met. But with him it was the real deal." She paused, took another sip of tea, and blinked against the moisture in her eyes. "Darn, it's just hitting me—that he's gone."

"Sorry," Sidney whispered.

"No," she waved a hand and wiped her nose with a napkin. "It's okay. I...you know I only saw the man a couple of times a year. Just seems like more, you know."

Sidney's cell phone began to chirp. "Excuse me," he said and got up from the table, holding the phone like it was an overripe banana, and walked away a few steps.

"Sidney, that you?" It was John Marr. Sidney swallowed and blinked. "Sidney, you there?"

"I'm here."

"It's John Marr."

"I know who it is."

"Yeah, okay." Marr hesitated. "I've been thinking, Sidney... thinking we need to meet up and talk this thing out. Where are you? I could come your way."

Sidney took in a deep breath, trying to fight off the tightness in his chest, and moved toward the front of the store.

"Sidney, you there?"

"I'm here."

"So like I said, we need to meet, you and me. Just tell me where you are."

Sidney stood at the front window of the shop and stared out

into the street. He watched a UPS delivery truck trundle by as his mind raced. "No need for us to talk, John," he said finally.

Marr emitted a nervous laugh. "Hey now, Sidney, sure we do."

"Why would I do that?"

"Why…because we need to…you know, clear the air. Give me a chance to set you straight on all of this. I mean, you got it all wrong, I tell you."

"Don't think so."

"No—"

"And now you've committed murder and arson."

There was silence on the line for a long moment. "What you talking about?" Marr said.

Sidney hesitated then plunged ahead. "You know damn well what I'm talking about." The phone was shaking in his hand. "How…how could you do it, you, you despicable piece of slime?"

"Still don't have a clue what you mean. Think you're losing it, Sid old man."

"The fire," Sidney answered. "The fire! They…died."

"You're crazy. Where are you, Sidney? We need to settle this."

Sidney tried to laugh, but it was only a squawk. "You can't settle this."

"You need help, Sidney. You are delusional. I can help you, but we have to talk so we can clear away these crazy accusations."

Sidney looked over his shoulder; Crystal Thompson was clearing the tea service. "Look, we both know they aren't accusations," he whispered with force. "You're sick. Now quit calling me or—"

"Or what?" John Marr's voice had cooled. "I'll—"

Sidney punched the phone off, his hand still shaking. He took in several deep breaths and winced at what he'd just done. Why did he have to spout off? When he turned Crystal Thompson was looking at him. "You okay?" she asked.

"Yeah, sure," he said and gave up a bogus laugh. "Argument

with my plumber," he lied. "Trying to get a leak fixed long distance."

She held out the order form. "I filled it out."

He nodded, took the sheet of paper and studied it without seeing it. "Thanks," he said "Any questions?"

She shook her head. "You sure you're okay?" she asked. "You look kind of pale."

"I'm fine." When she didn't seem convinced, he added, "Really, I'm fine."

Crystal Thompson eyed him for a moment more and then looked at her wristwatch. "So you going on south?"

"Uh, yeah," he answered, "heading on down the road."

"Won't be much left open this time of day."

Sidney blinked at her, still coming down off of his adrenalin fright over John Marr. "Probably right," he said.

A woman carrying a small fuzzy white dog in one arm entered the store and moved to a greeting card rack. Sidney glanced at her as one would a passing car and then back at Crystal Thompson, who was still staring at him with surprisingly green eyes, her big earrings swinging slightly. The bell over the door tinkled when the customer left without buying anything.

"Jonesy laid over here in Florence once in a while. Usually he stayed here." She smiled and reached out to touch a lighthouse figurine. "And you're more than welcome if you want."

"Oh, no," he stuttered, "I wouldn't want to put you out."

"You wouldn't be," she said, "just me and my husband. We have a couch that makes into a bed. John, he loves company. My husband."

After a moment of hesitancy, Sidney accepted. Crystal Thompson looked over her shoulder and told him that all he had to do was walk through the door marked Private at the back of the shop and he would be in their living quarters. When Sidney returned from the car with his duffel, Crystal Thompson was waiting on an elderly, stooped woman who was purchasing a fluted flower vase. She motioned for him to go on back.

He let himself in and disturbed a man who was napping in a wheelchair; a television with a huge screen was on—a nonstop news channel was chattering about the crises of the hour. The moment was awkward as the man was suddenly roused from his slumber—surprised, blinking.

Sidney stood stock still; the two men stared at one another.

-13-

The duffel hung from Sidney's right hand—a dead weight grounding his unease. "Sorry," he said. "I didn't mean to barge in. Your wife told me to—"

John Thompson lifted a hand, which hung from his wrist like an unstrung marionette's. "No, no," he said. His voice was but a loud whisper. "Crystal, she's always sending people back here without warning. Her little game. Trying to keep my people skills up. You're the third surprise visitor this week." He reached down and pushed a wheel, aligning himself more squarely on Sidney. "And who might you be—besides embarrassed? And sit, please—anywhere you like."

Sidney put the bag to one side and settled into a recliner covered in pale pink velour. The living space was like a long garage divided in half—a narrow living room and dining space on one side, a small kitchen on the other; compact like a mobile home but with high ceilings.

After some throat clearing, Sidney explained who he was and once more revealed that his predecessor had died suddenly. John Thompson merely nodded and gave up a small shrug of his shoulders. He then tried to put Sidney at ease when he volunteered why he was in a wheelchair—his *modus operandi* as he called it—that multiple sclerosis had put him there. He had been an attorney in Portland, a courtroom litigator, successful until his body began to let him down and he had to give it up—his re-vered life at the bar.

"So," John Thompson said, dropping his hands on the chair push rims, "this is my alter ego. This chair. We have this love-hate thing going." He coughed a dry laugh, raised a hand, and dragged limp fingers through a mound of thick brown hair.

Sidney thought he looked to be in his mid-forties, but maybe older. Except for a small potbelly, John Thompson was thin for a man who spent much of his time immobile.

"So Jonesy is dead," he said. "Can't say I'm surprised. Crystal, she put stock in the man for some reason. Stayed with us once or twice." John Thompson repositioned himself in the chair. "Seemed like a windbag to me, sorry to say."

Sidney smiled but made no comment.

"Just the way I felt."

They had run out of small talk by the time Crystal Thompson came in from the shop and stood looking back and forth between the men. Her husband had switched to the food channel while Sidney was thumbing through an old issue of *Newsweek*. Other than the lowered sound of the television, all was quiet.

She lifted up the pizza box she was carrying. "You boys ready to party or what?"

John Thompson raised the remote, and the television went black. "What topping?"

"What else? Old Towne Combo: the works, everything in the kitchen, you know."

John Thompson rolled his chair with practiced hands. "Sidney, you like pizza?"

"Been known to eat a bite or two."

"Good. There's beer in the fridge. Grab three bottles, would you?"

They gathered around a small table that sat astride an invisible line between living room and the kitchen. To Sidney, it felt like they were in a child's playhouse in one sense. The Thompson's lives had definitely been compressed.

Sidney brought the beer, twisted the caps off, and observed Crystal Thompson pull a slice of pizza from the box and put it on a plate for her husband. He looked up at her, smiling, and she leaned down to kiss him on the cheek. Sidney looked down so as not to witness John Thompson struggling to get a pizza slice up to his mouth. Crystal Thompson glanced at Sidney and smiled. They ate in silence until they had each taken their first healthy bites out of a slice of Old Towne Combo.

The Thompsons were an incongruous couple. She, slightly older, her showy bespangled presence contrasting that of a former attorney, even now dressed in a plaid sport shirt and gray slacks; his fair, lightly freckled skin was boyish in comparison. Sidney saw the Thompsons exchange eye contact and smiles. Finally John Thompson set his bottle down using both hands and looked at Sidney.

"So Sidney," he said, wiping his limp hands on a napkin. "You are a different one. By now old Jonesy would have filled the air with his verbosity. What say you?"

Sidney felt his face redden.

"Never you mind him," Cynthia Thompson prompted. "John, leave the poor man alone."

"Man must have something on his mind," said John Thompson.

"All right," Sidney said. "But mostly just say I'm curious."

"About?" John Thompson asked.

"You two. How you worked things out and why here?"

"Ah," uttered John Thompson. "You do have a bit of Jonesy in you. He was nosy too."

"John!" Crystal Thompson chastised her husband.

"All right, since I goaded you into it, I'll tell you. When the MS got the best of me, we had to pool all our resources and start over. Sold our house, my partners bought me out, and we cast about for a landing spot. Two years ago we found this business and building for sale: shop and living quarters all on one level, and here we are. Crystal runs the shop, and I do the books. That enough for you?"

Sidney nodded uncomfortably and moved to change the subject. "I noticed the picture of a young woman…on the shelf over there. That your daughter?"

The Thompson's looked at one another. Crystal Thompson eventually turned her head toward the picture. "Yes, that's our daughter, Sarah." There was a long moment before she spoke again. "We don't see her anymore."

"I'm sorry," Sidney said. "I didn't mean to—"

"She's a hooker," John Thompson spit out. "Turns tricks for a living."

Sidney swallowed his embarrassment; no one spoke. John Thompson pushed his wheelchair back from the table, spun it around, and rolled away into the living room. A moment later the television came on, and the announcers for a basketball game could be heard.

"Sarah," Crystal Thompson began slowly, "stayed in Portland when we came here to Florence. She was enrolled at Portland State University, at least she was for a while." Crystal Thompson paused. Sidney sat still and waited. "A little over a year ago, I guess, we lost contact with her. We made trips to Portland, several trips. She wasn't going to school. No one knew where she was. Then…then the police contacted us and told us she'd been arrested for soliciting. John had his former law partners take care of everything, but then…she would do it again, and again."

"I'm sorry," said Sidney. What else could he say?

"Finally," Crystal Thompson went on, "Sarah told us that that's what she wanted to do and to leave her alone." She sucked in a sob. "My baby, my god, what…" She cupped her hands over her mouth and cried soundlessly.

Sidney sat back and blinked back his own tears. The basketball game broadcast mumbled in the background. Crystal Thompson wiped her eyes and managed a sweet sad smile.

"You know," she whispered and looked toward the living room. "Jonesy, he looked for Sarah. John doesn't know this."

Sidney raised a hand to indicate she needn't worry.

"Somehow, he found Sarah—out in northeast Portland. He talked with her." She shook her head. "Sweet old Jonesy. It didn't do any good, but he tried, bless his heart. And you know he'd look her up every few months to see that she was okay—I mean as okay as she could be—and then he'd call me."

———•———

Sidney spent the night on the Thompson's hide-a-bed couch. He didn't really sleep, what with John Marr and Jonesy and a young prostitute running through his head. Slightly before six in the morning, he dressed in the light from a table lamp, left a note of thanks on the kitchen counter, and slipped out through the shop entrance into a chilling fog. In the quiet of the early hour, he crossed the street, empty except for the Caddy and a beater Ford pickup, and entered a tiny park that had a gazebo and wooden deck at the edge of the river. He looked out over the water; the current was slow, the river glassy. The graceful arches of a thirties-era art deco concrete bridge stood high in the mist and spanned the Siuslaw River. A blue heron soared by soundlessly on its huge wingspan and landed near the shoreline. Sidney stood quietly watching the bird in the cool moist air and considered who he was at that moment: a messenger of death, prey to a threatened predator, a salesman of trivia, and a master of false starts.

He pulled himself away from the river, found Clyde's Pretty Good Café open early up on the highway; the only other people in the café were an elderly couple getting an early start back to California. Sidney ate scrambled eggs and sausage and read a copy of the *Eugene Register-Guard* someone had left behind. He searched the paper to see if there was any more news about the fire that had killed Ginny Snyder and her husband. Four pages in among a collection of local stories was a short piece about the fire, which was still being considered accidental. It gave Sidney a chill to realize that he was probably the only person alive who really knew who was responsible. John Marr knew that, too.

After breakfast, Sidney washed up a bit in a tiny restroom, gave Clyde a thumbs-up on the way out, gassed up at an Arco station, and drove on. He had only gone a mile or so when he pulled off the road and parked on the paved lot of an empty building that had once been home to the Siltcoos Fish House restaurant. A For Lease sign proclaimed it to be a prime retail location. Sidney sat there for a couple of minutes, engine running, then turned off the ignition and pulled out his cell phone. She answered on the fourth ring with fuzz in her voice. Sidney eased her into a state of semi-alertness; she wasn't pleased.

"Sidney, it's barely seven o'clock."

"Yeah, it is. But you told me to call."

Ellie calmed. "Yes, but at a reasonable hour."

"You never said that."

She laughed, or maybe purred, "Okay. Where are you anyway?"

"Couple of miles south of Florence."

"You driving already? Aren't you the early bird."

"I got up early. Couldn't sleep."

"Poor baby," she teased.

"Ellie?" he said her name like a question.

"Uh-huh."

"You ever wonder if we should've had children?"

She was silent for a moment then spurted out a laugh. "What are you smoking?" When he didn't respond, she said, "Okay, what's going on?"

He reached down, pressed the power seat switch until the seat hummed back as far as it would go, and leaned his head back on the headrest.

"Sidney?"

"I'm here."

"So you're calling me at seven-whatever-in-the morning, from wherever on the bleeping coast, to ask this question? What's the deal—you get laid last night?"

"Ellie, for god's sake. That all you ever think about?"

Her laugh was breathy. "Whenever I'm talking to you, yeah. Thinking of that, when are you coming home? I'm—"

"Horny, I know. Seriously, it's complicated."

"Sex?"

Sidney inhaled, exasperated. "No. Children. Having children. Not all birthday parties and romps in the park."

"What happened?" she asked; her voice was serious for once.

"I stayed with a couple in Florence. They have this gift shop, live in the back, and they have a daughter, college-age daughter." He paused.

"And?"

"Like I said, it gets complicated. Their daughter, Sarah's her name. She was in college, PSU, then they lost her."

"Lost her? What do you mean? She's gone? She die?"

"Maybe that would be better, her just being gone. No, she's on the streets. In Portland."

"You mean homeless?"

"No, I mean the other."

Sidney could almost see Ellie's brow wrinkling like she would do when she was confused. "You don't mean she's a prostitute?"

"I do," he said. "That's exactly what I mean."

"Oh, Sidney, how awful for those people."

"Can't get it out of my head," he said. "I keep imagining what it would have been like if we'd had kids. You know, if we would be having...problems."

Ellie sighed. "Of course. Everyone with kids has problems. Comes with the territory. That's why I...well, I never wanted a Sarah." She stopped; neither of them spoke for a long moment until she said, "Understand? Sidney, do you see why now?"

"Uh-huh," he answered. "I know why you didn't want kids."

"You felt the same way," she said, "as I remember. Right?"

"Hell, that's so long ago, I don't know how I felt. Really."

"Oh come on now, Sidney, you aren't going to leave me holding that baton just because you heard a sad story. It was our pact, and you know it."

"I suppose," he said. "I guess I just needed someone I could say Sarah's name to, like it was my responsibility to spread the word." He chuckled. "You know old Jonesy tracked down the girl for her mother."

"Really?"

"Yeah, so she'd know how her baby was. Something, huh? Jonesy. His ghost is with me every bloody mile over here."

"Sidney, when you coming home? You're sounding down."

He took in a deep breath and let it out. "Not for a while yet. Miles to go and curios to show."

"Hmm, another slogan for another job. Think this one is going anywhere?"

"At least as far as Brookings," he laughed it out. She didn't say anything back. "You know me, Ellie."

"I do," she answered.

"So you know my track record. In general, my life has never really gone where I've aimed it. Misfires, too many misfires." A semi rolled by; its wake rocked the car. "Better, I guess, that we didn't bring kids into it."

"Sidney," she sighed.

"I couldn't have taken the looks of disappointment in their eyes...and yours."

"Please," she said, "come home."

"Can't, you know that. Even bad choices carry expectations." He sat up and pushed the switch; the power seat slid back into place. "Nope, Ellie old girl, I gotta keep the pedal down."

"What about what's his name, Marr?" she said. "He still pestering you?"

Sidney gave a little laugh. "It's way beyond pestering with

John Marr. Now he's trying to hunt me down."

"Sidney! This is getting scary," she said, raising her voice.

"He doesn't know where I am. I'll be okay," he said, accepting denial as a remedy. He talked soft to her for a bit longer then disconnected the call, turned the ignition, clicked the seatbelt back on, waited until a huge RV went by towing a Jeep Wrangler behind it, and eased out onto the highway.

He may have soothed Ellie, but not the thing that had set up housekeeping in his stomach.

-14-

There were only two stops between Florence and Coos Bay–North Bend: Coos Bay–North Bend, the towns that sounded like one but abutted each other and jousted over territorial bragging rights. Even driving below fifty, Sidney rolled into Reedsport, the next scheduled stop, in little over thirty minutes. It was only eight thirty-eight. He found a coffee shop open in a strip mall between Zesto's Pizza Parlor and Econo Cleaners. He settled into a far corner table with a small regular coffee and another maple bar and pulled out his cell phone for the second time that morning. He didn't want to make the call, but he knew he must. Nina Beeman answered on the third ring.

"Sidney!" she almost shouted. "Thank god you've finally called."

Sidney felt a chill. "Why—what's wrong?"

"Oh," she quieted, "nothing really. Sorry. It's just that I've had my hands full keeping Ned from calling you. We've been beside ourselves wondering how…Sidney, what did Lamont Courter do when you…you know, what'd he do?"

"I haven't seen him yet."

"What?" Her voice lowered, and she whispered. "Where are you—right now?"

"Reedsport."

"Reedsport? That's way south. But why—"

"Nina," he broke in, "I just wasn't ready to face this Courter. I've never even met the guy, and to just walk in and accuse him of...well, that."

"But—"

"I'll see him on my way back through. Promise." They paused. "It'll give me some time to think over my...how I'll approach him. Helluva thing, after all."

"I know," she said. "I'll keep Ned at bay somehow. Got the last orders you faxed—that was good. Keep sending them as soon as you get them. That will help me with Ned. I'm keeping him busy filling orders and doing the shipping. Does him good."

"I'll fax you what I get when I get it."

"Okay. By the way," she said, "that guy, that John Marr?"

"Yeah." Sidney sat up straight and put his half-eaten maple bar down on his napkin. "What?"

"He called again. Yesterday."

"And?"

"Tried to get outa me where you are. Don't worry," she said. He could almost visualize the frown she wore when distressed. "I didn't tell him anything. Heck, I couldn't, anyway, I didn't even know where you were."

"Thanks."

"Now that I know what he's up to, his smooth talking gave me the creeps."

Sidney inhaled slowly and let it out. "It's even worse than you know, Nina. You can't tell him anything—it's that serious."

She didn't respond.

"What?" he prodded. "Nina. Is there something?"

"No, not really." Her voice was small. "I mean, not about where you are I—"

"Nina." Sidney had a grip on his coffee mug; he picked it up and set it down hard. A very large, red-faced man in bib overalls lowered a big cinnamon roll and turned his head toward the sudden noise. "What is it?" Sidney pressed in a hoarse whisper.

"Well," she began and hesitated before going on, "he asked if you were still driving your old Camry. He said *junker* Camry actually." She tried to laugh.

Sidney looked out the window at the Cadillac sitting in the parking lot. "And you told him that I am driving the Cadillac."

"Sidney, I'm—"

"Just had to brag that Beeman's salesman has a nice ride. Huh? That it?"

"No, I...I'm sorry, I didn't think." He heard her blowing her nose. "It is that serious, Sidney? Really?"

"Afraid it is."

"But it's not really bad or anything, right?" When he didn't respond, Nina Beeman, pressed, "You're not...in real danger, are you, Sidney?"

"Best you not know," he said softly, but his heart was racing. "I'll fax more orders in when I have some."

He cut Nina off in mid-sentence, censoring the panic in her voice. Out on the highway a dump truck rumbled by, its empty box clanging when it hit a depression in the roadway. Sidney, oblivious to the noise, approached the car and felt the knot in his stomach harden when he looked at the vanity license plate: IGGY. He took in a ragged breath and got back into the car, set his hands at ten and two, and barked, "Shit!" Because of Nina's revelation to Marr, he might as well have had a neon sign on top of the car.

At ten o'clock, still in Reedsport, with John Marr floating in his head, Sidney called on Seahorse Gifts and Treasures, a small boxy little shop. The only thing the owner, a woman named Kelly, said of Jonesy's demise was, "No kidding." She hadn't necessarily bonded with Jonesy, she allowed, but appreciated the day he'd helped her move a monstrous display case when there was no one else to help her.

Sidney pulled out an order form. "You know something, Kelly? I've just about heard enough Jonesy-saves-the-day stories."

The woman laughed hard. "I'll just bet you have."

He left Kelly still chuckling and stopped by a jumbled shop that went by the name Heaven Sent Gifts, Antiques & Crafts owned by a woman named Charlie who touted that "You have to sell anything and everything to survive in this town". So she proved it by ordering bead charm bracelets, angel figurines, and Mexican design woven blankets. Four miles down the road it was Burt's Myrtle Wood Gifts in Winchester Bay, a village that boasted it was The Crab Capital of the Oregon Coast. Burt, near eighty and thinking of retiring, had carried Iggy products since the very beginning, in amongst everything myrtle wood. While the old man went on about his arthritis, Sidney sat in a myrtlewood rocker, pretended to listen, and imagined John Marr searching for a silver Cadillac with an iguana's nickname on its license plate.

———•———

When Burt finally ran down, Sidney bid the old man farewell, left with a hefty Iggy order, and drove back to Reedsport. He had decided what he had to do next. After he found a quick-print shop that would fax his orders to Beeman's, he headed east on Highway 38 along a beautiful stretch of the Umpqua River. He plodded along the curvy river highway behind an empty wood-chip truck until he hit the I-5 freeway and ran the car up to eighty on into Eugene. He took the city center exit and searched for a phone booth—a rare thing—found one with an actual phone directory attached, and thumbed through the white pages. Sidney was pretty certain that John Marr's ego would keep him from using an unlisted number, and there he was: John Q. Marr on Edgewater Drive.

The house was an impressive brick two-story structure with a massive front entrance, high French paned windows, a land-scaped yard, and a circle drive. Sidney drove by slowly on the first pass. There were no cars in the drive. But there was a four-car garage, so someone might be home. He was betting it wouldn't be John Marr. He finally quelled his butterflies, eased the car into the drive, and stopped adjacent to the front porch. After several deep breaths he got out and sauntered past nasty-neat flowerbeds brimming with purple crocus and emerging daffodils and approached the front door. Two sculptured black lions sat impassively on each side of double doors. Sidney stood on a thick cocoa mat with a big block M set in it and pressed the doorbell; a serial ringing of chimes arose, seemingly announcing the arrival of royalty. He stepped back and was looking over his shoulder when the door opened.

The woman had a narrow face, short blonde hair, and blue eyes. She was wearing beige slacks and a white polo shirt. Her expression at seeing Sidney was pleasant enough but somewhat wary.

"Mrs. Marr?" Sidney asked.

"Yes."

"You may not remember me. My name is Sidney Lister?"

The woman smiled benignly, but said nothing.

"Several years ago I took pictures of your new granddaughter... and your family."

The smile widened. "Which one?" she laughed. "It must have been Jennifer. We've had another granddaughter since then—Erin."

"Congratulations," Sidney said as enthusiastically as he could muster.

Mrs. Marr smiled some more. "Thank you. We're getting to be quite a crowd."

"Sounds like."

"So, Mr. Lister," she offered, a bit confused, "what can I do for you? If you're looking for John, I'm afraid he's out of town."

"I know, but I just took a long shot that he might be at home—you know, either coming or going." Sidney forced out a small laugh. "Well, I wonder...could I leave a message with you?"

"Of course," she stepped back. "Please come in. Would you like something to write on?"

Sidney followed her into the house and waited in a formal entry and stared at a grand staircase that seemed to have come straight out of *Gone with the Wind*. Mrs. Marr returned, handed him a notepad and a pen; he stood in place and scribbled the words he had drafted in his head on the drive from the coast. When he handed her the folded note, he smiled and asked if the Q in her husband's name stood for Quincy.

"Why, yes," she answered. "How did you know?"

"Not many Q names," he said. "Just took a guess."

She gave out a small laugh. "And it's Quincey with an *e*, I'll have you know. One best not forget that small feature." She seemed to enjoy that small moment of rebellion.

Sidney left Helen Marr—she'd offered her first name after he had addressed her as Mrs. Marr too often—standing on the elegant front porch, undoubtedly trying to remember an obscure portrait photographer but putting her best manners forward. He wondered if the woman was aware of her husband's act of retribution against him.

Back on the freeway, Sidney replayed the words he'd written to his adversary: *Dear John, Sorry I missed you. I just wanted you to know that the matter you are pursuing is more elusive than you originally imagined. I'm afraid that the goal you have in mind may now cost you more than is feasible. In fact, if you continue along this course, it may cost you more than you can imagine. Sorry, old man, but it's best you know.*

> *Regards,*
> *Sidney*

P.S. I enjoyed meeting Helen.

———•———

By mid-afternoon, Sidney rolled back through Reedsport and immediately south of Winchester pulled off at a viewpoint and killed the ignition. He retrieved an old baseball cap from the back seat, stepped out of the car into a stiff breeze, and zipped up the windbreaker he was wearing. The cool wetness against his face revived him but didn't erase all that was weighing on his mind. He looked out at the spectacular view of the ocean and a jetty that reached out like two rocky arms creating a seaway into the bay.

The uninterrupted miles of driving had lulled his brain into dull introspection, and introspection always punished him with his many *just-shorts*, as he came to call them. He hadn't actually been a failure; as a matter of fact, he had been very competent at most things. It was that for some reason he was never at the right place at the right time; he was repeatedly *just short* of success.

Now, not only was he taking table scraps from a dead huckster, a madman was after him as well. And, except for his ex-wife, he had no one to turn to. When had that happened? There had been friends over the years, hadn't there? If so, where were they now? Who were they? Family? His father had died suddenly eight years before, leaving his bewildered mother frightened and feeling so alone that she moved to California to live with her older sister. Sidney managed to call her on special occasions but never shared the real status of his life with her: *Everything's fine, Mom.* His only sibling was Sonia, a sister nearly ten years younger than he, who lived on the east coast. Sonia had gotten her doctorate in paleontology—after all, her name meant *wisdom*—and took extra effort to keep a significant distance between her and her underperforming older brother. *Life,* Sidney thought, *if you aren't paying attention it forgets about you.*

A sudden squall came in and drove him back into the car. He wiped at his face with a handkerchief, tossed the ball cap over his shoulder, and started the car just as his cell began to chirp. He dug it out of his coat pocket and lifted to his ear.

"You were at my house!" John Marr yelled as soon as Sidney said hello. "You fuck you!"

"Hello, John Quincey with an *e*. You got my message then," Sidney said calmly, even as his heart thumped.

"Listen you—"

"I asked if you got my message," Sidney broke in. "Did Helen give you my message?"

"I got it." John Marr panted into Sidney's ear. "Whatever the hell it means."

Sidney forced himself to laugh. "You know darn well what it means. Give it up, John Quincey. Just give it up, or you'll pay the price."

Marr was silent for a moment. "Nah, you're not going to keep quiet. How can I be guaranteed you won't talk?"

"You can't," Sidney said. He inhaled; they both breathed their tension into the phones. "Fact is, I could call the cops any old time. Might, too. How's it feel? Best you turn yourself in."

"Like hell. Look, okay, so you know what you know. What we gonna do about it? I have money." When Sidney didn't respond, Marr added, "I can set you up in your own business somewhere: California, Mexico, whatever."

"Does Helen know about any of this?" Sidney asked.

"Damn you!" Marr exploded.

"Does she, John?" Sidney said. "Does she know that she is married to evil?"

There was a moment of deadly silence before Marr breathed out, "You're going to pay for this, you son of a bitch. I'll kill you."

Sidney shuddered. He had no response.

"What's that?" John Marr asked. "That beep. You recording this?"

"Paranoia becomes you," Sidney answered. "No, it's my cell phone telling me I'm running out of juice—just like you. Time's running out, John."

Sidney ended the call and tossed the phone onto the passenger seat. He sat with his hands twitching on the steering wheel and stared into a renewed film of gauzy moisture on the windshield. The throb of a motorcycle engine roused him. A big candy red Honda Goldwing loped by; he watched a wide-bodied man get off the bike, pull some rain gear out of his saddlebags, and begin to wiggle into some rain pants. Sidney started the car's wipers, turned on the defroster to clear the fog off the windshield, and drove off glad he didn't have to straddle a wet motorbike.

But he knew his plight was worse than a wet crotch.

-15-

Around four o'clock Sidney crossed the McCullough Memorial Bridge spanning Coos Bay and drove on into North Bend. He called on a cluttered import gift shop next to the Sears store in the Pony Village shopping mall. The owner, a lean, bony woman who seemed at war with herself, aggressively retained her status of never having done business with Beeman's. Sidney gladly left her to her demons, treated himself to a tropical sunlight smoothie from the Orange Julius stand (only 250 calories was the promise) and, as an afterthought, bought a second one and walked back to the import shop. He handed the frosty drink to the owner, smiled at her incredulous expression, wished her a nice day, and drove across the invisible dotted line that separated North Bend from its larger cousin, the town of Coos Bay. The Courter's Curios store in Coos Bay sat in the heart of the downtown on Broadway. The manager, the first male Sidney had encountered at a Courter's store, was Charles Scott. He was a big man all around: tall, maybe six four, tree trunk body, bull neck, and a voice to go with his size.

Charles Scott looked at Sidney over metal-framed glasses set low on a wide nose and studied him for a long moment after hearing of the death of Oscar Jones. "The hell you say," he finally responded. "Gone then, just like that." He snapped a thumb and forefinger with a metallic pop.

Sidney nodded. "That's about the way it happened, I understand."

Charles Scott's laugh was a deep rumble. "And here you are—Sidney, is it?"

"Yes."

"Sidney, the bona fide carrier of bad news. Bet that's been fun."

"Not so much," Sidney said.

Charles Scott cleared his throat and laughed. "Not so much. Well hells bells, this calls for a toast to old Jonesy. Don't you think?" He looked at his wristwatch. "Near closing. I'll leave Trish to wrap up, and you and I can walk down the street to Jack's. Buy you a sour mash whiskey—that's what Jonesy always had."

Charles Scott gave his assistant manager notice that he was leaving and came back pulling on a Gore-Tex raincoat. He waved for Sidney to follow and pulled on a tweed English driving cap as they stepped out into the face of a whipping rain that had sprung up. They each lowered their heads and surged forward, arriving only minutes later at Jack's Anchor Bar & Grill only slightly drenched from the stinging rain.

Charles Scott whipped his cap off and shook it upon entering the small establishment. He looked into the bemused face of the man standing behind the bar and growled, "Blast it all, Jack, I'm wet on the outside again." He grinned back at Sidney. "My friend and I are ready to equalize that dilemma. What say?"

Jack, a small man, round of face and belly raised a hand. "Okay, Charles my man, what's your pleasure?"

Charles Scott pointed a finger at the bartender. "This here's a wake. So in honor of our old friend Jonesy Jones, bring us a couple of Jack Daniels on the rocks. We'll be at my usual address." He gestured toward a table in a back corner.

They hung their wet jackets on the back slats of some loose-jointed wooden chairs and lowered themselves onto seats padded with black Naugahyde. "Your second address?" Sidney said.

Charles Scott chuckled. "I do come here more than I ought to. Sort of my hang. Being unattached I need a place that serves as home base, I guess you'd say." He pulled a cigar case out of his coat pocket and extracted what looked to Sidney like a panatela. "Plus its one of the few places I can still smoke my cigars. Hell, I guess that's even going to change pretty soon." He used a lighter to fire up the cigar, leaned his head back, and exhaled. The smoke settled out between them.

"You're a bachelor then," said Sidney. "Never married?"

"Now I never said that. What I said was that I'm unattached. I've had my turn at the connubial state, more than once as a matter of fact." Jack the bartender arrived with their drinks, dropped a couple of paper coasters, and set down the glasses of amber liquid. Charles Scott nodded to the bartender and picked up his glass. "To Jonesy," he proclaimed loudly. Others in the room looked over and smiled; a couple even raised their glasses.

Sidney lifted his glass and, with less enthusiasm, said, "To Jonesy."

"And you, Sidney, are you married?" Charles Scott drew on his cigar again.

"Was," he answered.

"Ah, the most favored status in my humble opinion. So we are brothers under the skin after all," said Charles Scott. He raised his glass toward Sidney.

"Children?" Sidney asked.

"Oh yes," was Charles Scott's response. He raised an eyebrow. "A daughter. Daphne. God awful name, her mother's choice for a grandmother she adored." He fingered the smoldering cigar. "We are estranged, my daughter and I. Ah, Daphne. The result of the sewage of divorce. How about you?"

"No, no children," Sidney replied. He flashed back to his phone call just that morning with Ellie and again wondered if they both would regret having no offspring. Sometimes he felt a cold lump in his throat if he thought about getting old with no one to care much if he did, or having no chance to give a child better advice than he'd gotten about life. And sometimes he wanted to cuss Ellie out for denying him that right; other times, like right then hearing about Charles Scott's separation, he felt relief.

"Anyway," Charles Scott was saying, "Jonesy and I were simpatico on most things but marriage. He had this wife, you see."

"Her name is Mildred," Sidney said with an edge to his voice.

Huh? Oh yeah, Mildred. Sure. Too bad." Charles Scott leaned over the table. "But you see, Sidney old man, Jonesy had this natural liking for the opposite gender. And his job, while it could be a bloody bore, it had one supreme benefit: a buffet of women." He laughed and sat back. "Of course, I'm not telling you anything you don't know. Right? Am I right?"

Sidney sipped some bourbon and set the glass down. "It's a job. Like any other, I guess. Lots of driving, nights in motels—nothing glamorous, that's for sure."

"Come, come," Charles Scott said, lowering his head to stare over his glasses, "I know this business. How many men are managing those shops you call on? Huh?"

"A good number."

"Uh-huh. Sidney, I think you're yanking my chain. Jonesy had some tales to tell, wife or not. You run across any broken hearts on the trip down?"

"Most were saddened by his death," Sidney answered. He thought of Beulah Strong, the big-boned woman in Astoria, and her affair with Jonesy, and how she nearly had him in bed as well.

"Saddened," said Charles Scott. "More then likely they're missing a little man-on-the-road tickle." He raised his hand to the bartender for another round. "You must have seen Lamont Courter when you came through Newport. How was that for you?"

"No, I didn't see him. I plan to do it on the way back."

"Hmm." Charles Scott tapped the growing blunt end of ash into an ashtray. "You stop by the Courter's on the harbor in Newport?"

"I did, yes."

"Then you met up with Janis Hill, right?" Charles Scott was grinning. "The manager?"

Sidney felt his face warm. "Yeah, I met her."

"And?"

"Got an order."

"Got an order, he says. Is that it? Sidney, are you dead below the waist? Now you must admit that there is one fine-looking woman. Am I right?"

Sidney nodded. "I would agree. But I knew that. We went to high school together…in Portland. Grant High."

"You're kidding me," Charles Scott slapped the tabletop. "You know, I've made a couple runs at getting to know her, take her out, you know. We have these manager meetings several times a year up there, and I've put on the charm, but nothing. Like I was a rock or something. And now out of nowhere you blow into town and fall into old home week. So you got plans for her on your visit on the way back up the coast?"

"I'm old news," Sidney said.

"Hmm, too bad." Charles Scott pressed the stub of his cigar out in the ashtray. "Well, you have some order forms in your sales case there. Pull one out. I know your stuff almost by heart."

Sidney reached into his case, drew out an order blank, and handed it to him. "The items on sale are in red."

"Yeah, I see them," Charles Scott started rapidly entering numbers beside products. "Geez, still trying to push those dang starfish? Things are older than me. Looka that, you have a fire sale price on 'em. Why not? They're practically antiques—maybe I can get collectors interested."

"The Iggy items are blocked out on page three. Have a plush

toy version now, too. And take a look at the candle section. The Sand and Sea? They're sort of new and have a ocean sand finish and a Sea Breeze scent."

"What the hell is a Sea Breeze scent?"

"Got me." Sidney laughed. "Sounds nice."

"You must have a warehouse full of 'em."

"So how did you get into this business?" Sidney asked.

Charles Scott snorted. "You mean why don't I have a real job?" Sidney didn't take the bait. "If you want to know. I was a life insurance agent for a lotta years. Wore me down—wasn't my gig. Cost me my marriage, my sanity, and nearly killed me. The pressure to perform drove me to the edge. I had a mild heart attack and said that's it." He checked order box after order box, signed the form, and handed it back to Sidney. "So I found this cute little job and have been selling gifty stuff and geegaws ever since."

Sidney finished his second drink, begged off another round, and left Charles Scott to his second cigar and a switch to scotch; he had relocated himself to a barstool and was jawing with Jack by the time Sidney had pulled on his windbreaker. The rain had abated. Sidney drove around until he found a reasonably priced motel, checked in, and went next door to a local steak house and had the cheapest ground sirloin they had with a glass of red wine, baked potato, and salad. He was back in his room by eight o'clock. He plugged in his cell phone so it could recharge and turned on the television. The screen brightened into the long face of John Kerry, the newly anointed Democratic nominee for president being interviewed by CNN news commentator Wolf Blitzer.

"Let me tell you, Wolf," Kerry was saying, "today our national security begins with homeland security. The 9/11 commission has given us a path to follow, endorsed by Democrats, Republicans, and the 9/11 families. As president, I will not evade or equivocate. I will immediately implement all the recommendations of that commission."

Sidney recognized the words he'd heard Kerry state again and again. When Wolf Blitzer said, "But, Senator Kerry, how can you—" Sidney hit the mute button and smiled at the mouths opening and closing like fish feeding. After a minute or so of amusement over the silent yawping he flicked the set off and looked around to see if there was anything to read and found a curled paperback in the drawer of the nightstand atop the always-present Gideon Bible. It was an old Ed McBain 87th Precinct novel called *Poison*. The cover was a slash of ominous red lettering beneath the staring face and bare shoulders of a young blonde.

He propped up the pillows on the bed, took off his shoes, rolled back the pages, and had just read the first line when his charging cell phone began to ring. A chill ran up his back. He let it go, and it stopped after five rings; that's when it rolled to voice mail. With the book open on his chest, Sidney waited to see if whoever it was would redial.

The only sound was the rumble of a television coming from an adjoining room. Someone had just slammed a door somewhere when the phone began to ring again. Sidney got up and stood over it and waited until the fourth ring. He picked up the phone, charging cord still attached, and pushed the answer button but didn't say anything. After a moment someone said, "Sidney?"

"What?"

"Ah, there you are," said John Marr.

"So?"

"I'm zeroing in on you. Just thought you ought to know. Seems only fair."

"That right?" said Sidney. "Well, that's really good because the state police are looking for you. Where are you, John Quincey?"

After a pause, Marr chuckled. "Hey, that was a good one, Sid. Had me there for a second or two. But of course you wouldn't do that—call the police."

"That right?"

"Sure. What you gonna tell them? That some bad things happened, and you think I did them? They won't give up a cup of coffee for that. Fact is you're the only loose end I have, and I am going to tie that up real soon."

"That right?" Sidney repeated.

"Yeah, like I said, I'm closing in. I know you're south of Newport. Right?"

Sidney didn't respond.

"Well, I figured out that much. But then that leaves a whole bunch of territory yet to cover. But guess what I did, Sidney. Can you guess?"

Sidney remained silent.

"Okay, I'll tell you anyway." Marr giggled. "I thought, what the heck, I'd just start dropping in on the gift store places along 101 and ask about you. And, boy, has it been fun. I must say, old man, you've made quite an impression on folks. Yes indeed, quite an impression."

Sidney shuddered and sat on the bed.

"That little side trip you took to Eugene? That was a stroke of genius. Threw me, really did. But I've regrouped and have you in my sights. Hey, guess where I am tonight? Go on, guess."

"Up yours," Sidney breathed.

"You're no fun, Sidney. Okay, I'll tell you. Florence."

Sidney inhaled involuntarily.

"What was that sound? A little scary, huh, knowing that I'm closing in. By the way, the Thompsons at the Laughing Clam, they really liked you. Except for you sneaking out early that next morning. They felt bad about that."

"John," Sidney said softly. "Play your game, but you're not getting away with this."

"Think not? Better reconsider, Sidney. I've got a whole lot more to lose than you do, and I am desperate to protect what I have. For you, I'm an inconvenience. For me, this is the endgame." There was a pause. "I'll see you soon."

Sidney pushed the end button. Again the only sound was the muffled bass from a television in a neighboring room. He lay back on the bed and held a pillow over his head to blot out the sound and think. He had to think. What could he do to evade his pursuer? The foam pillow had a dank odor to it; finally he threw it aside, sat up, and reached into his sales case for the Oregon map he kept there. He spread it out on the bed, found Florence, and ran his finger down to Coos Bay—less than 50 miles.

Sidney refolded the map, put it back in the case, and snapped the latch. After pacing the room for a few minutes, he picked up his cell phone and dialed information; he was praying that her number was not unlisted. It wasn't. He wrote it down on the scratch pad provided by the motel. After several deep breaths he dialed and waited as his chest muscles tightened: three rings, four—she wasn't home. Then she answered.

"Janis?" Sidney's voice was tenuous.

"This is she."

"Hi, this is Sidney...Sidney Lister."

There was a slight pause on her end. "Oh, Sidney," Janis Hill said, her voice lighter and more open than when they had last spoken. "How are you?"

"I'm okay."

"Say, did your friend ever catch up to you? What was his name?"

"Was it John Marr?" he answered.

"Yes," she said. "Did he find you?"

"Janis, that's why I'm calling you." He cleared his throat. "Just when and how did he contact you?"

"Well, he came into the store actually, yesterday morning, and asked to see the manager."

"And what did he say? How did he get around to me?"

"Sidney, what is it? Something wrong?"

"Could be. So what did he say to you? I don't want to seem pushy, but I need to know. What did he ask you?"

"If I knew you," she said softly. "If I'd seen you. That he'd been trying to catch up to you. An old friend but that he didn't have your cell phone number and that your company didn't have an actual schedule of where you were at any given time."

"And what did you tell him?"

"He's not your friend at all, is he?" she said.

"No. What did you tell him?"

"That all I knew was you were heading south. Sidney, who is he?"

"My worst nightmare, Janis. Don't worry—he's not the law or anything." He paused. "He's worse than that."

"Are you in danger?" she asked.

Sidney walked toward the television set as far as the charging cord would let him and back before answering. "Yes."

"My god," she breathed. "What are you going to do? Call the police?"

"Look, Janis, if John Marr calls you again just say you don't have any additional information. Don't act as if you know anything. Play dumb so he won't consider you a source of how to find me. Do you understand?"

"Sidney, you need to call—"

"Do you understand what I just said, Janis?" He nearly shouted.

"Yes. I get it. Sidney, what is this all about?"

He lay back down on the bed and stretched his legs out on the faded yellow and brown checked spread. How could he explain in a few short sentences? There was no way to do that.

"Sidney, you there?"

"Yeah, I'm here," he said. "Let's just say it's best that you don't know."

For a moment she didn't respond. "Sidney." Her voice was tentative. "You're creeping me out. What is it?" She tried to laugh. "You can trust a Grant High alum."

Sidney looked up at the ceiling just as another door slammed;

then he heard a car engine start up and a vehicle back away. "It's, well, it's too convoluted to try and tell you the whole of it."

"So give me the Cliff Notes version."

"Well," he closed his eyes, "the short version is that the man you saw—"

"The guy who came into the store? The one I talked to?"

"That was John Marr, yes. He has committed some criminal acts. Some really bad stuff."

"Like what?" Her voice was more uneasy.

"Never mind. Not going to tell you." He inhaled. "The thing is, I'm the only person who knows what he's done. I know it all sounds very melodramatic, like a made-for-TV movie or something."

"No, it sounds awful. What are you going to do? What can you do?"

He sat up and put a hand against his forehead. "The only thing I can do," he said. "Double back and…uh wait—forget I said that. I don't want you to know my whereabouts. Not a good idea for you."

Neither one spoke for a long moment until she spoke. "Sidney, where are you?"

"I can't—"

"Forget that, where are you?"

"Coos Bay. I'm in Coos Bay."

"Coos Bay. Okay, you can do that in a little less than two hours, less if you have a clear road, which you should at this time of night. Were you planning on leaving tonight?"

"I…never mind."

"Come on now. Are you going to leave tonight?"

"Yes."

"Okay," she said, "when you hit Newport, call me. I'll give you directions to my place. You can stay here tonight. I have a hide-a-bed."

"Janis, that's not a good idea," Sidney said.

"Just get going," she said.

In twelve minutes, Sidney had thrown his clothes and toiletries into his bag, tossed the room key on the bed, left the room, and loaded his duffel and sales case into the Cadillac. He closed the car doors with a click, started the engine, and eased out of the motel parking lot.

He hoped that no one noted his departure.

-16-

Sidney topped off the gas tank, bought a large container of so-so coffee in an everything-but-nutrition AM-PM Arco Station store, drove out of Coos Bay, passed through North Bend, and gave the Caddy its head. Janis had been right; traffic was light, and he was able to make good time on a clear night and dry road. On the outskirts of Florence, he felt a chill, realizing that John Marr was in the town. He hoped Marr was sound asleep somewhere off the main highway; he shuddered to think Marr might be sleeping on the same couch bed that he'd slept on at the Thompson's of Laughing Clam. As he waited at a red light, a gunmetal gray four-door BMW turned onto the highway from the opposite corner and proceeded north. When the light turned green, Sidney accelerated slowly and stayed well back of the other car. He didn't know what John Marr drove, but a big BMW seemed the right fit for his self-image. The gray car drove at the posted speed limit through town then began to slow; Sidney did the same until the BMW finally turned off and drove into a residential area.

There were no other cars on the road. He accelerated, and the Caddy easily hummed up to speed. An old Willie Nelson CD, a leftover Jonesy artifact, provided background distraction. He slowed for all the small towns: Yachats, Waldport, Seal Rock, and passed the Newport city limits sign at eight minutes until eleven according to the dashboard clock. An empty supermarket lot served as a pull-off point where he tapped Janis Hill's number onto his cell phone keypad. She answered on the first ring and gave him directions; ten minutes later he found her small condominium complex on Coast Avenue and pulled into a visitor parking slot.

He stepped out of the car, stretched, and looked up—saw stars in the black sky, noted how calm the air was, and relaxed for the first time in several hours. She was waiting for him at an open door to her second-floor condo; they exchanged tight smiles. She stepped back, and he carried his gear inside.

"You made good time," she said.

"Not much traffic. Clear shot most of the way," he responded, still holding his duffel.

"You can put that down anywhere, unless you just want to hold onto it."

He smiled, set the bag down by a boxy couch, and turned to face her. They looked at one another in the quiet; it was an awkward moment. Sidney remembered how often he had viewed Janis Hill as unattainable, the one he and his male classmates had ogled and over whom they had made inane speculations.

And now he was in her space, both of them somewhat weathered by the passing years; she by far the least affected, Sidney observed. The promise for each of them, so clearly defined by the time they had graduated high school, had been tossed and tested, even mauled, into the reality that now defined them. In spite of the twenty-nine years that had passed, Janis Hill could still turn heads. But he sensed that no matter how the years had passed, she was comfortable being just who she was. She hadn't bothered to dress up for his arrival, and why should she? She'd thrown on a white chambray shirt with the tail out, wore blue pajama bottoms, a pair of clunky Uggs slippers, and no makeup and stood looking at Mister Most Likely to Succeed whom she had evidently never noticed. The cheekbones that most of the girls would have died for were still there, as were the blue eyes and the lovely mouth—all of it.

"Well," she said finally and raised her hands.

He blinked and came around. "Yeah. Thanks. This is a huge favor."

She shrugged. "After we talked I began to think about what you told me. Scared the hell out of me."

"I know. I shouldn't be putting you in this position. I can still go find a motel."

"No." She shook her head.

"Really, that's what I should do." He reached for his luggage.

"Sidney, no," she said. "You will *not* do that. Let's have a drink, get comfortable—then we'll talk about this, this...your dilemma." She waved a hand. "Wine, scotch, gin?"

He asked for a gin and tonic; she agreed and asked him to mix the drinks while she got a package of some kind of sliced white cheese out of the refrigerator and pulled a box of wheat crackers from the cupboard. They settled onto the couch with their drinks, and she watched Sidney put away a fistful of crackers and several slices of cheese while draining his drink. When he looked at her, she wore a teasing smile.

"Sorry, I guess all of this has made me hungry," he said. She merely shook her head. "Nice place." He looked around, nodding as if he were viewing architectural splendor.

"It's okay," she said. "Compact, that's for sure. One bedroom, tiny bathroom, everything else out in the open—just the way I like it. Lease will expire in two months. Have to decide if I want to re-up."

"For the job or the condo?"

She laughed. "Good question. Working for Lamont Courter can be a challenge."

"What's he like?"

"You mean you haven't met him yet?"

"Nope, been putting it off. Have to deal with a thorny issue between him and Ned Beeman." He raised his glass, took in the last dribbles over ice.

She studied him. "A thorny issue. He can be that, all right."

He sucked in a ragged breath. "Just what I needed to hear."

"Not your week, is it?"

"No." He set his glass down. "Definitely not. This week has been the most unbelievable blip of time I've ever dealt with. Flat out the weirdest ever. I mean, I've had some highs and lows, but this...this is surreal. I must be dreaming. Tell me I'm dreaming."

She smiled, slipped her slippers off, brought her feet up onto the couch, and sat on them. "I'll bet you wished you *were* dreaming," she said.

"How far back can I go?" he said and laughed. "Lot of ground to cover—about which parts of my life were dreams. I'd go for do-overs on a lot of it."

"Amen." She looked down into her drink tumbler for a long moment.

"Look, it's getting late here," he said, breaking the moment. "If it's okay, there's someone I need to call...."

She sat up with a start. "Sure. I'll get some sheets for the bed."

He stepped out onto the balcony and slid the door closed. The night was cool and quiet. Stars flickered. He took in a deep breath, pulled out his cell phone, and dialed Ellie. She answered after three rings sounding warm and sleepy.

"It's me," he said.

"What is it?" she asked, her voice suddenly clear and alert. "You okay?"

"Yeah, for the moment."

"Where are you?"

"Newport."

"Newport," she echoed. "So what do you mean: for the moment? It's that guy, John Marr. He's still after you, isn't he?"

"Yeah. He's getting serious."

"Now damn it all, Sidney, get on home," she scolded. "I told you."

"I know. I'm working on it. That's why I'm in Newport again. I need to clear some things up in the morning here in Newport. Then I'm outa here. But I need you to write something down. Get a pad and pencil, and I'll dictate it to you. Okay?"

Ellie hesitated. "Okay, give me a sec to find something to write on."

When she was ready, he told her the story of John Marr, in chronological order; he edited it but included the essentials. When he'd finished, neither of them spoke for a bit.

"You got it?" he asked finally.

"Yes." Her voice was a whisper. "What—"

"Hang onto it. Nothing's going to happen but... but if it did—"

"Like what?"

"Oh, I don't know, Ellie. If I turn up missing or something, then give it to the authorities, to the police in Eugene. Promise?"

"Sidney—"

"Promise?"

"Yes, but this is awful. I'm afraid. What if he finds you?"

"I'm going to do my damnedest to stay out of his way. But hell, he can follow me back to Portland anyway."

"Yes, but here we can protect you."

"Who's we? You?" He laughed.

"I'm tough."

"That you are, but this calls for a different kind of tough."

"Where are you now?" she asked. "Someplace safe?"

Sidney turned and looked back into the condo; he could see Janis stretching a sheet over the hide-a-bed. "Yes, I'm safe."

He said good-bye to Ellie and slid the balcony door open. Janis was spreading a blanket over the bed that had been pulled out of the couch. Sidney closed the door and went over to help with the final touches of bed making. They smiled at one another. She bid him goodnight and disappeared into her bedroom. A strange day had ended even more strangely with the most beautiful girl in high school in the next room and a demented predator threatening to kill him.

Sidney thrashed about on the thin hide-a-bed mattress, got up to pee once, and slept maybe fifteen minutes at a time. Around five he turned on a lamp next to the couch and wondered where John Marr was and how long he could evade him. A car door slammed shut down in the condo parking lot; Sidney rose up, heart thudding, but the car started and drove away. No way could he sleep, so he slipped into the bathroom and washed his face, shaved, wet his hair down to get rid of bed head, brushed his teeth, and came out to find Janis Hill in her blue pajamas standing at the kitchen counter pouring water into a coffee maker. She smiled as he stopped abruptly, still wearing only his Jockey shorts.

"Good morning," she said with a lilt and looked him up and down. "Coffee?"

He grabbed his clothes off the chair where he'd left them and walked back toward the bathroom. "Black," he answered, holding his shirt and pants in front of his exposed body.

When he came out fully clothed she was waiting with a red mug full to the brim with steaming black coffee. "Here," she said, handing it to him. "My turn?"

Sidney stepped aside and gestured for her to enter the bathroom. The hide-a-bed had been stripped of sheets and blankets and restored to its day job. It was still dark when he went out onto the balcony again and settled into a plastic chair. He sipped hot coffee and felt a shudder when he realized that it was Sunday. He wouldn't be able to call on Lamont Courter until the next day. He'd have to kill an entire day. A big diesel pickup started up in the small parking lot. It clattered its way out onto the street, and gradually the rattle of the engine faded. Her voice startled him.

"My noisy neighbor," she said. She was dressed in a gray pantsuit with a wine colored curve-necked blouse underneath, ready for work, holding a coffee mug of her own. "He works construction. That's the company truck he brings home every night. Nice, huh?" She sat in the white plastic chair opposite his and peered at him over the rim of her mug.

"Hope I didn't wake you up too early," he said.

"You did."

"Sorry, my head was full of distractions."

"Mine too. Can count on one finger the times I've had an old Grant High grad sleeping over."

"Yeah, Sidney Lister, big distraction huh?"

"Don't sell yourself short. After all, I've seen you in your underwear. Want some toast or a bagel?"

He stared at her for a moment. "A bagel would be great."

"Cream cheese?"

"You bet."

"Come and get it."

She slid two sliced bagels into a toaster oven and pulled a plastic tub of cream cheese from the refrigerator. Sidney poured himself a second cup coffee and watched her move quietly through several domestic steps before setting the bagels on the table and handing him a paper napkin.

"Been a while since I've had breakfast with someone in my own space," she said, smiling. "Not that this is a real breakfast—it's just usually my breakfast. The big switch is from bagels to wheat toast."

"Pretty much the same for me," he said. "Living alone makes it easy to cheat on cooking."

She spread cream cheese, put the knife down, and said, "Okay, enough trivia. What about this character—John Marr, right? He's actually hunting you?"

Sidney nodded, and they both bit into their bagels.

She wiped the corner of her mouth with a napkin. "So what did he do?" she asked; her voice was blunt. "Must be something heavy."

"Look, Janis," he was peering into her blue eyes, "I'm not...I... it's not a good idea to tell you all of it."

"Why not? I'm a big girl, and I've probably seen a lot more of the raw side of life than you ever have."

"Not sure about that."

"Believe it." They were staring at each other, chewing bagels and swallowing coffee; neither of them looked away. "So?" she said.

He licked at the cream cheese on his lips, took in a breath, and told her about John Marr. She never took her eyes off his and never said a word until he had finished.

"That's it," he said and raised the coffee mug to his mouth.

About halfway through the telling, she had stopped eating. When he finished, she took in a breath and looked toward the deck door and daylight. It was then that Sidney noticed the small lines at the edge of her eyes and mouth and the gentle fleshiness beneath her chin, all of which made her more attractive to him. A youthful body with none of life's stress marks, while nice to look at, proved nothing as to how someone would react to what life would throw at him or her. All was promise for the young; he knew how hollow promise could be.

Janis turned her head and caught Sidney studying her. He smiled and felt his face warm. "And so there you have it," he said to fend off the awkward moment.

She shook her head. "Incredible. The man is...is...he's evil. What can you do?"

He leaned forward on his elbows. "I don't know. What I know is enough to maybe get the police curious on a slow day. But I'm pretty sure it's all hearsay in a legal sense and would be filed away in a drawer labeled *Wild-Ass Citizen Accusations.* Then one day,

Sidney Lister might just be gone."

Her eyes widened.

"That is the worst-case scenario I've conjured up, anyway," he said, smiling sadly.

"You really believe it could go that far? My god."

"He's over the edge now, maybe even psychotic—nuts for sure. Like I said, he called it the *endgame* for him."

Janis put her hands around her coffee mug and pulled it back toward her on the table. She looked down into it as if she saw something floating there. "You need to fight back," she said. "Don't you?"

Sidney sat up and folded his arms across his chest. He inhaled deeply and said, "I've thought about it. Going after him, taking him on, but..."

"But what?"

"He's more desperate than I am, has more to lose. I've imagined an entire episode of me turning back on him, becoming the pursuer instead of the pursued. I've planned it all out...that is, right up to the point of facing him. Then what? Throw out a nasty quip? Challenge him to a duel? Bagels at thirty paces?"

She laughed and covered her mouth with both hands. "I'm sorry," she said, "it's not funny, not at all."

"But it is funny. Sidney Lister—hit man? No, I'll just have to stay ahead of him somehow, at least for now."

"But then what?"

"I'll think of something."

Janis reached over and took hold of his hands. "Get some help, Sidney. This guy sounds dangerous."

"Who?" he asked, laughing. "The Grant High football team?"

"That's the right idea," she said. "Seriously."

———•———

Before Janis left for a Sunday's business on the harbor, she offered Sidney another night's stay if he needed to; she left a key on the kitchen counter. With her gone, the condo didn't seem the place to be. He packed up his things, left them all next to the couch, and drove down to the Nye Beach parking lot. The sun was out, but the wind was cool and blowing hard. A seagull swooped low over his head as he took some stairs down to the beach and plowed through the sand, his loafer slip-ons filling some with each step. He finally got onto some firm wet sand and began to walk; the stiff wind was invigorating and served to mask some of his unrest. Ahead of him an elderly man wearing a heavy parka was throwing a stick for his black Labrador to chase down. The dog bounded after each throw as if it was the first time he had ever chased anything. Sidney enjoyed the innocence of the scene and wished he were back selling janitorial supplies, with his only cares being paying rent and buying groceries and not worrying about saving his very life.

When he returned to the parking lot, he sat on a bench and dumped the sand from his shoes and shook out his socks. Back inside the Cadillac, he looked out at the Pacific Ocean, at its constant motion and its endlessness. His cell phone interrupted his reverie; he held the device in his hand and felt the pulse as it rang again and again. He knew who it was.

"What do you want, John?"

There was no response for a moment. "Hey, Sidney, you knew it was me, huh? You got caller ID?"

"No, you're just the only sicko calling me this often."

"You'll think sicko when I catch up to you. I'm having breakfast in Florence, and soon I will be calling on all your customers. Let's see...Reedsport. Anybody in Reedsport who'll remember you? Bet there is."

"Won't make any difference, John Quincey. I'm not even in the state of Oregon anymore."

"What? Nice try, but I don't believe you."

"Hell, after your threatening call last night I packed up and hit the road. I could be in California, or headed to New Mexico, Texas, who knows? Maybe Canada. Anywhere to get you out of my life."

"Don't believe any of that for a minute," Marr said. "What about your job…and, and that company car? Nope, you're right here still in Oregon."

"Quit my job, and I'm buying the car from my former employers. Good-bye, you demented son of a bitch." Sidney hit the kill button and immediately dialed Beeman's. He got the weekend answering machine and left a message for Nina; he told her that if John Marr called he needed her to tell him that he'd quit his job yesterday and was buying the car from them, and they don't know where he was going. He confirmed that he would be meeting meet with Lamont Courter Monday morning and he'd get back to them on how that worked out.

He sat in the car for a while longer and watched the distant silhouettes of people walking, running, children digging in the sand, and dogs chasing things; but he felt no peace in the tranquil scene. When a big boat Oldsmobile pulled in next to him, he jumped, heart pounding, only to see an elderly man and woman slowly extricate themselves from the car. He watched them hold onto one another and shuffle off to the parking lot viewpoint. They stood shoulder to shoulder and looked out to sea, obviously no longer able to enjoy a stroll on the beach. *I should live so long,* Sidney thought.

He spent the rest of the day knocking around the town, going from viewpoint to viewpoint; the most interesting being the Fisherman Memorial park, *Dedicated in loving memory of all Lincoln County based fisherman lost at sea since 1900.* Inside the memorial was a chapel-like room containing photos of many of those lost, along with flowers and candles. Artifacts of remembrance were displayed, everything from watches to padlocks and seashells, even a TV remote.

He ate lunch at a Subway then went down to the historic bayfront and dropped by Courter's Curios to let Janis know that he'd be staying over. He offered to bring in an oyster fry, coleslaw, and garlic bread from a local favorite, Ocean Boy's Fishery, so they could eat in. She grinned her acceptance.

It was nearly seven when she arrived back at the condo looking exhausted. Sidney had kept the oysters warm in the oven. He ordered her to sit; he would serve. She kicked off her shoes, sagged into a chair at the table, and willingly let him be her waiter. They consumed the oysters plus a bottle of chilled chardonnay, chatted briefly about their day—hers had been busy, lots of weekenders shopping; his had been quiet, a footloose tourist—before Janis yawned, begged off, and went to bed. Sidney pulled out the hide-a-bed and lay in the dark.

Where was John Marr, and how was Sidney going to approach Lamont Courter?

-17-

Courter's Curios corporate offices, if one wanted to call them that, were in an older boxy office structure down near the Embarcadero on the harbor. Sidney was sitting in the reception area slightly before ten o'clock Monday morning, waiting his turn to see Lamont Courter. Two other salesmen were ahead of him. The receptionist, an older woman with white hair pulled back and held in place with a set of combs took his name and pointed to where the coffeepot was; he passed on the coffee and thumbed the usual assortment of worn magazines. He was skimming a copy of *Gift World* when the white-haired woman said his name.

He stepped forward, stood while she made him wait, and smiled into her discourteous eyes when she finally said, "Mr. Courter will see you now."

Lamont Courter was sitting behind a huge desk piled high with papers, catalogs, sample products, and assorted other debris. A football sat on one corner of the desk, signed, it looked like. He was stubbing out a cigarette in a big glass ashtray when Sidney entered. He motioned, and Sidney took a seat.

"Beeman's," he said in a raspy voice. "Where the hell's Jonesy?"

Sidney studied the fleshy red face and buzz cut of white hair and said, "He died. Thought maybe you'd heard."

"He what?" Lamont Courter sank back in his chair and looked at Sidney. "No one told me. Died! You shining me on? He and I were supposed to play golf this weekend. No wonder he didn't show."

Sidney smiled; he hated the guy already. "I doubt that Jonesy had a fatal heart attack just to get out of a golf game with you."

The man raised a hand and pawed the air. "Sorry. That's just the first thing that came to mind." He rubbed a hand over his face. "Can't believe it, Jonesy dead. I'll be. So who the hell are you? A quick replacement, I gather."

"Very quick," Sidney answered. "I'm Sidney Lister. Filling in."

Lamont Courter laughed. "And you got the call to make Jonesy's run down the coast in March. Some fun, no doubt."

"Not really."

"I'll bet not really." He leaned forward, grinning wide, yellow teeth showing. "I'd guess you're finding out some pretty peculiar things about our friend Jonesy."

Sidney noticed the purplish splotch on Courter's neck below his right ear. It was a port-wine stain. He remembered an uncle, long dead, who'd had one and how as a small boy he could never take his eyes off the strange purple mark on the man's cheek. Thinking about that he missed Lamont Courter's question.

"How's that?" he asked.

"Jonesy," the man barked. "I said you probably found out some strange things about him along the way."

"Like what?"

"You tell me. He could be a wild man. How about the women? They heartbroken over Jonesy dying?"

"Folks were saddened," Sidney said.

"Horse pucky. Saddened, my ass. The man was a rake of the first order."

"What makes you say that?"

Lamont Courter sat back and eyed Sidney. "You kidding me, fella?"

"What do you mean?"

"Jonesy Jones, that's what I mean. The stories he told me about his days on the road would fill a book—a very raw book, I must say."

"Seemed that he had a gift in dealing with people."

"A gift," Lamont Courter grunted. "What's that supposed to mean?"

"Well," Sidney began, "at one store the manager lamented her loss of an origami partner. At another—"

"Ora got what?"

"It's the art of Japanese paper folding, Jonesy was a master at it. Another woman recalled how he helped her get through her husband's death. And—"

"I get it." Lamont Courter dropped a hand onto his desktop and narrowed his eyes. "I'm the letch who just wanted to hear his stories about fucking women."

"I didn't say that," Sidney responded.

Lamont Courter folded his arms and studied Sidney for a long moment. "I don't much like you style, mister. And let me tell you something, I have a special arrangement with Beeman's. If you want to know the truth, I have old Ned Beeman by the balls. Something between him and me that gives my company here favored status. And I intend to continue exercising that status. Understand?"

Sidney smiled.

"Something funny?"

"Mr. Courter, I understand—"

"Good. Now we can get down to cases. I expect—"

"Sorry," Sidney interrupted. "I meant to say that I understand what you would like to be your status. However, you didn't have such privileges with Jonesy, did you?"

"What do you mean?"

"As I've been advised, you and Jonesy negotiated a special agreement when he came to work for Beeman's. That agreement has worked well for both parties, and Beeman's will continue to operate on those same terms."

Lamont Courter's face had taken on a reddish hue, almost making the port-wine stain invisible. He rose up in his chair. "Who the hell do you think you're dealing with, mister? Listen up good. Jonesy and I had a fine working relationship. You might even say we were friends. But he's dead, and the agreement—call it an understanding—well, that just died with him. It's rescinded. Get it?"

Sidney retained his smile. "I hear what you're saying. However, as I said, we will continue to operate under the same agreement as before, Jonesy or no Jonesy."

"Are you deef?" Courter punched at an old intercom box. "Yeah, Gert, get me Ned Beeman on the line, Beeman's International. Yes now!"

"Wait, Mr. Courter," Sidney broke in. "No need to do that."

"Hold it a minute, Gert," Courter said into the box. "So you agree with me, Mr. Lister."

"I didn't say that. We'd better talk some more." Sidney nodded toward the intercom.

Lamont Courter stared at Sidney for a moment then said, "Gert, I'll get back to you. Now what the hell do you think you're doing?" he said to Sidney.

"I think we know, don't we, Lamont?"

"I have not a clue what you're talking about." But the man had sagged back in his chair, and his tone was less aggressive.

"Nice football you have there," Sidney said. "Signed, I see."

Lamont Courter didn't take his eyes off Sidney. "Yeah, Jonathon Smith. He was quarterback for Oregon State. Signed that for me in 2001, his senior year."

"You a big fan of OSU?"

"Uh-huh."

"Big donor, too?" Sidney asked.

"I do what I can." Lamont Courter reached for the pack of

155

cigarettes on his desk, tapped one out, and lit up with a butane lighter.

"May I?" Sidney gestured toward the ball.

Lamont Courter nodded and watched Sidney go to the corner of the desk and pick up the football. He rolled it in his hands, examined the signature, and put it back down.

"Play football yourself, Lamont?"

"High school."

"Go to all the OSU games in Corvallis, do you?"

"Most."

"How many years, would you say? More than five or six?"

Lamont Courter exhaled a cloud of smoke and tapped the cigarette over the ashtray. "I've been a season ticket holder for over twenty years."

"Really. That long."

"Yeah, but what's this got to do with the price of bologna in Brazil?"

Sidney sat back down and crossed his legs. "Oh, a lot, really. I understand that Jonesy was a football fan, too—at least when it came to your interest in the game, especially in OSU football. Am I right?"

Lamont Courter didn't respond, but his eyes were boring into Sidney's.

"Are we beginning to have an understanding here?" Sidney asked.

"No idea what you're talking about. But, I'll tell you, I'm not liking your attitude. So if you want to continue to do business with me, you'd better—"

"Home game," Sidney cut in. "October 31, 1998, OSU and California. The Beavers lost 19-20. You and a friend consoled one another at a local watering hole. Got a buzz on."

Lamont Courter stood up at his desk and leaned on his fists. His eyes were wide. "How the hell…Jonesy was the only one who knew. Promised me."

Sidney kept going. "On the road home, west of Philomath on Highway 20—"

"Stop!" Lamont Courter yelled. He put his hands over his ears and slumped back down in his chair.

When the man took his hands down, Sidney went on. "There was a boy, on a bike, and you hit him. But you and your friend drove away that night, didn't you?"

"It was an accident—I didn't see him. Really, I didn't see him…I didn't mean to—"

"But he's dead anyway. And Jonesy knew all of that, didn't he?"

Lamont Courter looked up at the ceiling. He nodded. "How did you—"?

"Jonesy kept his word. He never said anything about this. But men tell their wives everything, Lamont."

Lamont Courter closed his eyes. When the intercom buzzed, he hit the button and told the one called Gert that he couldn't be disturbed. "So what do you want?" he asked.

Sidney stood and walked to a window that overlooked a parking lot. The window needed washing. Sidney put his open hand against the cool glass and thought of being Lamont Courter's worst nightmare. He knew how that felt. After all, he had his own demon. He couldn't help wondering at that moment where John Marr was and if his ruse was working. When he turned back, Lamont Courter was still seated, looking his way; he had fired up another cigarette. Sidney walked back and sat down again. The two men studied each other for a long interval. Sidney was uncertain of where to begin, and undoubtedly Lamont Courter was hesitant to say anything in the face of the renewed threat.

"Where to begin," Sidney said finally.

"Hell," Lamont Courter croaked, "just spit it out. How much hide do you plan on taking off me?"

"No, it's not that. I'm sure you and Jonesy had a gentlemen's agreement."

"Gentlemen's agreement as long as I kissed his ass."

"I can imagine. No, I'm caught up with just how much life is about 'gotcha.' And you've been a player." Sidney pointed at Lamont Courter. "Who knows, if you hadn't played gotcha on Ned and leveraged what you knew to threaten him, maybe Jonesy wouldn't have had to do a turnabout and essentially terrorize you in return. It was terror you felt, wasn't it?"

Lamont Courter drew on his cigarette and squinted as smoke rose up. He studied Sidney but didn't respond.

"And maybe you are feeling it again. No statute of limitations on killing someone, I guess. Now there's a new Jonesy standing in your office talking about football. Your guts must be churning. Mine would be."

"There a point to all this?" Lamont Courter said. "How long you gonna gloat? I've got a business to run. If you're going to turn me in, do it for all I care."

Sidney leaned forward. "Lamont, you're not a nice guy. Are you?"

Lamont Courter clenched his teeth but didn't respond.

"Okay, I guess we're agreed on that," Sidney said. "So here's the deal. We'll go on doing business like before under the Jonesy agreement, and your secret is safe with us. The only problem for you is that several more people know the story now. The Beemans didn't have a clue about the deal between you and Jonesy, but now they do. You should be treating Ned Beeman with a tad more respect, and business will go on as usual. Agreed?"

Courter did a stare-down with Sidney then said, "Agreed."

"By the way," Sidney asked, "how on earth did Jonesy find out?"

Courter glowered. "My football buddy," he grunted, "the one with me when I hit the kid. Turns out he was Jonesy's brother-in-law. Died of stomach cancer a while back. Guess he needed to get the thing off his conscience, so he told Jonesy. Couldn't believe it. I wished to hell I had missed that lousy game. Over and over I've wished that."

"I'm sure."

The man sniffed at Sidney and reached into a desk door, brought out a bottle of Jim Beam and a dirty glass, and poured himself a drink.

———•———

Sidney left Lamont Courter smoking another cigarette, sipping his bourbon, and staring at nothing. When he walked out through the reception area, the woman, Gert, looked at him as if he was from the CIA. He smiled at her and wished her a nice day; her response was to glower even more.

Outside it was cool, and the day had clouded over; a mist was in the air. Sidney pulled the collar up on his jacket, headed for the Cadillac, sat in the car, and called Beeman's on his cell. Nina answered as usual and got Ned on the line at Sidney's request. He could sense their anxiousness from the tone of their voices and the fact that neither one started chattering at him. He started by telling them that he had just come from meeting with Lamont Courter.

There was silence; then Ned asked, "How was that? Did he try to kill you?" He laughed over his own joke.

"Not funny, Ned," said Nina. "Behave now. What was his response, Sidney? Did you tell him about...well, about what we know?"

"Yeah, I told him. Almost sad in a way."

"Sad?" Ned broke in. "Nothing sad about that creep. Has it coming."

"He's not alone on that, Ned," Sidney said. "We all have a piece of that."

"So what now?" Nina asked.

"Just go about your business with Courter's. And never bring this matter up, never. You hear me, Ned? Never. Ned?"

"Yeah, I hear ya."

"You understand? Do not ever mention it to anyone, let alone to Lamont Courter. We're skirting the law here, probably breaking it, so keep your trap shut unless you want trouble."

"We'll do as you say," Nina said. "Now what about you and your devil? John Marr? By the way, I got your message off the answering machine this morning."

"Okay. Did he call you?"

"Yes, about an hour ago," she said. "Asked if you were still employed by us."

"What'd you say?"

She laughed. "I turned on a real snot, you know, madder than hell. Cussed about you just up and quitting on us in the middle of a sales trip."

"He believe you?"

"Who's to know? Maybe. And, like you said, he asked about the car, actually said: *What about the Cadillac?*" She laughed some more. "I cussed again about you just taking the car and lying that you are going to pay for it. Threatened to call the cops on you."

"You really laid it on. Good job. Hope it works. So what do we do now about the rest of the south coast? I have the stretch from Coos Bay to Brookings that I haven't covered. Still want me to do it?"

"I don't know," Nina said. "I'm afraid for you. Ned?"

"Hell yes, we need that business."

"Ned," Nina said, "for heaven's sake, Sidney's in real danger here."

"Yeah but...okay, you're right. Sorry, Sid."

"How do the orders look so far? Any good compared to Jonesy's numbers?"

"Yes," Nina said, "stronger than we figured. We appreciate your hard work, don't we, Ned?" Ned grunted.

"Tell you what," Sidney said. "I'll hang around Newport for another day or so, rent a car, and finish up down south on a blitz run and head back. How's that sound?"

"Rent a car?" Ned said.

"Yeah, park the Cadillac out of view and use a rental. Less likely that Marr can spot me in another car if he didn't buy Nina's story and is still roaming 101."

"We made a payment on the *MasterCard*, so you should use that one," Nina said.

Sidney ended the call with Ned moaning about using the credit card and Nina reminding him to be careful. He drove down to the harbor to find Janis. She was in the store when he entered, talking with a woman about hand-knitted scarves. She spotted him and smiled as she wound a red scarf around her neck in a stylish manner. The woman she was waiting on smiled and nodded and probably thought the scarf would look as good on her as it did on Janis Hill. It wouldn't.

After the happy customer left, Janis came over to where he was fiddling with some shot glasses with NEWPORT OREGON etched on them. He had to smile because she looked so good and was smiling at him.

"Those are a hot item," she said, looking at the glasses.

"Be better if they had scotch in them," he said.

"Maybe something could be arranged." She smiled wider. "How'd your meeting go with Courter?"

"The man's a piece of work."

"Told you."

"I did all right with him," Sidney shrugged. "Don't think I made his day, though."

"So, you going back to Portland?"

"No. I'll be here for a day or two then finish my run down to Brookings."

She lost her smile and searched his face. "Is that safe? What about that creep?"

"I've made a few maneuvers, see if they work. I was thinking more about asking you out to dinner."

She studied him for a moment.

"Unless you'd feel at risk, me being hunted down and all. Or you don't want to be seen with the most likely to succeed male graduate of Grant High's class of '75."

She laughed. "That's it—being hunted by a nut who wants to kill you doesn't faze me. But the Grant High thing could be a real embarrassment. When and where?"

"You tell me."

She looked at her watch. "Seven, and let's do Italian but not down here. There's a place up on the highway in a strip center, believe it or not, good food. Jim's Great Italian. I know, not an inspiring name, but it is very good food. Look it up. I'll meet you there."

He intended to enjoy the moment and shrug off John Marr— could he?

-18-

Sidney left the shop, passed the fish processing plant with its tangy aroma, and strolled on down to a boardwalk where he could see the fishing fleet at rest, huddled in their berths. Seals barked incessantly as they lazed on the rocks of the jetty just off the fish plant. It was cool, but he sat on a bench anyway and watched the gulls fly about and a couple of boats chug into their berths. Even with the picturesque distractions of the harbor, the aggregate of the past week's lunacy swarmed into his mind, and he couldn't keep from sorting through it all, episode by episode: the faces and lives of those he'd told of Jonesy's death flashed by like old friends; the anguish on Lamont Courter's face when he realized his secret was out of the box—again; the pleasurable chance meeting of Janis Hill. But the threat to his life hovered above all those things.

A seagull circled in and let go with a large white dollop that hit with a rude splat on the bench inches away from Sidney's leg. It then had the temerity to waddle around on the boardwalk as if a food offering would be forthcoming. Sidney laughed and decided that the avian insult along with a growing chill was enough. He left the bird eyeballing him and found a coffee shop nearby in an old house, ordered an Americano and a bran muffin, sat in a soft armchair, and picked through some left-behind remnants of the daily paper. The headlines above the fold on the front page spoke of more trouble in the Middle East and a court order to halt same-sex marriages in San Francisco. He tossed the paper aside, concentrated on his muffin and coffee, and without warning was hit by a feeling of invisibility, like he was there in that place but not really.

He looked around him. He was used to being a stubborn loner and had convinced himself that he liked it that way, even preferred it. So why now was he feeling this hollowness? The sense that he could walk out of that coffee shop, go down to the harbor, slip down into the water and disappear, and after a few days of inconvenience to the locals and fuss and feathers by the few who knew him—be history.

The voice roused him. He looked up into the face of a smiling young woman who was wearing a blue knit hat and had a silver stud sparkling on one nostril of her nose.

"Yes?" he said.

"I was wondering, are you done with the paper?"

He assured her he was; she smiled some more, thanked him, and walked away with it. For an instant, Sidney thought of inviting her to join him and discuss the news of the day. Even buy her a cup of coffee. But the idea made him laugh to himself, and considered that the young woman would likely cringe at the thought of it. *The guy was old enough to be my father,* he could imagine her telling a friend. A few minutes later, he gathered up his empty cup and plate and took them over to the bus bin. On the way out the young woman who had asked for the paper happened to look up. He smiled, but she just went back to her reading; he left fully assured that she had only wanted the paper.

———•———

He stepped out into the mist and walked back past Courter's, looked in through the displays in the window and toyed with the idea of going in, but went on. Since Janis' offer of a bed hadn't been left opened-ended, he went searching for a motel and found the Eight Bells Economy Inn up on the highway; it fit his needs and budget. He checked in, showered and shaved, and laid out his freshest shirt, slacks, and blue blazer then stretched out on the bed and promptly fell asleep. He woke at six forty-five, jumped up, washed the sleep from his face, wet his hair and ran a comb through it, dressed in a rush, and sped off.

Jim's Great Italian wasn't hard to find. It was like Janis had said, in a strip center between the Ace Hardware store and Smythe's Furniture Emporium. For a Monday night the place was busy. Sidney parked in among a crowd of cars and followed a young couple into the restaurant; the foyer was four deep with people waiting. He looked around for Janis but didn't see her, and then she was at his side grabbing his right hand and pulling him along to a table in a far corner. She gestured for him to sit.

"Best table in the place," she said. "I hope you are impressed."

Sidney smiled at her over the candle flickering between them in its faux crystal glass holder. "I am. A cozy table away from the furor—very nice. Busy place. Must be good."

"It is. You'll see. It would be good even in Portland."

He thought she looked terrific and could tell she'd gone to some extra effort to dress for the occasion. Her hair was different, like she had put something on it to give it more body or something; whatever, it was beautiful. She was wearing a dark blue dress with a scooped neckline and a thin gold band necklace and matching earrings. He was enjoying all of that when she spoke.

"Sidney, what are you doing?"

"Admiring you," he said. "Is that okay? You look lovely."

"Of course." Color rose in her cheeks. "Thank you. It's nice to have a reason to dress up a little. This is not a dress-up town. Part of its charm."

A young man wearing a black apron with JIM'S GREAT ITAL-IAN stitched on it in yellow lettering appeared with menus and a wine list; he poured ice water and asked if they were interested in ordering a drink. Janis took the initiative and ordered a bottle of Oregon pinot noir.

"My favorite," she said, "from the Sokol Blosser winery up in Yamhill County. You'll love it. Now tell me about your meeting with old man Courter. You said something about a thorny issue, so must have been fun." Her smile was a tease.

"No," Sidney began, "it was interesting, but it wasn't fun. And I can only tell you that after a difficult time of give and take, we came to an understanding."

"About what?"

Sidney saw the question in her eyes and retreated from answering while he considered what to say.

"That serious?" she said.

"No," he started, "it's just that…well…yes, it is serious, and I can't tell you the whole of it." He raised a hand. "On my honor."

She laughed lightly. "So what can you tell me?" Her eyes were dancing with mischief. "Other than the *big* secret."

Sidney couldn't help but smile. "I guess you could call it a game of pin the tail on the donkey. My employer and your employer have been taking turns being pinned or doing the pinning. The ouch factor is what we cleared up today."

"The ouch factor?" She laughed. "What's that?"

"Let's just say that if you're the one saying ouch, things are not going in your favor. You are the one being pinned. My errand today with Lamont Courter was to make sure that my employer isn't saying ouch."

"And…is he?"

"No. He is not."

"But Courter is."

Sidney nodded. "I would say so, yes."

She studied him intently for a moment. "Boy, you sure know how to get a girl's curiosity up. That's all you are going to tell me?"

"All I can tell you. Believe me, Janis, it's all you want to know."

The waiter returned with the wine, forcing her curiosity aside while he opened the bottle with a flourish and poured a small portion into her glass. She tipped up the glass for a taste, winked at Sidney, and nodded her approval. After the pour, Janis told the waiter they needed more time before ordering and lifted her glass.

"To the class of 1975," she said. Their glasses clinked, and they each took a swallow of the lush red wine. Sidney smiled his appreciation. "Only the best for a fellow grad," she said. "So that's all I get to know about you and Courter?"

"Afraid so."

"Okay, man of mystery and drama, what about the other guy, the one on your trail? Do you know where he is?"

"I did until today. I tried to put Marr off my trail by some lying and maneuvering. Hopefully he bought it."

She shook her head. "Where will it end?"

Sidney said, "Good question. Can we talk about something else?"

Janis smiled as the waiter returned. "Sure, let's order some great food. I recommend the crab ravioli or the clam linguini. Both are wonderful."

They both chose the ravioli with garlic broccoli and a mista salad. They continued to enjoy the wine with a basket of olive bread and managed to chat about days gone by instead of Sidney's dilemmas.

"Janis, I've always been curious about what happened to you after high school," Sidney was saying when their food was placed on the table.

She examined her plate, studied the presentation of the food, but didn't answer his question. "This looks lovely," she said.

He agreed. They began to eat, humming their pleasure and adding swallows of wine. Every time Sidney got ready to restart the conversation, the waiter would come by to top off their water glasses and pour more wine until the bottle was empty.

"You're right," Sidney interjected when the waiter had once

come and gone. "Great food. Best ravioli I've had—ever."

She smiled. "I became someone else, but I guess you know that?"

"What?"

"You asked what happened to me after high school. I said I became someone else. Do you know who I became?"

Sidney blushed. "Janis, I didn't mean to pry. I was only—"

"It's okay, Sidney." She reached out to touch the hand he had laid on the table. "I haven't talked about it for a long time, is all. When I think about it, it's like another person lived that life, not me. You ever feel that way?"

"Oh yeah," he answered. "Flashbacks. You have flashbacks? I do. They're like a book of short stories. They're in the same volume, but each chapter is different—but the ending is always the same."

The waiter reappeared, handed them each a dessert menu, recommended the tiramisu, then left to let them think about it. Janis read the menu and put it down.

"I don't want any dessert. You?" she said.

"I'm pretty stuffed," Sidney answered.

She looked at her wristwatch. "It's still early. Let's go to my place. I have a fair bottle of brandy only partly gone. Want to help me finish it off?"

Sidney agreed easily and followed her blue Honda Accord to the condo. He settled in on the couch and watched her move around effortlessly: getting glasses, the brandy, and bring everything over on a tray—simple acts, but he took pleasure in just watching her. She smiled and handed him a snifter; he poured and they sat back to sniff the aroma and sip the brandy.

"I'm not a connoisseur of liquor. I just bought this for price. Hope it's okay," she said.

"It's fine. Thanks."

"Sure," she said. "Nice having a guest. I'm not very social."

"Really? I always thought of you as…I don't know—"

"A party girl?"

Sidney's laugh was self-conscious. "Something like that."

"I know everyone thought that." She rolled her eyes. "Not true. First off, I was really shy, and then none of you guys ever asked me out."

"No way," Sidney said. "Come on, I don't believe that for a moment."

"It's true. I swear." She raised a hand.

"Never would've thought that."

"That's because of what came after high school. My showgirl days."

"When you became someone else, you said."

She stood suddenly, spun around, raised her arms, and kicked one leg up, laughing. "Meet Electra Bly," she announced.

Sidney laughed and clapped his hands.

"Wow, I haven't done that in years," she said, laughing hard. "I think I hurt myself." She put a hand in the small of her back. "I used to be able to kick nearly vertical with either leg for three shows a night, day after day. I was in great shape back then."

"You look in great shape now," Sidney said.

"Oh sure." She sat back down on the couch and reached for her glass.

"Electra Bly. Your show name. I'd forgotten."

"Yep, my alter ego. We lived together in New York and Vegas and finally Reno for over twelve years. She and I, we laughed, loved, and cried together until we couldn't anymore."

"Couldn't?"

"I should say until they wouldn't let us do it anymore. You know who *they* are, don't you? *They* are always around, wherever you are. In my case, they were the ones who watched the hourglass. Hourglass that was a joke among the chorus girls, what with being judged by our hourglass figures and the hourglass of time. When the sand ran out of one or the other *they* pulled the plug."

"Sounded like an exciting life to those of us who clocked in at a routine job every day. One of our own had hit the big time. We talked about you at every reunion."

She looked at Sidney and reached out to pat his arm. "I know. And it was exciting for a long stretch. When I was still young and naïve. The music, the crowds, the stage—showtime! Nothing like it. Then it becomes a job like any other, only with feathers and leg kicks. But..."

"But what?"

Her smile was sad. "You don't want to hear my *poor me* tale, Sidney. Let's just sip our brandy and relax. The end of a nice evening."

"Maybe we can trade tales of woe."

"Now that sounds like fun. Okay," she turned toward him, "you go next. Tell me the Sidney Lister tale."

"It's going to tower over your story," he laughed. "Mister Most Likely to Succeed will blow you out of the water. Ready?"

"I can handle it."

He began with the marriage, job of promise number one, and then gradually on through the trail of possibilities and a spiral of mediocrity right down to when he walked into her store. When he had finished, they sat in the quiet for some time and finished off the bottle of brandy.

"That's not the way it's supposed to go, is it, Sidney?" She spoke softly.

"I don't know. I made my own choices."

"Me too. And here we are, the remnants of the brightest shining examples of our class. So you still see Ellie, then."

Yeah." He chuckled. "Like I said, we have this special arrangement."

"At least she still cares about you."

"There's that. We just can't live together."

"I was married," she said. "First time I was only nineteen."

"First time?"

170

"Three times all told. Each one sadder than the last. Number one was twenty years older than me, an ardent fan—with money. He was also a drunk who'd push me around some then weep about it—that old story. Number two tried to save me from number one. He was a young guy who fantasized about being a big talent agent and used me to jump-start his own big plans. That's when I moved to Vegas. The *big plans* sort of worked because I could still sing in those days, and that got me more work. For a while it did. Then number two saw a younger version of me and decided he had big plans for her. After that I moved on to Reno to see if I could rediscover my career. Did some chorus shows and met up with number three, a sweet guy. A stand-up comedian. He was trying for a comeback, too, so we were attracted to one another for that reason. We had this two-week romance and got married. Then I learned that he was getting himself wired for his gig each night with a snort. He talked me into trying it, too. Took most of what we were earning for the habit."

"My god," Sidney said.

"Yeah. Anyway, one morning while the comedian was sleeping it off, I packed up and used what money I had to get a flight back to Portland. Stayed with my folks for a few months until they'd had enough. I'd found a job at a dress shop selling high fashion but making peanuts. Hard to believe, looking back on it, but I worked there four years. But I kept looking for something else and saw an ad about managing in a gift shop on the coast. So here I am. Been here a long time, longer than I was Electra Bly."

"You divorced now?"

"Oh yeah, the comedian was good about it. We split, and last I heard he's still telling jokes somewhere."

"Any children?" Sidney ventured.

She didn't answer, just looked down into her empty snifter. Then she moved her head side to side slowly. "No. No children."

"Me either. Ellie was adamant about that," he said. "Having kids was not on her life agenda, never would be." He chuckled.

"That was made painfully clear to me from the moment I had lust in my eyes."

"Not for lack of possibility," she went on, as if she hadn't heard Sidney. "Lost two. One because a twenty-year-old dancer couldn't…make that mustn't…lose her figure. The next time, my body paid me back."

They fell silent. A car door slammed down in the parking lot. Janis excused herself to use the restroom, so Sidney stepped out onto the balcony deck and breathed in the nighttime ocean-borne air. The mist had finally let up. He was looking down over the railing, listening to a couple arguing about something Sidney couldn't figure out. When the door to their condo shut, Janis was at his side.

"Those are the Wilsons," she said. "The *Warring Wilsons* as they are known among my neighbors. Almost makes one happy to be solo."

"Almost?"

"Until pleasant occasions like this."

"Yes."

"How about a walk on the beach?" she said. "Since I live here I don't very often do that anymore."

"I don't have any beach-walking shoes," Sidney said. "Last time out, I filled my loafers to the brim with sand."

"Think I may have some old shoes you could fit into." She smiled. "I've had a couple of male visitors."

"Ones who left clothing behind?"

"Be nice."

Sidney pulled on an abused pair of Adidas running shoes that Janis pulled out of her front closet; they were a size too big, but he cinched them up tight. It was cool, the sky was clear, and there was no wind. They put on coats and walked several blocks to the Nye Beach turnaround, past the Yaquina Art Center, and took the stairs down to the beach. Lights from the houses and businesses cast enough illumination to see where they were going. The tide was still in, so the surf foam shown a phosphorescent white in the indirect light from the shore. They slogged in loose sand until the footing firmed up on damp sand and walked for a distance with the sound of the waves breaking.

Janis pointed to a big driftwood log that was resting high up on the beach, a third of its body settled into the sand; they backed up to its smooth gray surface and sat facing the surf, their shoulders touching. Two figures came out of the darkness and passed by in front of them, a young couple holding hands and laughing. Suddenly the woman pushed her partner abruptly, and he plopped over onto the sand. She ran off, broadcasting a joyous peel of laughter, and soon her boyfriend was up and in hot pursuit, growling playfully. They faded into the darkness.

"Don't get any ideas," Sidney said. "I'm not running anywhere in these galoshes. Besides, you'd have to help me up."

Janis laughed and shoved an elbow into his ribs. "You mean you wouldn't chase after me? What about the Sidney who coveted me in high school?"

Sidney hesitated, uncertain, and then put an arm around her shoulders. "He's right here," he said.

Instead of pulling away, she leaned into him. "Good," she said. "That's good."

"Yes." A lean male runner came out of the dark and went by on long, smooth strides. Sidney followed him with his eyes and said, "Do you ever feel lonely?"

She didn't answer right off. "I guess everyone does at some time," she said after a moment. "Why?"

"How does it affect you?"

She reached over and took the hand in his lap and held it between her hands. "What is this? Sidney?"

"There was a moment today, after I saw you in the store, when I felt invisible. When I had this hollowness in me, like there was nothing there. It was strange. I was in a coffee shop with people all around me, and I…this sense of being no one came over me."

She squeezed his hand. "Being in a crowd can be one of the loneliest places on earth. I ought to know."

"Yeah, but it was a realization that if I were gone tomorrow… what difference would it make?" He got up off the log and took a step. "Nothing," he said to the black.

"Hey," Janis said, stepping to his side. "Let's go back." She took his hand.

It was after midnight when they returned to her condo. They undressed slowly in her bedroom with a lamp from the living room casting a dim light. Sidney saw her body and felt the pleasure of seeing her shapes: her neck and the hollow beneath it, the breasts he'd always wondered about as a teenage boy, her waist, her hips. It was unlike Ellie and he playing their sensual games. And it wasn't how he'd imagined the unattainable Janis Hill when he was seventeen, or how his dufus male friends had discussed her dimensions, complete with hand movements, and then laughed like fools.

Sidney shivered and reached out; she came to him. They touched and kissed gently before slipping between the cool sheets of her bed and holding one another. With no shyness they explored and stroked and made love easily.

It was as if they had done it together many times before.

-19-

Just as first light was seeping in, Sidney slipped out of Janis' bed and stood looking down at her sleeping form. Her hair was partially covering her face; her breathing was deep and rhythmic, the way of a sound sleeper. He gathered his clothes from the various places they had landed and dressed quietly in the living room. He wrote her a short note and left it on the kitchen counter: *Mister Most Likely still covets you—Sidney.* He wrote his cell phone number beneath his name.

He drove back to the Eight Bells motel, showered, packed, and dressed in a pair of khakis, a plaid sport shirt, and his blue blazer, and checked out. The clouds were high and dry. He found a café open for breakfast, enjoyed a short stack of buttermilk pancakes with a couple of eggs and coffee, and picked up a discarded copy of the daily newspaper from Eugene. There wasn't any more news of the fire, which gave Sidney a foreboding that John Marr might get away with the crime unless he took the step he'd considered but shied from—contacting the authorities.

At the motel front desk he had asked where he could rent a car on the cheap, and the jowly woman manager with a smoker's voice recommended Carson's Cars. He found the place at the south end of town on the highway. The cramped lot held a mixed array of used cars. A huge billboard rose above a squatty sales office building. In a splash of letters red and black it read: CARSON'S CARS: WE SELL 'EM • WE RENT 'EM • WE BUY 'EM. The owner, Charlie Carson, agreed to let Sidney park the Cadillac on the back of the lot for a few days in exchange for renting him a well-preserved 1998 Hyundai Elantra sedan. He loaded everything he needed into the rental and headed south. Twenty-four miles out of Coos Bay he drove into Bandon—or Bandon-By-The-Sea as the Chamber of Commerce billed it—known for its cranberry bogs and array of craggy volcanic sea stack rocks in the surf at Bandon Beach.

Sidney's first stop was the local museum gift shop; it wasn't open, so he slid an order form and catalog under the door. The customer log indicated they always ordered the same two items anyway: logo hats and rubber magnets. Down by the harbor in Old Town, the owner of a bait, tackle, and gift shop, a jolly fellow with a grey crew cut and gold-rimmed glasses, was surprised to see an actual over-the-road salesman. He didn't remember anybody named Jonesy, never heard of Beeman's, but was so delighted to do business face to face rather than on the Internet that he gave Sidney a substantial order. The other stop in Old Town was Hazel's Card & Gift. The shop had been a Beeman's account for a long time, and orders had been consistently above average.

Hazel Truitt was in her early forties, slender, had short blonde hair and a pleasing face. She was having a cup of tomato soup and a homemade tuna sandwich out of a plastic sandwich bag when he found her at the back of the shop. She apologized for being caught eating her lunch.

"I'm a one-person gang here," she said. "Grab my food when I can. Let's see, you're selling something—can tell that. What's your game?"

Sidney laughed. "First, I'm a messenger," he said.

Hazel Truitt set her soupspoon back down in the cup. "Now that's an intriguing opening line. What's the message?"

"Well," Sidney put his sales case on the floor, "to begin with, my name is Sidney Lister, and I'm from Beeman's International." He reached out to her with one of his hand-lettered business cards.

She looked at it and dropped her smile. "But there's more."

"Yes. I'm replacing Oscar Jones as your sales rep."

"That so?" Her smile was wary. "Replacing Jonesy. Why's that?"

Sidney studied her face and tried to gauge what her reaction would be. "He passed," he said. "Jonesy died."

Hazel Truitt sat stone still and stared at him, her eyes unblinking.

She picked up her sandwich, took a bite, chewed it, and washed it down with a spoonful of red soup. After a moment she smiled. "You know, I can see his big smile and his big body in my mind's eye. He would barge into the shop and boom out a big hello to me—and my mother. She's Hazel, too. Retired last year. Wait, I'd better call her."

Sidney stood back and watched as she dialed the phone on the sales counter and listened to the one-sided conversation as two women shared unpleasant news. When she hung up the phone, her eyes were wet, and her smile was sad.

"Silly," she said and wiped at her eyes with a hankie. "Us getting all weepy over a traveling salesman. What I mean is…that didn't come out right, sorry."

Sidney shook his head. "That's okay. I've had a lot of responses to Jonesy's death. No two were alike."

Hazel Truitt shook her head. "What a bummer."

"You name it, I've likely heard it," he said.

She stepped around the counter and came up close to Sidney. "Jonesy was on my preferred list of certain traveling gentlemen."

Sidney felt his face grow warm. "Is that right?" he said. "Preferred list?"

"Uh-huh." She smiled with a tilt of her head. "We had this understanding, one we both enjoyed, I must say."

"Okay," he responded, stringing the word out as far as it would go.

She reached out and brushed something invisible off Sidney's blazer. "Now tell me, Sidney, have you seen my order record with Beeman's? I know you have. Pretty healthy, wouldn't you say? I'm not stupid—you'll see that I order just the good stuff from your line. It's just that I also order according to other priorities." She raised her eyebrows.

Sidney widened his smile but didn't know what to say so said nothing.

"Want to know how it works?" she said with a twinkle. "My preferred list?"

"Have a choice?"

"Not if you want to hold Jonesy's place on the list. Do you?"

He shrugged. "Spell it out. Guess I can choose to opt out."

"Sure enough." She laughed. "Okay. First there's dinner."

"Dinner."

"Yes. And that would be at the George Sand Bistro. Jonesy's favorite, mine too. Great food. You'll love it."

"Okay." Sidney was thankful that Nina had made a payment on the MasterCard account.

Hazel Truitt was enjoying herself. "Then after dinner we'll adjourn to your motel room for after-dinner drinks and an afterglow of conviviality."

"Afterglow."

She nodded. "By the way, you should get a room reserved over at Cecilia's Armitage Inn."

"I should? Cecilia's?"

"Yes. They can fill up, but it shouldn't be a problem this time of year. Oh, and Jonesy always asked for room 202. Second floor, view of the beach—his favorite." She pulled a thin phone book out from behind the counter and tossed it at him. "Here, you make reservations at the restaurant and the motel. Not right for a lady to do that." She chuckled at his uneasiness. "Now pull out an order form. I'll take care of the dreary business part while you make those calls."

Sidney made reservations; and, after Hazel Truitt filled out a more than respectable order, he left and checked into room 202. He enjoyed the view while he considered how to respond to Hazel Truitt's expectations for the evening ahead. As agreed, he picked her up at the house she and her mother shared, a small bungalow not far from the gift shop. They had reservations at George Sand Bistro for eight o'clock; the food was indeed quite good, and she proved to be fun company and a good conversationalist. At around ten o'clock, they left the restaurant and walked to Sidney's rental. She complained a second time about missing out on riding in the big Caddy but allowed Sidney to hold the door for her and endured the short ride to the motel.

Sidney used the magnetic key card to open room 202; it felt too warm and almost airless when they entered. Hazel Truitt strode to the sliding door to the balcony and shoved it open. The drapes surged back as a gust of wind blew in. She took in a deep breath.

"That's better," she said. "Don't like stuffy."

Sidney studied this woman he'd only met at the most seven hours ago. She wore nice leather sandals, light beige brushed denim slacks, and a linen hemp-looking blouse that had a vee neck and wasn't tucked in, along with a necklace made out of small seashells; they looked nice against her tan neck. She stepped out onto the balcony then turned, came back in, and dropped into the only upholstered chair in the room.

"So, where's the wine?" she said.

Sidney shrugged. "Didn't think about it. Sorry."

Hazel Truitt laughed and reached into the large shoulder bag she carried. "Figured as much. Here." She pulled out a bottle of white wine and an opener. "Open this and pour me a glass, my dear sir. A nice buttery Chardonnay from up the coast at Otter

Crest, the Flying Dutchman Winery. I carry their wines in the shop."

Sidney took the bottle from her; it still held an earlier chill. "So this is a commercial?"

"No, it means I splurged, but at my cost. Here." She handed him a wine opener and brought out two wine glasses. "I don't fancy drinking that fine wine in a throwaway plastic glass from the bathroom."

Under her watchful eye, Sidney managed to open the bottle without shredding the cork and gave them each a generous pour. They touched glasses and raised them in a toast to Jonesy. Hazel Truitt took a swallow and stepped out onto the balcony again. Sidney joined her, and they stood looking out into the dark, listening to the surf.

"You know," she said. "Been thinking about Jonesy. Remembering little things. Usually you don't do that—think about someone much who drops in and out of your life but isn't really a part of your life. You know what I mean?"

"I guess so," he answered. "Of course, to us road warriors, the people we see along the way really are part of our lives."

She turned to face him. "Really. Hadn't thought of it like that. Makes me feel sad in a way. I mean, to me the traveling people who call on me are...what would I call it? A diversion, I guess. A break in the routine."

"Like the carnival coming to town? Cotton candy and the freak show?"

"No!" she said loudly, her eyes squinting. Her voice lowered. "Why? Is that how you think of yourself?"

Sidney emptied his glass in one swallow. "No," he answered, "but I guess we're all a little freaky at times."

She laughed. "Meaning me, I suspect."

"Didn't say that."

"I know what you're thinking. Lonely gal in Bandon, one you've never met before, pokes a finger in your chest and tells you to rent a motel room and take her to dinner if you want to get what you came for."

Sidney smiled. "It's been a nice evening." He stepped back into the room and brought out the bottle of chardonnay and poured what was left between them. "So," he said, looking into her waiting eyes. "You have a special someone in your life?"

Hazel Truitt turned to face the ocean, sipped from her glass. "What do you think, Sidney? Take a guess. I'm curious."

He inhaled and let out his breath slowly. "Not a lot to be gained by my taking a wild guess about your love life, I figure."

"You think my only hope for a love life is hitting on traveling men in trade for my business. That about right?"

"No, wouldn't say that."

"Okay, what about you? You have someone in your life who's waiting for you to get on home?"

Sidney smiled. In an instant he had images of Ellie and Janis in his head. He knew that neither one would fit Hazel Truitt's question, not in the way she meant. "I have no one who fits that definition at the moment."

"Well I do," she said.

"Must be a special relationship," he said.

"It is." She laughed. "My mother can't wait for me to get home."

They both erupted in laughter and ended up hugging one another as they laughed and laughed some more. When they stopped and stepped apart, Hazel Truitt wiped a tear from one eye and said, "So maybe there's no one waiting on you at home, but I have this feeling that there's someone causing you an itch."

Sidney smiled. "Could be."

"Well so did Jonesy. His wife."

"Mildred," Sidney said.

"Oh," she said, sobering. "I never knew her name. I just knew she was out there...somewhere. Mildred. I'm sorry to know that."

Sidney shrugged. "I have never met her. Frankly, I didn't really know Jonesy. He was just the big guy who rode off in the Caddy smoking cigars."

Hazel Truitt shook her head. "Those cigars. Part of the package." She looked at her empty wine glass. "Sidney, this has been fun, and, honestly, I didn't intend to coerce you. Wasn't my plan. Don't think I could, anyway."

"No," he said, his voice soft.

"So tell me, how were you going to get out of sleeping with me?"

"Hadn't figured that out yet."

"You were cutting it close, then." She reached out and put an open hand against his chest. "Let me tell you, Mr. Sidney, the woman in me would like you to know that I do have a someone who thinks warmly about me."

"I'm glad to hear it," he said.

"Well, like I say, I'd *like* to tell you that." She smiled sadly. "He thinks of me, all right, thinks of me as his little old gal, available whenever he's ready to go out for a beer with the boys or a roll in the hay."

"He have a name?" Sidney asked. "This fella?"

She looked into his eyes. "Let's just say he's all I got."

"Fair enough. I shouldn't have pried."

"No harm. But it's been nice…this evening. It's what I counted on when Jonesy would come to town, a man who saw more than my tits. Truth is, we only did it once. More than anything, it was nice to be listened to and to actually be treated like I have a brain. My guy…oh, I care for him, best of the lot I run with around here, but I sure wish I could see it in his eyes."

"What's that?"

"Come on, Sidney, what every woman wants, a man that looks into her and…and cherishes who she is."

Sidney fumbled his thoughts and smiled lamely. "I can understand."

She smiled back at him. "Before you take me home, will you do me one favor?"

They lay on top of the quilted bedspread and he held her and they slept. At around three in the morning, she roused him and he drove her home to her mother. She kissed him on the cheek before she left the car; he promised to see her again and wished her well.

Right then Sidney decided to write a journal of this unique trip he was on, maybe end up creating a record of Jonesy's world.

-20-

Sidney awoke with an eyeball headache the next morning and barely made it in time to partake of the motel's borderline continental breakfast. A glass of watery orange juice from concentrate, a hardboiled egg that didn't want to be peeled, and weak coffee did little to spark a comeback. Mouthing the egg, he started his Jonesy journal, scribbling on a scratch pad he'd taken from the motel room—the first entry being his recollections of Beulah Strong, the big woman from Astoria; he decided to change names to protect the innocent. And what he wrote was a sympathetic account of Beulah and the pitiful affair she'd had with Jonesy, which led him to rewind his own close call with Hazel Truitt the night before. After extracting more awful coffee from a sputtering pump pot, he carried the paper cup and his duffel to the parking lot and pointed the Hyundai south.

Just before he hit Port Orford, Sidney's cell phone let him know he had service again and two messages. He pulled the phone from its position in the cup holder. As soon as he heard John Marr's voice he hit delete. The second message was from Janis; she wanted him to call her and recited her cell number. She answered right away.

"Sidney, where are you?"

"Just coming into Port Orford. Is something the matter?" he asked.

"What? Oh, no, just wondering if you're okay out there," she said. "Anyone chasing you? Exotic women hitting on you? Stuff like that."

Sidney tap-danced around his nap with Hazel Truitt. "No, no one chasing me—at the moment. Turned down three gorgeous women, though." He drank in her airy laugh. "Don't know where Marr is. Maybe he's given up."

"We can only hope," she said. "I was just wondering, are you coming back through Newport on your way home?"

"Yeah, I have to turn in my rental and pick up the company car. Why?"

"Oh nothing, really, it's just that you left your blue windbreaker at my place."

"I haven't even missed it," he said, somehow expecting something more from her.

"I'll have it at the store. You can drop by and get it there. Oops, gotta go, bye."

Before Sidney could respond she had disconnected. He held the dead phone in his hand and felt a twinge in his stomach; the windbreaker message was an *Oh nothing* that was the sound of something hoped for sliding away.

He had driven another couple of miles when the phone chirped again. He pressed it against his ear said, "It's me," expecting it to be Janis again. It wasn't.

"Really?" It was John Marr. "Well this is me, Sidney, and I found the Caddy right here in Newport. Can't hide those Iggy license plates. You lied to me."

Sidney kept his eyes on the road and didn't respond.

"You there, Sidney? How do you like driving that breadbox on wheels? Clever," he went on, "switching cars on me."

Sidney held the cell phone out in front of him, hit the end button, and drove on to Port Orford. When the phone began to cry again, he ignored it; after five rings it kicked over to voice mail, where John Marr's irritating baritone would be waiting for him.

He was still angry when he parked on a side street off 101, known as Oregon Street when it passed through Port Orford, and called on Earl of Orford Gifts & Niceties. The shop was positioned in the middle of the building between a natural foods store and a real estate office.

In typical fashion, a bell tinkled above the door, and a waft of the familiar smells came at Sidney one more time. He exhaled, looked about, his feet planted in blue-green shag carpeting, and spotted a nice array of Iggy items—maybe all was not lost. A thick, wide woman, evidently a customer, with a purse hanging from one arm, was sorting through a pile of closeout placemats, tablecloths, and napkins; a background of soft indecipherable music was playing, and an orange tabby cat came forward to rub against Sidney's pant leg.

At first he just heard the voice but saw no one. Again he heard, "May I help you?" Then he saw her. No more than four and a half feet tall. A petite woman, fine featured, short black hair, big blue eyes, and a smile revealing teeth that appeared too large for her mouth.

"Hello." Sidney spoke with show-time cheerfulness. "I didn't see you."

She laughed like she didn't mean it either. "I get that all the time—as you can imagine."

"No, what I meant was….are you Doris Cadwell?"

"I am, and this is all of me." She lifted her arms and smiled.

Sidney set his case down and held out a hand. "I'm Sidney Lister. With Beeman's International?" He had taken to saying Beeman's as if it were a question because he knew there would be one right after.

"Beeman's? Is that right?" She blinked at him then spread her lips again, showing her teeth. "Sorry, I'm just—"

"I'm not the right person, am I? You're used to seeing Jonesy."

"Uh-huh. I mean, yes. Are you taking his place?"

"That's right." He saw the confusion in her eyes. "You see,

Doris, Jonesy passed away."

She raised a hand to her mouth. "Oh my god. He's...Jonesy is dead?"

Sidney nodded and put on his sympathy face. "About a week and a half ago."

She stared at him and kept staring until she finally lowered her hand and looked away. He waited while she digested the news.

She looked back at him. "How did—?"

"Heart," Sidney said quickly.

At that moment the customer walked by carrying an arm-load of assorted closeout items; Doris Cadwell smiled sadly at Sidney and went off to ring up the sale. She was about to return when another customer came in looking for a birthday gift, and Doris Cadwell went off to help the young woman choose something for her mother. Sidney stepped to the front window and looked out onto the highway wondering if John Marr was closing in.

He started when Doris Cadwell spoke. She had come up behind him. "I'm so sorry about Jonesy," she was saying to his back.

He spun around and looked down; her face was pinched with sorrow. "Yes, we all are," he said.

She twisted her hands together and squeezed. "I've been expecting him, actually."

"I'm a little behind," Sidney said. "Being new to the route, I'm not—"

"No," she said, "it's not that. Not about, you know, buying product or anything."

Sidney waited for her to say what it was. "You see...well," she laughed nervously. "I have this little problem, and I told Jonesy about it last time he came by. Oh... this is silly—you don't need to be bothered, not with him dying and you having to take his place. It must be hard. Are you all right?"

Sidney nodded. "I'm fine. What is it? You can tell me."

Doris Cadwell suddenly choked up. She raised a hand to ward off Sidney's concern and ran to the back of the shop and disappeared into a tiny restroom. When she finally came out Sidney was rearranging the Iggy items.

"We still sell Iggys pretty well," Doris Cadwell said. "But as far as ordering, I really need more Earl of Orford tee shirts."

"Okay." Sidney went to his sales case and pulled out an order blank. "By the way, who is or was the Earl of Orford?"

"Want my thirty-second elevator speech? Okay. There was this English officer, George Vancouver, the one whose name is plastered all over the Northwest and Canada? Anyway, he explored the Northwest Coast, including right here where Cape Blanco is. Well, George Vancouver had a friend named George, George the Earl of Orford, whom he greatly respected. So wa-lah: Port Orford."

"And so here you are, you and the Earl."

She smiled, but then tears formed.

"Doris, what's the problem?"

"My landlord," she said after a moment. "He makes my life miserable. I…I'd move, but I have so much invested in this place, and I have two more years on the lease. I'm stuck."

"Tell me."

She laughed. "You name it. The roof leaks. There are the rats, big rats. Earl, my cat, is even afraid of them. They chew up stuff and scare the wits out of customers. On top of that I want to replace my sign, but he won't give me permission, says what I want to do is too big or doesn't fit the building standards—he gives me a new excuse every time I ask."

"Sounds wretched."

"And he's even stomped into my store and ranted at me in front of customers about what I terrible tenant I am."

"Who is this person?" Sidney asked.

"John Beagle."

"Like the dog?"

"Exactly, like the dog."

"So what was Jonesy going to about this?"

Doris Cadwell shrugged. "He said that if the matter hadn't resolved by the time he came by again that he was going to make Beagle an offer he couldn't refuse." At that she laughed nervously. "I don't know what Jonesy meant for sure."

Sidney looked down into her face. "Where can I get in touch with him? This Beagle?"

"He lives out on Cemetery Loop Road. Doesn't have any office I know of, just owns a bunch of buildings he rents out. Why?"

"Maybe I'll just drop in on him, see what he has to say."

Doris Cadwell screwed up her face. "I don't know. I sure don't want him to get any nastier."

Sidney smiled. "I'll be nice. At first, anyway."

She wrote down an address on a slip of paper and handed it to Sidney; her hand was shaking. "Don't worry," he said, "I won't make things worse. If it looks like it's heading that way, I'll back off."

———————•———————

It wasn't hard to find John Beagle's place. He had his name painted in big black letters on an oversized mailbox out by the road. The house sat at the end of a long dirt lane; wood fences ran on each side of the drive. It was a big rambling wooden structure with a sloping barn-like roof called a gambrel, as Sidney recalled; it had a big wrap-around porch, upstairs bay windows, and was covered with wooden slat siding painted white with windows and shutters trimmed in black.

After several minutes and two pushes on the doorbell, an elderly man with a mane of white hair and a prominent nose opened the door. He was dressed in blue bib overalls and a bright red flannel shirt. He eyed Sidney but didn't say a word.

"Mr. Beagle?" Sidney said.

"That's right." The man's voice was reedy in an unpleasant way.

"My name is Sidney Lister. I understand that you are the landlord for the building where the Earl of Orford gift shop is located. That right?"

"What if I am? You wanting to buy the building? Anything's for sale if the money's right."

"No, nothing like that. I was just visiting with the lady who owns the shop, Doris Cadwell. Very nice lady."

"What, you buying her out? If you're wanting to squeeze me on that lease, forget it."

Sidney folded his arms across his chest. "Mr. Beagle, I am not selling or buying anything, but I do have a question for you."

John Beagle pulled his arms out from behind the bib and shoved them into his pockets. "What question is that?"

"Very simply, sir, what do you have against Doris Cadwell?"

The old man withheld his response for a moment and studied Sidney's face intently. "Who says I have anything against that woman?"

"It's common knowledge."

"What's common knowledge?"

"That you are an abusive and unresponsive landlord to her," Sidney said in a calm, even tone.

John Beagle was nonplussed and made no response to the accusation.

"Why is that, sir?"

"You'd best come on in," John Beagle said finally.

Sidney followed the man into his house and on into a large kitchen in the back, where he had Sidney sit at a big walnut plank table. John Beagle went to a cupboard and came back with two glass tumblers and a bottle of Knob Creek bourbon. He put a glass in front of Sidney, sat across the table from him, and opened the bottle.

"A taste?" he said. Sidney nodded and watched him pour them each a generous serving. "Here's to tomorrow, may we rise to see it." They each took a swallow and set their glasses back down.

"First, let me ask you if you are a lawyer?"

Sidney said he wasn't. To that, John Beagle nodded and took another drink and leaned back in the ladder-back chair he was sitting in. "From the day I leased that space to Doris, I wished I hadn't. So you're right in your assessment—I never give the woman a break. Why? Because I can't stand her being there."

"Why? Seems like a nice person. Store is clean, well run, and seems to complement the other businesses there."

"You're right on every count."

"But the leaky roof, the rats, the obfuscation over better signage—why your belligerence on all those things?"

John Beagle picked up his glass, drained it, and poured another slug. "I don't want her there."

"But you agree that she is a good tenant. That makes no sense."

John Beagle took another long drink, set the glass down firmly, and leaned over on his elbows. "I loved her," he said.

"Who?" Sidney asked, bewildered. "Doris Cadwell?"

"My Missie, my little Missie." John Beagle drank again.

Sidney said nothing more; he decided to wait. He sipped from his glass and watched John Beagle closely.

The man looked up. His eyes had reddened, and his face was cast with grief. "I saw it from the day I first met Doris. I should have stopped it then, denied her the lease, but I didn't. I've hated myself for going ahead ever since." He sat back and took in a deep breath. "Missie. She was my little sister. Missie was our nickname for Millicent. She drowned on Agate Beach many years ago. She was only twelve." He sniffed. "I couldn't save her. I tried but..." He closed his eyes.

"What is it?" Sidney asked.

John Beagle opened his eyes. "Doris...she is Missie. Her face, her eyes, even her voice resembles Missie, all that I remember and imagine she would be like today. I have thought of buying Doris out of her lease, but...then I'd lose her. Wouldn't I?"

"My god, man," Sidney said, "this can't go on. You're making yourself crazy and making her life unbearable. Is that what you want?"

"No, no of course not. But—"

"Have you thought of talking to her, to Doris?"

"What?" He sat up straighter. "Oh no, I couldn't. No, simply couldn't."

"Why not?"

John Beagle took one more drink. "I'd be afraid."

"Of her?"

John Beagle nodded.

Sidney followed John Beagle's pickup back to the Earl of Orford, and they entered the store together. He held the old man's elbow when they went in and could feel him trembling. Doris Cadwell was waiting on a customer and looked at the two men with some alarm but continued to smile as she rang up a sale on the cash register.

When the three of them were alone in the shop, Doris Cadwell came out from behind the counter. She looked up at Sidney, her eyes questioning. It was quiet. The men stood facing her, looking down into her eyes, wide and blue.

"Well," Sidney said finally, "I guess you two know one another. Right?"

They both nodded—John Beagle looked down, and Doris Cadwell looked up at Sidney.

"Doris, John has something he wants to share with you," Sidney said. "That right, John?"

"Guess so."

"Well, do you or don't you?" Sidney pressed.

"Yeah," John Beagle answered. "I guess. I mean, yes I do."

"You willing to hear him out?" Sidney asked Doris Cadwell.

She turned to John Beagle, looked up at him until he met her gaze, then nodded and said okay.

"Tell you what," Sidney offered, "I'll watch the store while you talk in private in the back. I think I can handle your cash register."

He watched as they walked together to the tiny office; the door clicked shut, and everything was quiet. Sidney took up his position behind the counter on a cushioned stool and waited. He picked up Earl the cat when it came looking for attention, and they settled in, Sidney stroking, Earl purring.

The only customer was a man needing a tee shirt, any tee shirt. He'd come for the weekend and hadn't packed what he called his beach shirt. Sidney sold him an Earl of Orford shirt in extra large—just one more Doris Cadwell would have to re-order from him.

Nearly an hour passed before the door opened and Doris Cadwell and John Beagle came out. Sidney studied their faces for trouble and anger but saw neither. They came over to him.

"Everything all right?" Sidney asked.

"You mean did we fight?" said Doris Cadwell, smiling.

John Beagle laughed. "Well, Doris, I'd best be going. I have some animals that need feeding. But, like I said, I'll have Hector over here tomorrow to get to work on that roof."

"And the vermin?" she said.

John Beagle laughed. "That too."

"Thank you, John." She stepped up to him, and they gave each other a hug. "And you can call me Missie anytime you need to."

John Beagle looked at Sidney, smiled, and gave him a wave. When he'd gone, Doris Cadwell grinned and said, "He's even going to pay for me to have a new sign. Can you believe it?"

Sidney accepted an on-her-tiptoes hug plus a nice order, left Doris Cadwell to imagine better days, and drove the twenty-eight miles to Gold Beach.

-21-

Daylight had mostly slipped into the ocean by the time Sidney hit Gold Beach. The Beach Budget Motel stood on the highway beckoning like an aging call girl, wearing a sorry paint job, promising low rates, free HBO, and just maybe a flash of what she used to be. He did the ritual check-in, toted his gear into room 112, where he mopped his face with a warm washcloth and brushed a day on the road from his teeth. He stretched out on the bed, breathed in the familiar tired-room smell, and immediately the threat of John Marr re-entered his head. Regardless of whatever else Sidney was doing, he knew Marr was hunting for him—out there trolling the streets and highways. *You need to fight back,* Janis had prodded. Sidney again considered the idea of going chest-to-chest with John Marr, a man filled with rage, a desperate man who had forty pounds on him, who was perhaps a borderline psychotic—forget the perhaps. Janis had also said: *Get some help. This guy sounds dangerous.*

Dangerous.

Sidney sat up on the edge of the bed, reached for his cell phone, and entered the number for information. First he called the Eugene Fire Department and asked for the fire marshal—not in, gone for the day. After Sidney listened twice to prerecorded fire safety admonitions, a deputy chief came on the line and told Sidney what he knew about the fire that killed Randolph and

194

Virginia Snyder—nearly zilch. The fire had been judged accidental, started by a faulty electric heater in a bedroom. The Snyders had died from smoke inhalation; the bodies had been burned beyond recognition—end of story.

When he called the Eugene Police Department, he managed to sound cogent enough to be forwarded to whoever might have information about the fire that killed the Snyders. After a brief wait, a Detective Miller came on the line, laughing about something before sobering and saying "This is Miller, how can I help you?" In fact, Miller had been on duty and drew the short straw the night of the fire; they had no permanent arson investigation unit. His take was the same as the fire department's: accidental, deaths by asphyxiation, bodies unrecognizable. Suspicious? No, nothing suspicious, he responded, and wondered why Sidney was inquiring. Sidney had his lie ready: that he lived nearby and had always wondered what really caused the fire, but it sounded like the same thing he'd read in the paper.

He thanked the detective, disconnected before he could get any more curious, and went to find something to eat. The kid running the front desk at the motel mumbled that a good place to eat was Wally's. By the time Sidney drove the mile to the place, the skies had opened, and it was pouring so hard the car's wipers threatened to stall. He decided to stay in the car, wait for a letup, and called Ellie.

When she answered, the rain was pounding on the roof so hard that he had to yell to be heard.

"Ellie," he shouted, "you'll have to speak up. I'm sitting in the car, and it's raining so hard I can barely hear you."

"Where are you?" she yelled back.

"Gold Beach."

"Are you all right? Are you safe?"

"So far," he said.

"What about that guy, Marr?"

"He found me. Well, not me, he found the car I left in Newport, the Caddy. Thought I'd throw him off my scent if I weren't driving it. Rented a car. But somehow he sniffed it out."

"Sidney, Sidney," she said at the top of her voice. "He's not going to let up, is he?"

Suddenly the downpour stopped as if someone had shut off a faucet. He could speak normally. "Guess not, guess he won't. Called me on my cell again today."

"Oh," she moaned. "What'd he say? This is so horrifying."

"What'd he say? At first, when he realized that I knew everything he'd done, he wanted to talk, to work things out. But now that he's figured out I'm not going to look the other way, he's trying to find me—"

"And do what?" She cut in. "Kill you? That's what he wants to do, right, Sidney? Damn it all. Call the police. Then get in your car and come home. Playing catch me if you can is stupid, stupid, stupid."

Sidney could hear her breathing hard. He opened the window a few inches and felt the rain-cooled air filter in. "Well, it's time to reciprocate," he said with feigned bravado. "Give back as good as I'm getting."

"Oh really?" Her voice dripped with sarcasm. "And what's that mean? Challenge him to a duel? Cream pies at ten paces?"

"I can protect myself." He paused. "I'll get a gun."

"And what do you know about guns?" she challenged. "You've never owned a gun. Right?"

"Still, maybe I should get one—for protection."

"That's asking for trouble." She laughed. "You'll end up shooting yourself."

"Come on, Ellie, this isn't a schoolyard shoving match. I've got to be ready."

"Like I said, come home," she answered.

"Think he couldn't find me there?"

"Maybe, but here we can circle the wagons."

"Forget that. I'd be too predictable there. Over here I have wiggle room. Besides, I know this guy. He's no fighter either. In fact, he's a big bowl of Jell-O."

"A bowl of Jell-O who wants to kill you."

Sidney didn't respond.

Ellie let out a long sigh. "And you're no fighter."

"What choice do I have?" After a pause between them, he said, "I'll be okay. I'm just sounding off. Don't worry—I'll do everything I can to stay out of his way. I'm still a self-preservationist. My motto is *Run away to never fight another day*."

Ellie gave him a laugh of relief even though both of them knew he was glossing over the real risks.

"But now I'm hungry," he said. "I was just waiting the rain out until I could go into this café and eat."

She laughed. "So that's why you called me, just to fill time until the rain stops. Gee, I feel so special."

"You are special."

"Well, show it by coming home."

Before he disconnected he promised her one more time that he would be careful with John Marr. Whatever he meant by that he couldn't tell her. He didn't know himself. Wally's was a basic foods place; it was about half full with the kind of eaters who order fast, eat fast, and don't talk while downing their food.

He ordered a meatloaf sandwich and a beer and pulled out a notebook he'd bought from Doris Cadwell. He had transferred his entry about Beulah Strong into the new notebook and was working on Paige Peterson from the Courter's in Seaside and recalling her tale of suicidal despondency. A young waitress with terminal acne brought his sandwich and a cold bottle of Hamm's beer. By the time he had finished both, he'd also finished with Paige Peterson. He closed the notebook, and his thoughts returned to Ellie's admonitions.

What would it look like, his taking the fight to John Marr? He felt a chill between his shoulder blades at the thought of actually coming face to face with the man. What was John Marr capable of? Did he really intend to do away with Sidney? Of course, what other choice did he have? A mother with a big family suddenly yelled "I told you, Timmy. Now stop it!" Sidney stared at the red-faced woman and at the cowering child, got up, paid at the counter, and left. It was raining again. He ran to the Hyundai, drove back to the motel, sat in the dark, and tried to imagine coming face-to-face with John Marr. When would it happen? How would it happen? How would he react? He closed his eyes, breathed slowly, and attempted to force a picture into his head—to conjure a likeness of the man intent on killing him. But he could only recall a shadowy representation of Marr, one that would suddenly appear, and then fade away when Sidney's heart started to pound.

When he'd had enough of that futile exercise, he stepped out of his room into the cool night air and stood by the door. At first, he scanned the parking lot and studied the shadows before laughing at himself and setting off on a walk to clear his head. There was no one about: no strangers standing outside for a smoke, or unknown persons staring out from one of the other rooms, watching his movements.

After twenty minutes of circumnavigating the parking lot, he returned to his room, turned on the television, ignored whatever was on, muted the sound, and slept hard.

———•———

The next morning at first light, someone started up the Harley motorcycle that had been parked next to the Hyundai the night before; its beastly rumble shattered Sidney's sleep. While he lay rubbing his eyes, the cyclist revved the bike with three short blasts before backing out and roaring away—so much for sleeping in. Sidney sat up on the edge of the bed, burped meatloaf, and lurched off to the bathroom for a pee and a shower. The Beach Budget Motel didn't offer a continental breakfast, so he ended up at Cal's Home Cooked on the main drag. He ordered a Denver omelet, which was surprisingly good; Sidney made a mental note to come back when next in town—if ever.

He had two stops in Gold Beach. First was Confluence Gifts, located on Harbor Way where the Rogue River joined the Pacific Ocean. His sales roster listed a Reggie "The Rogue" Olinger as the owner. Olinger remembered Jonesy, liked him well enough it seemed, and was sorry to learn of his death. He sent Sidney on his way with a passable order; according to the sales log, it was the first time he'd ordered anything in three years. Rack up another score for Jonesy.

"You're not serious?" was the response he got from Sylvia Jolly at the Jolly Beans Sweets and Gifts on the Ellensburg Avenue stretch of 101. Plump, dyed blonde, about fifty, Sylvia Jolly was dumbstruck about Jonesy's passing.

"If that don't beat all," she said, shaking her head. "You know, he's up and ruined my record. It's been over five years since anyone I know has died. This is not a good omen. No siree bob."

Sidney just smiled, wondering how he should respond to someone's no-deaths record being broken.

Sylvia Jolly pointed to a calendar hanging behind the counter. "See that big X right there? April 23rd? That'll be my hubby and me's twenty-fifth anniversary. We're going to Hawaii, and I was just sure we'd do that with my death record intact." She saw Sidney smile. "No, I put great stock in such things. There was a stretch in my family when there were no deaths for over twenty years."

"Some things can't go on forever," Sidney said. "Life is one of 'em."

"Well sure, but…just ruins my day is all," she laughed.

He left Sylvia Jolly with a *Why the hell not* order in hand and with her still complaining about the end of her run of deathless years. The sporting goods store just happened to be on his way back to the car, but he froze in front of its display window at the sight of the words GUNS • AMMO • ACCESSORIES painted on the glass. He looked around as if he thought someone might be watching before strolling casually into the store. The display case holding handguns was next to the cash register. Sidney stood back and looked at the array of weapons, the likes of which he had never even held in his hand: Colt, Beretta, Glock; small, square weapons, black, chrome, beautiful even. He stared at the arsenal and considered if he could ever use one, even if he was under attack by John Marr.

"Can I help you?" The man who spoke was leaning on the glass countertop. He had a silver mane of hair, mustache to match, and aviator glasses with rose-colored lenses.

Sidney blinked and flashed a nervous smile. "Not sure."

The man studied Sidney for a moment then pulled a handgun out of the case. "Here, hold this little baby."

He held out a small, black matte pistol. Sidney hesitated but took it in his hand and instantly noted the weight, the coldness of the metal, and the feel of the strange object in his hand. He smiled nervously, hefted it and handed it back. "Nice," he feigned. "How much?"

The man pushed up on his glasses with a pudgy forefinger. "That's a trade-in. Beretta Bobcat. I can let you have it for one ninety-eight. Great for personal defense."

Sidney smiled again. That was more than he had in savings. He nodded and said, "Thanks, I'll think about it," and walked out of the store. After all of his bravado talk with Ellie, he couldn't do it.

He drove into Brookings a little after noon; Brookings and its smaller neighbor to the south, Harbor, were the last stops before the California border. The area is known as Oregon's Banana Belt due to its temperate climate all year and because it's famous for growing the majority of America's Easter lilies. But not that day—it was overcast, and a chilling wind hit Sidney when he exited the car to quickly consume half a foot of turkey and ham at a Subway. He had decided to hit the three shops on his list, make no cold calls, and head back to Newport as soon as possible.

A character name of Randolph Potts, a man with buckteeth who owned a shop called Potts-a-Luck, greeted Sidney's announcement of Jonesy's death with a raucous bellow of laughter.

"I told him," he gasped and laughed some more. "Told him he was too damn fat."

"Don't see the humor," Sidney said.

"I know, I know," Randolph Potts said, waving away his laughter. "But Jonesy and I, we had this bet. Look at me," he said, "skinny as a rail, right? I smoke four packs of cigarettes a day. Jonesy smoked a few cigars, but mainly he ate like a whale— hell he was a whale." He laughed hard and took a deep breath. "Anyway, one time me and Jonesy nearly came to blows over our health habits. So our bet was..." he started to chuckle again, "who'd die first. I know, sick, but we were both drunk as hell. He swore that lung cancer would do me in the way I smoked. And I was just as sure his heart would seize up the way he put the food away. We both drank, so we voided that part out."

"So how much was this death bet?" asked Sidney.

"Five hundred bucks," he said. "Two-fifty each. Got it in a little savings account down at the credit union. Still sitting there. Might even have some interest by now."

Randolph Potts stared at the counter top. "Big blowhard, he went and died first. Blast his hide."

Sidney had pulled out an order form. Randolph Potts looked up. "So guess you want me to give you a big order in memory of old Jonesy. Why the hell would I do that?"

Sidney smiled. "How are you going to claim that five hundred? Any provisions to assure that you have claim to it?"

Randolph Potts grinned a toothy smile. "Crafty you are. Yeah, I'll need a copy of the death certificate. We didn't trust each other a dime's worth." He waved a forefinger at Sidney. "You, you're cut from the same cloth as that asshole Jonesy."

Sidney came away from Potts-a-Luck with a big order and his promise to get a copy of the death certificate sent to Randolph Potts ASAP. He was sitting in the Hyundai on Chetco Avenue in front of the Brookings Courter's Curios going over his sales sheets when Nina Beeman called. She sounded tense, asked where he was and how things were going, all with little enthusiasm or real interest.

"I'll finish up here in Brookings in another hour or so," Sidney told her. "I'll fax in the orders before I leave town."

"Then where you going?" she asked.

"Back to Newport. Have to pick up the company car. I'll stay the night before heading back to Portland. Why, something wrong? You okay?"

"Yes," she answered. "Yeah, we're okay. Why? Don't I sound right?"

Sidney laughed. "Now that you asked, no you don't—sound right, that is. What is it?"

"Oh, just checking in, see how sales are going. Ned, he's his usual self, fussing and all."

"Wondering if I'm maxing out the credit card, is he?"

Nina coughed a laugh. "Not this time. He spent all day yesterday figuring how we can afford to exhibit at the Seattle Gift Show in August." Sidney thought, *why bother?*

"So what is it, Nina?"

She sighed. "Got a call from Lamont Courter. Rather, Ned did."

"And? He giving you grief again? If he is I'll—"

"No," she cut him off. "No, not that. He wants to see you again. Wants you to come by his office when you're back in Newport."

"That right? What for? He say?"

"Nope, just said he needed to see you again," she said. "You all right with that? Ned, he said the man sounded like he'd just woke up from a bad dream."

"More like living a bad dream," Sidney said.

"So anyway, you'll do it? Go see him?"

"Sure. Tomorrow. I'll see him tomorrow."

"Don't think I trust him," she said. "Be careful."

"It's okay, Nina."

She disconnected after another sighing hum.

202

-22-

Sidney stared at the phone in his hand and replayed his first face-to-face meeting with Lamont Courter; it had been almost surreal. After dredging up the darkest, most tragic mistake of the man's life, it had been like watching a death, witnessing long-held agony come out from where it had been secreted away. And now Lamont Courter wanted to see him again. Why?

He dropped the cell phone into a cup holder and stared out through the windshield for a bit before entering the Courter's store. The usually tiresome array of colors and scents in the shop was somehow comforting right then. A young clerk told him that the manager, a Dixie Gottschalk, wasn't in the store but was expected soon.

A splash of sunlight had broken through, so Sidney left his sales case by the door and went outside to take in the warmth. He sat on a bench, which had been cleverly positioned to take in a view of the highway, tipped his head back, and felt the sun on his face. He'd nearly dozed off when heard a female voice saying "Hello?"

He opened his eyes, looked up into the face of a woman with short brown hair, brown eyes looking at him through narrow glasses with red plastic frames; she had a slender face, which at the moment carried a questioning frown.

"Were you looking for me?" she asked. "I'm Dixie Gottschalk."

Sidney smiled and rose from the bench with as much dignity as he could manage. "Decided to take in the sun while I could," he said.

"Yes," the woman said, disinterested.

"I'm Sidney Lister," he said and held out a hand. With a degree of wariness, she grasped his hand lightly then pulled her red-nailed fingers away. "With Beeman's International?" he added.

She looked at the small watch on her wrist. "Yes, well, I don't have much time. I've just returned from a meeting at the Chamber of Commerce. I'm on the Tourism and Marketing Committee."

Sidney just nodded and smiled.

"But if you will come in the store, I can give you a few minutes," she said and marched off.

They met in a back room that was used for a limited amount of storage, a coffee maker, and a small desk. Dixie Gottschalk sat at the desk, and Sidney stood. She thumbed through several pink phone message slips that had been left for her and picked up the receiver from the phone on the desk. She glanced over her shoulder at him.

"This will just take a minute," she excused herself.

Sidney stepped back and leaned in the doorway and eavesdropped while she chatted with someone named Glenda about an art show. She set the receiver down firmly and turned in her chair, her mouth set in a hard line.

"Sorry," she said. "I'm on the planning committee for the Azalea Festival. One of our big events of the year: 65th Annual Azalea Festival. Not until May, but time flies, and then there's the Kite Festival in July, and finally the Festival of the Arts in August."

"You're busy," Sidney said offhanded.

"Yes, spring and summer are when we make hay on the coast," Dixie Gottschalk responded. "So you're with Beeman's, you said."

"Yes."

"So where is he?"

"You mean Jonesy?"

"Uh-huh. Bet he's dodging me."

Sidney raised his eyebrows. "Why would that be?"

Her eyes narrowed. "I'm sure you know very well why."

"Sorry, not a clue."

"I doubt that," she said. "After all, it ended up being dealt with by the owner of your company."

"I'm just a flunky in the system, I'm afraid. So what happened?" he asked.

Dixie Gottschalk studied Sidney a moment before taking her glasses off and cleaning them with a tissue from a box on her desk. She settled the glasses back on her nose and dropped the wadded tissue into a wastebasket by her feet. "He took liberties," she said, her voice softened for the first time.

"By liberties you mean…?"

"Liberties," she repeated. "He…it wasn't proper." Her voice became a hoarse whisper.

Sidney looked at her ring finger and saw a gold band there. "I'm sorry," he said.

"Yes, well, it's history now. I just thought he'd be man enough to—"

"He's dead," Sidney said. "He's passed. Sorry."

Her imperious expression dropped away. "What did you say?"

"Jonesy, he died a little over ten days ago. Heart attack."

She stared at him, her mouth partly open. Suddenly she stood and stared at him open-mouthed. "Well then," she said, "that's it." She slumped back down and looked at nothing. "He's gone."

"Sorry," he said. "It happened suddenly, so I've had to let people know as I go."

She didn't look up, but nodded.

"If you like, I can come back later," Sidney said.

Dixie Gottschalk looked up. "No, you've come all this way. Besides I need to make an order," she said and gestured for him to sit down.

He sat, pulled out a catalog and order form, and waited for her to say something.

She held out a hand and wiggled her fingers for him to hand her the catalog. "I doubt that you have anything new to offer."

"Not much," Sidney responded. "Some things, though."

"What, I'd like to know."

"Well, some new Mexican jewelry—on page 23 there. Yeah, see…right there."

She pulled the catalog closer to look at the images.

"Earrings are nice," he went on, "necklaces and bracelets." He reached into his case and brought out the plastic bag with samples in them. "Here." He opened the bag and let her examine the jewelry.

"He never should have done it," she said while holding up a necklace.

Sidney put his hands together and massaged them. He had no interest in reviving the woman's ire by saying the wrong thing. He waited her out.

"Jonesy, I'm talking about," she said, raising her eyes from the page. "What he did."

Sidney nodded but said nothing.

"You don't know what I'm talking about, do you?"

He shook his head. "No."

"Put down a dozen each of the jewelry items," she said, "Yes, those." Sidney marked the order form. "I was vulnerable." Sidney held the ballpoint pen over the page and kept his facial expression as neutral as he could. "What else?" she said.

"How about these picture frames?" he responded, pointing. "Doesn't show in the photos, but they come in bright colors, have wooden frames, good price. The one second from the top has seashells on it."

She looked at the pictures. "Okay, six each of the small ones, three each of the larger ones—make it ten of the small ones with the shells."

Sidney penned in the amounts.

"I'm a widow," she said. "Ten years."

"Sorry," Sidney commiserated.

"He knew that. Jonesy did. Not a secret around here." She took in a slow breath. "Twenty-two years, me and Harv. He liked his motorcycle, his metallic blue Harley Road King. He loved that bike. More than me at times, it seemed."

Her eyes moved from the catalog to Sidney. He gave her his *I'm listening* smile.

"He called it the O'Brien run." She held a hand up and began drawing a line in the air with her forefinger. "He and his two riding buddies, they would drop down 101 into California, just north of Crescent City, hook onto U.S. 199, and ride through the northern part of the Redwood Highway to the little place called O'Brien, Oregon. They would gorge themselves at Matlock's restaurant and head back home. At least once a month they'd do that."

"Must've enjoyed it," Sidney said.

"Yes," she whispered, and her eyes watered. "That they did. But it killed him…that little ritual. Slick road. He hit Bambi. They both died right there."

Sidney crimped his mouth and shook his head in sympathy. He looked back down at the catalog and thumbed through a few pages.

Dixie Gottschalk said, "He took me to dinner. Jonesy. To Claudia's…a seafood place." Sidney kept his eyes on the catalog. "Better put down a set of three each on the Iggy items, too," she interrupted herself. "And a dozen of the stuffed toy."

Sidney nodded and entered the order.

"Drove me there and back in that Cadillac of his. The car reeked of cigar smoke. So did he." She paused. "My Harv, he used to smoke a pipe, so it was kind of like that, I guess. Familiar smell. Comforting, in a way."

She stopped talking and stared down at the floor. Sidney

waited and pretended to go over the order again.

"Parked in my driveway," she said. "He'd been nice, a gentleman actually. Opened doors, held my chair, helped me on with my coat—I liked it. Hadn't been treated like a lady in a while." She wasn't really talking to Sidney; he was just there. "He leaned over to kiss me...I didn't resist. Seemed the right way to end the evening—in a way it did. Then..." She stopped, looked past Sidney at nothing, then went on.

"I don't know, I...we...right there in the car." She took on a look of alarm. "I didn't intend to...just let it happen." She held a hand up to her mouth; then her eyes turned cold. "In spite of how it may have seemed, he had no right. No right."

"I understand," Sidney offered.

"No you don't. Don't tell me that."

"Okay, you're right, I don't. Don't know a thing about...whatever happened."

She blew her nose on a tissue. "Now he's dead."

Sidney fiddled with the order form some more, clicked the top of his ballpoint open and closed over and over, and considered how best to bring the cathartic session to a close. He leaned back in his chair, inhaled, and said, "Well, is there anything more you want to—"

"I gave him the wrong signals, I suppose."

Sidney put the order form in front of her. "Here, he said, "sign this." He stood over her until she handed it back, said good-bye, and left without any further comment. Dixie Gottschalk just watched him walk away.

———•———

Sidney found Redwood Florist and Gifts down on Boat Basin Road and went in with the intent of a quick hit-and-go for his final stop. And that was the way it worked out. The owner, a young woman by the name of Rebecca Rice, was in a frantic work mode preparing an assortment of floral sprays for the funeral of a local teenager killed in an auto accident.

"Six sprays," Rebecca Rose lamented, "I have to have six ready by tomorrow morning. Funeral's at eleven." She swiped at an errant curl drooping on her forehead. "I'll be working late."

Sidney wished her well, and while she worked, looked around the shop and prepared an order for her to consider: mostly vases, candles, and decorative knick-knacks. She said that sounded good. Then she asked what happened to the other guy and froze in the midst of cutting flower stems when she heard.

"Geez, that's sad," she said. "And here I am working on these... for a funeral." She grimaced.

Sidney left the shop after only twenty minutes. He put his sales case in the back seat of the car, settled in behind the wheel, and massaged his face with both hands. It's over, he thought. He found Seabird Mail Services out on the main highway, faxed all the orders he had, gassed up, and pointed the Hyundai north. When he cruised into Gold Beach and was back in cell phone range, he called Janis.

"Hey there," she breathed into his ear. "Where are you?"

"Just coming into Gold Beach, heading your way," he said. "I'll be in Newport in a few hours. What you up for? I have my jammies."

She laughed. "Don't think you used them last time."

"If you insist."

"We had fun," she said.

"I'll say."

"It was nice, Sidney. I hope you will remain a friend."

Sidney heard it and knew what it meant. "Friend," he said.

"Yes, friends. You know, good friends. Do you have good friends, Sidney?"

"Not so many, no. You?"

"No fair throwing my own question back at me," she said. "But, yeah, I have friends, all sorted and filed by category."

"Category? Sounds a little sterile. Where am I in your filing system?"

"Under old Grant High, of course."

"How many in that file?"

"One."

Sidney passed a slow-moving elderly Volkswagen Beetle, came back into the right lane, and said, "So, close but no cigar—is that it?"

After a moment she answered, "I wouldn't call it that. How about a lovely interlude?"

The only sound for a moment was the hum of the engine and the tires on the road. Sidney drew up behind a FedEx tractor and trailer, slowed, and rested a wrist on the steering wheel.

"Sidney, it was nice," Janis said finally.

"But."

"I really enjoyed myself. You are a great guy."

"Ooh, the great guy line is a killer," he laughed.

"Come on now."

He sat up more in the seat. "I guess it's bye, bye, Miss Electra Bly," he said, "right?"

"Sidney."

He hesitated then held the end button down and accelerated around the FedEx truck, nearly doing a header with an oncoming pickup. Horns chastised him from all sides as he veered back into his lane and continued on.

A mile or so later his phone began to ring. He didn't answer.

-23-

Tired and fighting sleep, Sidney pulled onto Carson's car lot in Newport around eight-thirty; the place was shut down, office dark. He grunted, rubbed the fatigue from his eyes, and set about unloading everything belonging to him and stuffed it all back into the Cadillac, which was sitting right where he'd left it—still with the familiar ambience of cigars. He shoved the Hyundai's keys through a mail slot in the office door, turned, and was hit by a ferocious frontal attack.

John Marr body-blocked Sidney, shoved him back with two hands to the chest, then hit him in the face. Sidney cried out, staggered, and fell onto asphalt; the grit chewed into his hands— he tried to crawl away, but Marr was on him. He yanked Sidney over onto his back again, seized him around the throat with both hands, and began to squeeze. Sidney struggled for air and shoved against Marr's chest, pushed as hard as he could, but Marr was bigger and in a rage. The man's breaths came in gasps, his eyes stood out, and he ranted hoarsely into Sidney's face. Sidney understood nothing of Marr's guttural oaths; he was fighting for his life: legs thrashing, arms flailing, trying pry the constricting hands from his around his neck.

Just as he was about to pass out, Sidney brought his knee up as hard as he could into Marr's groin; he heard Marr grunt and felt him pull away. Sidney came to gasping, his head spinning, and gradually gained back his senses. He struggled to a sitting position and reached up to rub his throat. Marr was leaning against the Cadillac, staring at him and holding his crotch. He was panting and looked like someone who'd been sleeping in his clothes for a month: heavily wrinkled suit pants, a crumpled dress shirt with the tail hanging out, wild hair; and his fleshy face had a three-day growth of beard. The two men stared at one another until Sidney rolled over on a knee and started to get up. Marr lunged forward awkwardly, drove a shoulder into Sidney, knocking him back down, sat astraddle of him, and smashed a fist into Sidney's face. He pulled up on Sidney's shirt collar, raising him up, and glowered at him. Sidney reached up and clawed at Marr's face; the bigger man slapped his hand away.

"You son of a bitch," Marr said. Spit flew out of his mouth and splattered onto Sidney's face. "You god-damned son of a bitch—you've ruined my life." He hit Sidney again on the same cheekbone. "You've ruined me," he yelled, picking Sidney up again by his shirtfront and slamming him to the ground. Sidney made a hapless swing with one hand, his fist glancing off Marr's forehead.

When lights flashed across the struggling men, Marr sat back on his haunches as a car came onto the lot; then he crab-crawled away before staggering upright. "This isn't over, you bastard," he bellowed and staggered off. A moment later Sidney heard an engine start; there was the sound of vehicular maneuvering and tires spinning. Then a car sped out of the opposite end of the lot. The car that had entered the lot pulled to a stop, its headlights shining on Sidney, as he lay crumpled on the pavement.

He rolled over and tried to sit up. His face was throbbing; he was woozy and tasted blood in his mouth. He started to drift off but was roused by someone shaking him. At first he thought John Marr had returned to finish the job, but it was Charlie Carson, the owner of the car lot.

"My god!" Charlie Carson was yelping. "Oh my god. Are you all right? Hey, are you okay? Mister. Wait right here—I'll get help."

———•———

The EMTs from the fire department treated Sidney's facial lacerations, looked at the redness on his throat, asked him what day it was, looked into his eyes, and helped him stand and walk around to check his balance to assess whether he'd had a concussion. They wanted to take him to the emergency room to be examined, but he refused, said he was okay. A police officer asked Sidney a lot of questions. He answered with a pack of lies: attacked by an unknown assailant, couldn't describe the man who did it, must have been a robbery attempt, Charlie Carson's arrival must have prevented it, he was just returning a rental car, must have been a random thing. The policeman put everything down and gave Sidney a business card with his number on it in case something else came to mind.

Charlie Carson, a thin, almost cadaverous figure, hovered in the background, smoking one cigarette after another and continually trying tell anyone who would listen how he had come to find Sidney: "I left my cell phone on my desk, just coming back to get it—otherwise...." He waited and watched as the emergency people and the policeman did their jobs. When Sidney seemed ambulatory and claimed to be clearheaded again, Charlie Carson followed him to the Cadillac and asked again if he was sure he was okay.

"Charlie, I'm okay. Don't worry, I'm not going to sue you. Wasn't your fault, a random thing for sure," Sidney kept the lie alive.

Charlie Carson patted Sidney on the back and said to call him if he needed anything later—in case he didn't feel well. Sidney promised he would and went in search of a motel for the night. He found an Econo Lodge on 101. After assuring the young woman at the desk that in spite of his bruises he was all right, he checked in, stripped, and took a very long hot shower. Afterward he downed several ibuprofen pills, pulled on some fresh boxer shorts, and lay atop a bedspread decorated with an array of blue seahorses. His swollen right cheek was turning purple; his head and body ached. He felt like a hammered steak.

He tried to sleep, but the throbbing headache kept him from reaching deep slumber. When he heard his cell phone ringing, he wasn't sure what time it was or how long he had been dozing. He rose up on an elbow and realized that he'd left his cell phone in the bathroom; he cursed, wobbled across the room, and snatched the phone off of the sink counter.

"What?" he muttered hoarsely. There was only breathing into his ear. "Who is this?"

"Where are you?" asked John Marr, his voice tentative.

Sidney hesitated. "In the hospital emergency room, you prick."

"No you're not. I checked."

"So what're you going to do now, John?" Sidney went back to the bed and sat down, his head swimming. "You're leaving scorched earth behind you a mile wide. Might as well toss in the towel."

"You tell the police about me?"

"What do you think? They grilled me pretty good. I gave 'em the full story."

Marr was quiet for a moment. "Don't think so."

"Sure I did." Sidney coughed. "You think I want you out there trying to kill me? They'll be looking for you. Still driving the Beemer?"

"Mercedes, you asshole."

Sidney laughed. "That was a trick, John Quincey. You're slipping. A Mercedes. Must be silver to match your big-as-a-barn ego. See, your options are already diminishing."

"Yeah, well then you should be afraid, Sidney," Marr said; his voice was a frozen rope. "Got nothing to lose, now do I?"

Sidney felt his heart flutter. "Might have something there, John. Except that you'll get caught sooner or later. By the way, I had a nice conversation with a Detective Miller of the Eugene Police Department about the fire and all. I spoke with a deputy chief at the fire department, too. Just yesterday."

"Don't believe you," he said after a moment's pause.

"Why's that?"

"Because. You want to keep this personal."

"Well," Sidney said, "I may have miscalculated on that point. I hadn't figured on you becoming a psychopathic serial killer." He heard Marr inhale with a hissing sound through his teeth. "The thing is, John, I really did call the police and the fire departments in Eugene. Not sure if my inquiries will revise their thinking or not, but never can tell."

"You started this," Marr said. His voice was not as loud, as if he'd pulled the phone back a bit.

Sidney tried to laugh. "That going to be your defense? Your honor, Mr. Lister is to blame for my sexual abuse of a child, her death, and the incinerating of a former employee and her husband. The premise being what? Oh, he owed me money and wasn't paying me off fast enough. Yes, he was paying regularly, just not as fast as I wanted, your honor. You know how horrible that can be. I had to kill those people and assault him."

"You're a fool," Marr said.

"You'll get no argument from me, but I'm the fool who may have a life to live. What will your brilliant self be doing life-wise in the very near future?"

"I will find you again, you bastard. And this time, I *will* finish things."

Sidney shuddered and took in a deep breath. "Well, John, I'm no hero. And you did give me a wake-up call tonight. With my head aching and my bruises throbbing, I got your message. You are serious."

"So?"

"The policeman who came to the scene of my beating tonight gave me his card. It has his phone number. I'm going to call him—now. I thought I could play the mind games with you until such time as the authorities caught up to you or you turned yourself in, but this has gone even farther than I imagined."

John Marr uttered a guttural murmur.

"Have his name right here," Sidney said. "Officer Rudy Johnson. Think I'll call Detective Miller in Eugene again, too, give him all the information I have."

"I'll kill you."

Sidney put a hand to his forehead; the pain had increased. "Maybe, maybe not, but whatever happens to me you are going to be history, John Marr, former candidate for Citizen of the Year." He disconnected and fell back on the pillows.

———•———

Officer Rudy Johnson of the Newport Police Department left the motel room just after midnight. He was carrying a notebook that held his notes from a lengthy interview with Sidney Lister. Officer Johnson's eyes had widened when he began to take in the scope of what Sidney was telling him. This was not only a local case of assault and battery; it had tentacles that reached into another jurisdiction and into crimes of abuse, arson, and murder. Officer Johnson asked Sidney to stay in town if he could until one of the detectives from his department could talk with him. He said that an APB would be put out for John Marr with all local, county, and state authorities. He also chastised Sidney for withholding what he knew about John Marr at the time of the assault. Sidney claimed he was stunned and confused from the beating. Officer Johnson looked at him with skepticism but said nothing more.

Sidney moved the Cadillac to the rear of the motel, as far from sight as he could find, locked the door to his room, and wedged a chair under the doorknob before falling into bed.

———•———

He awoke around six the next morning. His mouth was dry and crusty, his head felt like lead, and his body ached as if pummeled by several NFL linemen. He took another shower, shaved his tender face, and brushed the scum out of his mouth. Purple and yellow and rosy bruises glared back at him from the bathroom mirror; he cleaned his nails and discovered what he assumed were bits of John Marr's face beneath them—he'd gotten a piece of the man, after all. He dressed in a pair of chinos and a checked sport shirt, both being worn for the third time with perhaps a few days of freshening in between, and decided to call Ellie— the one person he could call; who else was there? He unplugged his cell phone from the charger and entered the familiar number. She was up and answered on the second ring.

"Sidney! Are you ever coming home? I can't wait—"

"Ellie."

"I know you—"

"Stop. I have something to tell you."

"You miss me."

"Listen now," he admonished. He waited a moment then said, "I was attacked by John Marr last night."

"What? Sidney!"

"I'm okay. A little banged up, but I'll heal."

"Sidney! Heal? Are you hurt? What happened?"

He told her all of it, and when he'd finished she asked if he had someone in Newport that he could turn to. He hesitated and thought of Janis Hill before saying no—other than the local police. Ellie said "My god" in between his pauses and exhorted him to be careful and get back to Portland. Her feisty protectiveness made him smile. She had always been tougher than he had from the very first day they met. They ran out of things to say, but even with lapses in their conversation Sidney could tell that Ellie didn't want to disconnect. But finally he told her he had to go and that he'd call her later. She put in one more plea for him to be safe.

There was a line waiting at the Navigator Café, which was bustling with the breakfast crowd, but Sidney decided to wait for a spot at the counter, deciding that a busy place was safer. Besides, the café was a quick walk from the motel, so he didn't have to bring the Caddy out of hiding. When a stool opened at the counter, Sidney slid in, and before he could wiggle his butt in place a waitress had poured him a cup of coffee. She studied his bruised face but didn't comment on it and asked him what he wanted as if he had the menu memorized; he just said eggs, sausage, and hash browns—no, no juice.

While he waited for his food, he pulled out his notebook for a bit of needed distraction and opened his salesman's journal. He was jotting down what we remembered about Molly Maguire, manager of the Courter's in Cannon Beach, when his food arrived and his cell began to ring simultaneously. A Detective Arnold from the Newport Police Department was on the phone. He wanted to follow up on the incident of last evening. Sidney thought: *Incident? It was a beating.* Sidney agreed to meet him back at the motel after he'd finished his breakfast.

He had just emerged from the café, blinking in bright sunlight and wincing at a stiff breeze, when his cell phone began to ring again; he figured it was the detective, but it was Janis.

"Sidney, are you all right?" she almost yelled. "It was on the radio, about you being assaulted last night. It was you, right?"

"Yeah. It was. I'm pretty good, few bumps and bruises."

"But you're still here, in town."

"Yes." He cupped a hand over the phone and his ear to hear. "I have a few things to clean up, and then I'll head back to Portland."

"Things? What things? And where is this guy Marr?"

"No idea, Janis. Could be in Mexico for all I know. If it was me, I'd be long gone. But who knows?"

"He's crazy, don't you think?"

"I'd say. Over the edge for sure."

As he neared the motel, he saw a plain dark blue Ford Victoria parked in front of his room. When he approached, a square-built man, thin hair, buzz cut, wearing khakis with a blue blazer and obligatory button-down blue shirt and rep tie, stepped out of the car. Sidney raised a hand and got a nod in return.

"Janis, I've got to go. A detective from the police is here to talk to me."

"But you'll call me?"

Sidney hesitated. "Lot going on, Janis. I will if I can. Bye."

He ended the call and approached the man from the blue car. They shook hands. Herb Arnold was his name. Sidney unlocked his room; they went inside and sat at the little table by the front window. Sidney pulled on a cord and opened the curtains. Arnold pulled out a notebook and a ballpoint pen and asked how Sidney was feeling.

"Better than the bruises would indicate," Sidney answered.

Herb Arnold nodded and pulled a leg up over his knee. "So I read what Officer Johnson got from you last night, but I need to go over it again." He eyed Sidney. "If what you said is true, we may have quite a case on our hands here. But this John Marr. I've run a check on him, and frankly he comes out as a stand-up citizen: owner of an impressive business in Eugene, nominated for Citizen of the Year, family man, no violations—clean as a whistle."

Sidney bobbed his head. "All of that is true."

"But then you say that he is the man who attacked you last night at...on the...Carson's Cars lot." Herb Arnold checked his notes again. "And you say he did that, attacked you, because you know all of this, which you declare to be true." The detective looked directly into Sidney's eyes. "You allege that he had sex with an underage girl a... Heather Cole?"

"Yes."

"And that she later died, or rather you say committed suicide because she was pregnant from this Marr?"

Again Sidney said, "Yes."

"Further you stated that you found out about this from a woman...let's see." He flipped a page. "Virginia is it? Snyder, Virginia Snyder?" Sidney nodded as Arnold went on. "And because this Marr assumed that Virginia Snyder, who used to work for Marr, had been the one to tell you about the Cole girl...that because of that he torched the Snyder house in Eugene in which Virginia and Randolph Snyder perished. Is that your assertion, Mr. Lister?"

"Yes." Sidney felt his face redden because when spoken out loud by a policeman the story sounded far-fetched. "Hard to believe, I know."

"Well," Detective Arnold said with a weak smile, "it's quite a set of allegations—that's for sure. However, except for the assault on you last night, it's all out of our jurisdiction."

"So that's it then?" Sidney leaned back in his chair, frowning.

"No," Detective Arnold said calmly. "No, we'll write all of this up and continue to look for this John Marr as a person of interest in your assault. As far as the other allegations, I'm going to make a call to the Eugene Police. I know a detective over there I've had dealings with and will run all of this past him. Get his take on it. See if they want to take things any further."

Sidney leaned forward on his knees. He pursed his lips and squeezed his hands together. "Person of interest," he said. "That person of interest is out there just waiting for me. Like I said, he even called me last night after the...after he beat me up." Sidney laughed coarsely. "Said he's going to kill me."

The detective locked eyes with Sidney and nodded.

"By the way, he drives a Mercedes."

Detective Arnold jotted that down in his notebook. "You know its color or anything else about the car?"

"No."

"Well, we'll keep looking for him. Of course he may have left the area. Would seem foolish for him to hang around here knowing that you've talked with the police."

"You don't know this guy," Sidney responded. "For him, this is a reckoning."

Detective Arnold considered Sidney's last comment, nodded, made some more notes, and flipped his notebook closed. "I'll have a patrol car come by the motel a few times during the night," he said.

When asked, Sidney told the detective that he'd be in town for one more night before going back to Portland.

Unless the worst happened—whatever that would be.

-24-

After Detective Arnold had gone, Sidney sat in the stuffy motel room and considered throwing everything into the car and getting the hell out of town. It had been a cold dose of reality to find that what he knew about John Marr's crimes constituted hearsay to the authorities and might never be proven. One corner of his brain even postulated that the only answer was for John Marr to be gotten rid of; otherwise he'd never be free of him. He remembered holding the black Beretta pistol in his hand, the heft of it, and right then wished he'd gotten it. Finally he called Beeman's and told Nina and Ned what had happened to him and that he had decided to head home, that he wasn't going to see Lamont Courter. They were shocked and worried for his safety, but even at that Ned whined and implored him to see Lamont Courter even briefly before driving north. After all, he had specifically asked to see Sidney.

Lamont Courter saw him right away, no waiting, much to the chagrin of two salesmen who'd been cooling their heels in reception. The gatekeeper, Gert, studied Sidney with the same hostility as she had at his last visit. Courter was seated behind his cluttered tennis court of a desk again, wearing another wrinkled white shirt and smoking a cigarette. The two men looked at one another without speaking until Courter waved for Sidney to take a seat.

"You look the worse for it," he said to Sidney. "You the loser?"

Sidney raised a hand to touch the bruise on his cheek. "Matter of fact, I am."

Lamont Courter sucked on his cigarette and blew out a thin stream of smoke. "I heard about it on the news this morning. So some guy just up and thumped you last night on some car lot. Carson's, wasn't it?"

"Small town," Sidney said.

"What was it? Attempted robbery?"

"I don't know," Sidney lied. "Random attack. Could have been robbery, I guess."

Courter stubbed out his cigarette in the glass ashtray and leaned back. Sidney waited for him to get around to whatever it was he had on his mind. He also noted that the signed football was no longer in its place of honor on the desk.

"Except for getting beat up, how'd the trip go over all?" Courter asked with little feeling. "Fun being Jonesy?"

"Not so much."

"You said that last time."

"Guess I meant it."

Courter reached up and massaged his face with both hands. A growl rumbled out of his chest. He looked at Sidney, reached for the pack of cigarettes on his desk, and lit another one with his butane lighter. With the first plume of smoke he said, "I can't do this anymore."

Sidney didn't say anything, just looked at the man: at the pasty skin of his face, the port-wine stain on his neck, and the watery blue eyes.

"I'm going to turn myself in," Courter said, catching Sidney off guard. "I don't give a shit anymore. Six damnable years of guilt, waiting for the phone to ring or some cop to walk in and cuff me." He drew on the cigarette until his cheeks caved in and seemed to swallow the smoke. Eventually it began to curl out of his nostrils. He leaned on his elbows and stared at Sidney. "You sleep at night?" When Sidney nodded, he said, "I don't. Haven't slept since it happened. Cat naps, that's all. Afraid I'll dream. I can still see the kid and hear the crunch and see the crumpled heap in my rearview mirror. I can remember that anytime, but I can't stand to have it come to me in a dream." He flicked the ash off his cigarette. "Sit up most nights. Watch TV, drink myself stupid, wake up with a screaming headache, and start all over again."

Sidney listened without comment but felt his heart beating as he assimilated the wretchedness that had been this man's life since his moral lapse. Listening to another man's confession of something dreadful was chilling.

"I've retained the best criminal lawyer I could find in Portland."

"Why tell me?" Sidney asked finally.

Courter sucked his cigarette down to a nub and put it out in the ashtray. "Who else can I tell?" he said. "My wife doesn't even know. She just thinks I'm just a stinking drunk—which I am. You're my test run, Sidney," he laughed, using Sidney's name for the first time. "I needed to say it out loud to a live person, to hear my voice saying *I'm going to turn myself in for killing a boy on a bike*." With that he put a hand over his eyes and began to gulp in sobs. His torso shook. He began to strike the desktop with a fist.

Sidney felt rigid; it was hard to breathe. He didn't think he could tell his body to move. He inhaled slowly and let his breath out as if by inches; then he'd inhale again until he'd gained control and began to relax. He couldn't make out why he was having such a visceral response to the agony of someone so little known to him, and yet he was.

Finally Courter gained control. He sat up, pulled a handkerchief out of his back pocket, and dabbed at his eyes. He blew his nose and took a deep breath. A small smile came onto his face.

"You know," he said, "that felt pretty good. Best I've felt in... hell, in years. I guess it's true what they say, you know, about getting something off your chest. Thanks."

Sidney gritted his teeth, but he nodded anyway. "So when you going to do this? See the lawyer?"

"Got an appointment next week. Was the soonest I could get in. Besides, I need time to organize things here."

"You going to tell them?" Sidney asked. "The people you work with?"

"No. I'll tell my wife, of course. Then again, it will become common knowledge soon enough. I'm putting together a management plan. Just hope my daughter is man enough to carry on with things." He leaned back suddenly and clapped his hands together. "God, I feel like a million tons have been lifted off. Just making a decision and telling somebody. How about a drink?"

Sidney hesitated. "Okay, I guess."

"Not to celebrate, for god's sake," Courter said, "just to facing up to it."

———•———

Sidney took one short swallow before he rose slowly, gave Courter a nod, and left the man leaning back in his big chair smiling wanly at nothing. He strode past the scowling receptionist without a sideward glance, feeling an edgy sadness in spite of the man's transgression. He slipped behind the wheel of the car and sat transfixed for several minutes before coming around and activating his cell phone; there were two messages. He decided to listen to the calls later and turned the phone off again.

The Samuel Case Pub & Grill was a snug eatery on the south coast highway. Sidney parked out back on the blind side of the restaurant's Dumpster and settled in. He sat at the bar, had a greasy and amazingly good Reuben sandwich, and washed it down with a pint of local microbrewed SKW Valley Fog brown ale. The waitress, name of Cleo, came up to take away his empty plate and asked if he wanted anything more.

"Another one of these," he said and held up his empty glass. "Tasty."

"That it is," she said. "My personal favorite."

Over the course of an hour, the other stools at the counter were filled and emptied as working men tromped in, ordered a quick hamburger or sandwich, along with Diet Cokes, pints of ale, or coffee, wolfed their food down, and left as quickly as they had come in. Sidney had attempted a conversation or two but, except for one chatty UPS driver, got mostly grunts in return. He stayed on, not anxious to leave the warm confines of the pub.

After his third pint of Valley Fog, Cleo asked, "Hey, hon, you want something more to go with that? Chips, fries, nachos?"

He shook his head. "No. By the way, who the heck is Samuel Case?"

"Was," she answered. "Founder of Newport and its first postmaster. That's him up there." She pointed to a framed faded black and white photograph of a long-bearded man, with deep-set eyes and a prominent nose.

"He looks like a teetotaler."

"Who knows, might have been. That'd be a hoot."

Sidney raised his glass. "To you, Sam," he said. "I'll have another Valley Fog."

When his fourth pint came, Cleo set a big plate of fries down with it. "Here, hon, you put some food in there with all that Fog. Okay? On the house."

Counting the whiskey with Lamont Courter and the ale he'd been drinking, Sidney hadn't consumed that much alcohol so quickly in a very long time. He felt light-headed and a little uncoordinated when he wandered off to the men's room. A cup of black coffee was sitting on the counter when he came back to reclaim his stool. Cleo breezed by carrying a beer order on a tray; she nodded, said, "Drink up," and winked.

Sidney took a few sips of coffee and fired up his cell phone. Janis answered after four rings.

"It's me," he said, his tongue thick and barely responsive.

"Sidney," she said, "where are you? Are you okay?"

"No," he laughed. "Can you come get me? Hey," he said to Cleo, who was filling a glass from a tap, "where is this place?"

Cleo reached for his phone. He handed it to her, smiling like a goof. "Hi," she said. "He's here at Samuel Case Pub & Grill. Yeah, on 101. Okay. Good idea." She grinned at Sidney. "She's coming for you, says to stay put."

Sidney gave her a salute. Janis arrived twenty minutes later. She was carrying his blue windbreaker. "Here," she said and handed it to him. "So, what have you been doing?"

He smiled. "Guess."

"Gee, that'll be tough." She laughed, gave him a gentle punch on the arm, and sat on the stool next to him. Cleo came by again. The two women smiled at each other and rolled their eyes. Janis ordered a glass of white wine and sat quietly while Sidney finished off his second cup of coffee. "So what brought all of this on?"

He shrugged.

"Wait, look at me, let me see your face. Turn your head. Wow, that's a real shiner, turning yellow and green. Hurt?"

"Not much."

"The police, they catch the guy?"

"Don't think so. At least they hadn't when I talked with them last." He smiled. "You know, you look really good."

"I'll just bet," she said, plucking at her hair. "After a day of unpacking freight, stocking shelves, building new displays—I must look really special."

Sidney nodded. "It's a fact."

"So, tell me, what are you doing sitting here getting loopy? You hitting on Cleo here?" Cleo was refilling Sidney's coffee.

"You caught me. And I was just making some headway, right Cleo?"

Cleo reached out and patted his arm. "You betcha, hon. I only have eyes for you now. Guess I'll have to call my old man. He'll be relieved." She walked off carrying the coffee pot and gave her rear end a wiggle.

227

Janis smiled, took a sip of wine, and turned serious. "Okay, what are you going to do? You have a man who wants to kill you."

"That's what he says. That's what the man says."

She shook her head. "Sidney, this is serious. It's a nightmare."

"How about I put out a contract on him?" Sidney grinned, his eyes still glassy.

"Sidney, come on now."

He inhaled and swallowed a burp. "Marr's attack on me—all fact. Verifiable. The really bad stuff: the girl, the fire, and the deaths—hearsay. My hearsay. To the police, Mr. John Quincy Marr is a fine, upstanding citizen. They weren't around when he was foaming at the mouth and trying to strangle me."

"God, do you think he's running or still around?"

"Don't know."

"That is scary. What can you do?"

His laugh was metallic. "Stay low, keep moving, and cower when cornered. Dial 911. Say King's-X. Hell, I don't know."

"It's not funny, Sidney." She twisted her wine glass on the counter and looked down. "So when are you leaving?"

"Tomorrow," he said. "Around mid-morning so I'll have some traffic to blend into in case my predator should be out there waiting. Cover, I'll need cover."

"Where are you staying?"

"Econo Lodge."

She nodded. "So think you're sober enough now to drive?"

"Yeah, Cleo's got me sloshing black coffee. Thing I need now is the john again."

He slipped off the stool. When he returned she was gone; only his windbreaker remained. He picked it up and replayed Bye, bye, *Miss Electra Bly* in his head. The Cadillac was still hiding out where he'd left it. He drove to the motel, parked in the out-of-sight spot he had used before, and walked quickly to his room. He locked himself in and stretched out on the bed. Sleep came in an instant and lasted until he awakened nearly two hours later lying crossways on the bed with a suffocating foam pillow over his face. He snorted awake, sat up quickly, wondering where he was, and was rewarded with a stab in his head as payback for too many pints of Valley Fog ale.

It was going on seven o'clock, too late to eat at the Navigator Café, which didn't do dinner. He ended up at the Canyon Way Bookstore and Restaurant, where a man and woman sitting across from him recommended the crab cakes. They were very good; he enjoyed them without the benefit of any more alcohol and topped off with a serving of bread pudding with rum sauce. Afterward he wandered the bookstore side and picked up a paperback copy of *The Da Vinci Code*. He figured that he would be the last person on earth to finally read it.

She called when he had just finished the first chapter.

"Checking to make sure I didn't drive off the road?" he asked her.

"Something like that. So you got back to the motel okay?"

"I did. All comfy on the bed here reading *The Da Vinci Code*. You read it?"

"Yeah. It was okay. It will keep you wondering."

"Good," he said. "I like to be kept wondering."

They were silent for a long moment.

"Still leaving in the morning?" she broke the quiet.

"Yeah."

"Suppose your ex—Ellie, isn't it? Suppose she'll be anxious for you to get back."

"Yeah," he said. "She's my buddy."

Janis laughed. "That what you call it these days?"

"Well there's that, too, but she's my only friend, really."

"Really? Only friend."

"Yeah, like I said before, I'm in the dark zone when it comes to a social network."

"Sounds lonely."

229

"Can be, especially when I don't much like myself."

"I've been there," she said.

"So, what you up to? In your jammies yet?"

"No, just watching some TV."

"Anything good?"

"Watching an old movie."

"So you wanting company, or is this just a social call?"

She hesitated. "Just checking in. So, see, you have more than one friend."

"What kind of friend are you?" When she didn't respond, Sidney felt the tightness that comes when rejection isn't spoken; it's just there, hanging. "You're the kind that'll come get a guy out of a bar," he said, filling dead air. "Thank you for that."

She chuckled, so did he, and that's how they left it.

-25-

Sidney sat in the car in its hiding place, gripped the steering wheel, and watched raindrops hit the windshield, cling for a moment, and then wiggle down the glass. He knew he was being ridiculous. How many ways must someone signal that your innermost wish is not hers? How many times before the message is received and accepted? He didn't know the answer; he just knew it was not yet—at least not for him.

He hooked up his seatbelt, drove the car away from the shadows, and cautiously pulled out onto the highway. Traffic was light. The dash clock reminded him that it was getting late, near eleven. He should have pulled this stunt earlier, or not at all. What was going to be his opening line? Go Grant High Generals?

He parked on Coast Avenue. Her lights were still on. It was as if he was young and foolish again, agonizing over Ellie after they'd had a fight. He remembered Mr. Conway coming out onto the front porch one time and walking out to where Sidney was sitting in his old Ford. He had leaned over and asked how the car was running. Fine, was the boy's answer. After nodding and studying the car, he said to Sidney that he used to buy only Fords; probably would again, they were good cars. Then he said, *You know, son, this is just what she wants. You mooning for her out here.* Sidney recalled looking into the man's kindly face, saying thanks, and driving away grateful for a way out.

But there was no one to warn off a full-grown male who hadn't heeded life's previous setbacks, so what the hell. He stepped out of the car and closed the door with a quiet click. The rain had stopped. The smell of marine air came to him as he walked across wet asphalt; its shiny blackness rose up beneath the blueness of vapor streetlights.

She answered his knock, and they stood in the open doorway. He felt something in his chest just looking at her. She was wearing jeans, a bulky knit off-white sweater, her hair was gently mussed, and she had on heavy gray socks. She held on to the doorknob.

"Sidney," she said, not smiling.

"The same," he said and held his arms out.

"Why are you here?"

He gave a little laugh. "What if I said I couldn't remember the words to the Grant High fight song?"

The flicker of a smile dropped from her face quickly.

He could hear the muted sound of her television. "So how's the movie?"

She folded her arms. "It's okay. An old Gregory Peck western."

"Love Gregory Peck."

Janis looked down at her feet. When she looked up, she said, "Look, Sidney, I meant what I said and—"

"I know," he said, raising a hand. "And I don't mean to be that person who won't take no for an answer. But for what it's worth—no, wait, let me finish. Please." When she nodded, he relit his smile and went on. "And, believe me, this isn't about a high school fantasy. For the record, you were lovely to look at back then but too remote and aloof."

"Gee, thanks." She managed a tight smile.

"Sorry. But the thing is, neither of us has lived up to the predictions of the high school yearbook editors. Right? I mean, life has cut us off short more than once."

232

"There a point to this? Because you're making me feel exceptional here."

"Yeah there is…a point. It's that twenty-nine years later this Janis Hill isn't that girl. She's a woman who I—"

"Sidney, I can't—"

"Wait." He reached out and put a hand on her shoulder. She didn't pull away. "Look, we've both hit the wall…any number of times. I'm not sure I'm up for another try any more than you are. But if you ever decide to, and I'm on your short list—"

"There's no list." She reached up and gently lifted his hand off her shoulder. "I've had my three strikes. I'm out of the game. Now it's about survival and taking care of me." She folded her arms again.

Sidney looked into her eyes but saw nothing for him there; he smiled, but she didn't reciprocate. After an awkward moment, he swallowed, nodded, backed away and walked down the stairs. When he looked back, she had already closed the door. In the car, he rewound what he'd just done, and pulled out his cell phone with the thought of calling her, just to—just to what? He didn't.

The phone registered an unretrieved message. It was from Detective Miller, the detective he had spoken to anonymously before. He listened to it:

"Mr. Lister, this is Detective Everett Miller with the Eugene Police Department. I'm following up on a call I received from a Detective Arnold of the Newport Police Department. This is regarding matters we are pursuing that may relate to the assault on you yesterday in Newport. If you could give me a call at your earliest convenience, I would appreciate it." He recited his personal cell number before ending the call.

———•———

The white four-door Mercedes appeared in his rearview mirror a block or so after Sidney had pulled out onto the highway headed back to the motel. At a stoplight the big car butted up against the

Cadillac and began shoving it out into the intersection. Sidney cried out and jammed on the brakes and slowed the slide, but he was already out in the middle. A small red car suddenly appeared coming from the opposite direction and barely slid past the nose of the Caddy, its horn blaring; a male face distorted in angry amazement mouthed unheard obscenities as the car passed.

Sidney could only see the silhouette of the person driving the Mercedes, but he knew it was John Marr. Not waiting for a green light, Sidney floored the accelerator and roared off with the other car in pursuit. Before he could collect his thoughts about what to do, Marr rammed him again, sending the car into a swerve that Sidney barely pulled out of. The town was bottled up for the night; except for a big semi, heading north, there were no cars on the road. Sidney fumbled with his cell phone to dial 911 but couldn't manage that and evade the onslaught of the other car. He was nearing eighty miles an hour, but the Mercedes stayed with him and slammed into him twice more. Sidney barely noticed when he sped past his motel; everything left and right was a blur. Marr's car gained even more speed and hit Sidney with such force that the Cadillac veered and sideswiped a parked minivan, which slowed his car and gave Marr a better shot as he swung out and came in on the left and hit the driver side door.

Sidney yelled but gained some control of the car and accelerated with everything the big engine had and managed to pull away as the Mercedes struggled to right itself after the collision. The car was reaching ninety-five on a road where cross traffic could emerge at any time, but Sidney had no choice. He raced past cars coming toward him; some of them pulled off, and he heard a chorus of rancorous horns rise then fade as he roared on. He approached the Yaquina Bay Bridge and accelerated as much as he could handle. The Mercedes came on and gradually gained on him. After the two cars roared off the bridge, Marr pulled alongside, his car's engine howling, and turned into Sidney again, colliding in a scream of metal. The cars were welded together. Sidney jammed on the brakes and was able to break loose and bring the Cadillac under control; he skidded off the highway to a jarring stop on the off-ramp leading to the OSU Hatfield Marine Center.

The white Mercedes had flown past, lurched over a low concrete median separator, and stopped down the highway. Sidney saw that Marr was turning around to come back; he tried to move the Caddy, but it had stalled. After three grinding attempts to get the engine going, he gave up and tried to open his door. But it was jammed shut, so he crawled over the console and got out on the passenger side. He stood behind the car to shield himself and watched as the big white car headed back toward him. But instead of jumping the median strip and coming at the disabled Cadillac, the car flew past, headed north; a part of its front bumper hung down. Then Sidney heard the sirens and could see flashing blue and red lights in the distance and turned to watch Marr's car slow and turn off onto a side road as the police cars approached, north and south.

Sidney came out from behind his car and began waving as the patrol cars caught him in their headlights. A state police car coming from the north and a city police car coming from the south both slid to a stop, and policemen sprang out of the cars, standing behind their car doors, weapons out. He was ordered to get on the ground, which he did. As he went down on his knees he saw John Marr's Mercedes nose out onto the highway and head north back over the Yaquina Bay Bridge. He waved a hand and pointed but was told once more to get down. He lay flat, arms out, and inhaled dust from the shoulder of the road.

————•————

By the time Detective Arnold of the Newport Police had been summoned and arrived, Sidney was exasperated, and John Marr was long gone. Arnold cleared things up with the officers on the scene, and Sidney was free to go after giving an extensive account of what had happened. Detective Arnold was savvy enough to immediately order an APB for the Mercedes and order John Marr held for questioning. Once again, Sidney could only tell his version of the chase; there were no witnesses to corroborate his story. Those who might have seen the chase would only be able to say they saw two cars driving at high speeds; some would say they saw one purposely hitting the other. But no one would be able to say who was driving either car.

After being questioned by all the official parties on site, he was free to go; but then the Cadillac couldn't be moved. The last hit by John Marr had rendered the car undriveable. After a tow truck had carted the car off to the local Cadillac dealer, Detective Arnold gave Sidney a lift back to his motel. Sidney sat in the dark at the plastic laminated table by the front window and peered out through partially opened drapes. It was quiet. No doors were slamming. No television noise filtered in from adjoining rooms. After rewinding the wild ride in his mind a couple of times, he went into the bathroom, washed his face, took a long drink of cold water, went back out, and turned on the television. He found CNN, sat on the end of the bed, and watched with the sound down, just reading the crawl at the bottom of the screen. Look at that: another congressman was tearfully confessing to being bad with a woman other than his wife.

He stared at the flickering screen until his mind shut down, then crawled up on the bed, pulled the bedspread over him, and slept in his clothes until the whine of an engine jarred him awake. His eyelids flicked open; he stared at the ceiling and wondered where he was. When the noise faded as the vehicle backed away, Sidney rose up on one elbow blinking. The television was still on; the talking heads still mouthing an endless stream of the ridiculous and the titillating.

He groaned, swung his legs around, and sat up. A slash of bright light streamed in through the gap in the drapes and found his eyes; he blinked and turned away. Then it all flooded back into his head: the terrifying chase, the scream of metal against metal, the crash, and John Marr's big car speeding away. He ran his tongue around a dry mouth and raised his arms up in a stretch before answering the call of his pleading bladder. It was nearly eight o'clock. He showered, shaved, brushed his teeth, dressed in the least wrinkled khaki pants he had and the most forgiving sport shirt, and walked to the Navigator Café. All he could handle was orange juice, a cup of coffee, and a bran muffin. He picked up someone's cast-off morning paper from Eugene and scanned the front page. Saw among other news that Medicare was predicted to go broke by 2019 and that the Terry Nichols trial for the Oklahoma City bombing was beginning. Sidney studied the picture of a tense Terry Nichols dressed in jail orange and shuddered to think that John Marr might never be held accountable for Heather Cole or Ginny Snyder.

He was on his second cup of coffee when his cell phone started ringing in his pants pocket. It was Detective Arnold; he needed to see Sidney again, said he'd pick him up at the café. He wouldn't say what it was about. Sidney was waiting out in front of the when the dark blue unmarked car eased into the parking lot. Sidney slid into the front seat; Arnold was drinking coffee from a travel mug.

"Morning," he said. "Get any sleep?"

"Guess you could call it that," Sidney answered. "I feel like a mud wrestler who lost."

Arnold chuckled.

"What's up?" Sidney asked.

"We're going for a drive. Buckle up."

Sidney clicked on his seatbelt. "Where to and why?"

"Think they found your friend." Arnold stuck his coffee cup into a cup holder and headed north on the highway.

———•———

Devil's Punch Bowl State Park is eight miles north of Newport and about half a mile off Highway 101. The main attraction is a large bowl naturally carved in a rock headland. Waves enter the bowl and often violently churn, swirl, and foam. The bowl was supposedly created when two caves carved by the ocean collapsed. But geology was not on the minds of Detective Arnold or Sidney when they drove into the parking area overlooking the punch bowl. A huddle of official vehicles from several jurisdictions formed a collage of confusion. Detective Arnold pulled up to the vehicular gathering and exited the car. Sidney got out slowly and looked around bewildered, squinting in the brightness of a beautiful sunny day on the coast. Then he saw the battered white Mercedes sitting askew in among the official vehicles.

Arnold looked at him. "That it?"

Sidney nodded. "Yeah, think so. Where's John Marr...the driver?"

"Follow me." They approached a state trooper who seemed to be in charge. Arnold caught his eye. "Sergeant Hollister, this is Sidney Lister."

The one called Hollister was tall, lean, and wore the traditional blue on blue uniform and Smokey trooper hat. He had been in a conversation with an EMT with the ambulance that had been dispatched from Newport. The assemblage included a county sheriff's deputy, several local firefighters, and a couple of petty officers from the Coast Guard. All eyes turned and looked at Sidney quizzically. He felt like a specimen.

Detective Arnold leaned in and said to the state trooper, "He's the one who was involved in the chase."

"Oh, yes," Hollister said, staring at Sidney. "Can he identify the victim?"

"I don't know," Arnold said, "but I would guess so."

Sidney stood back. It felt odd having people talking about him within earshot. Sergeant Hollister came over. "Mr. Lister, I'm Sergeant Tom Hollister. Understand that you were involved in a high-speed chase in Newport last night."

Sidney nodded. "That's right. Well, I was the one being chased. He rammed me, too."

"That's what I've been informed. Do you recognize that car?" He pointed at the Mercedes. Every official head turned as one to look at the vehicle.

"Yes, that's the car," Sidney said.

Hollister jotted something in a notepad he carried. He turned back to Sidney. "Did you know the man who was driving that vehicle?"

The word *did* hit Sidney. "Yes. His name is John Marr."

Hollister made another jot on the notepad. "That's the name on the car's registration. John Q. Marr." He looked at Sidney. "So you could identify him? This Marr?"

Sidney nodded. Hollister led him over toward the rim of Devil's Punch Bowl; the Pacific Ocean surf rolled in, white and frothy, on the beach below the bluff. They stood up close to a Cyclone fence at an angle where they could look into the bowl. Sergeant Hollister pointed down. After a moment Sidney could see a body down on the rocks on the floor of the hollow sandstone formation. It was clad in a white shirt and dark pants; he could see that the feet were bare. Four men were standing over the body; one was wearing a state police uniform, and Sidney figured the others, clad in fluorescent vests, were from the fire department and ambulance crew. From that angle and that distance, it was hard to tell, but Sidney thought it was John Marr. He told the officer that he couldn't really identify the body from that distance.

"I understand," said Hollister. "The paramedic has confirmed that whoever he is, he's deceased. The man is dead. It appears that his body became wedged among the rocks and was kept from being moved when the bowl filled and emptied with the tides. Of course, the tide is out at the moment. We're lucky in that regard."

"Did he jump?" Sidney asked.

"Seems like a good bet," Hollister said. "But he could just as easily have slipped and fallen. Take an autopsy to determine cause of death. As soon as we get a couple more men down there, they'll carry the body out in that basket you see—through the northern opening and up a trail from the beach. Once we get the remains up here I'd like you to take a close look and see if you can positively ID the body."

Sidney nodded his agreement and followed Hollister back toward the damaged Mercedes, with the official entourage following. He turned to Sidney again. "Mr. Lister, where were you last night after the incident, the chase?"

"Well, Detective Arnold took me to my motel. I don't know— it was after one, maybe two in the morning. Can't be sure. Late anyway. My car was too damaged drive."

"So I understand. And you stayed at the motel? Didn't leave at any time?"

Sidney looked at Arnold. "Not until this morning. I grabbed some breakfast. Right after that, Detective Arnold came for me. What, about nine?" Arnold nodded.

Hollister made more notes. A sheriff's deputy came up and whispered something to Hollister. The sergeant nodded. "They've found a pair of shoes and socks in the car."

"Suicide," Arnold said to Sidney.

Hollister looked over. "Maybe. We'll leave that to our CID officer when he arrives. Meantime, let's lock this down, tape it off, and secure the scene."

———•———

Finally, Sidney stood over the body; the skin was bloodless and sallow after hours in saltwater, but it was John Marr. The last time Sidney had seen him that close, Marr had been trying to strangle him. *John, you happy now?*

Sergeant Hollister cleared his throat. "Can you identify the body? Is that John Marr, Mr. Lister?"

"Yes, that's him," he said, and watched as they zipped up the body bag and transferred John Marr's remains into the funeral coach of the county coroner. Sidney gave all of his contact information to Sergeant Hollister and Detective Arnold drove him back to the motel. He watched until the unmarked official vehicle cleared the motel lot and eased back onto the highway, then he called Ned Beeman; he dumped the whole story on him: the car chase, his near-death experience, John Marr's actual death, that he needed wheels to get home, and that he was quitting. Ned swallowed all of it while expressing a variety of reactions with each new pronouncement from Sidney: "Oh my god. Oh no. I can't believe it. Sidney, that's awful. Don't worry, we'll get the car fixed. You can rent whatever you want to get you home. Now, don't overreact. We'll talk this all out later. Just get home and be safe."

Be safe, Sidney thought. The monster was dead. What more could he do to him? Ellie listened to all of it without saying a word.

"So it's over," she said when he finished.

"Yeah."

"Gives me the chills to think of someone jumping into the bowl. I've been there before, seen that big old hole. But he killed himself for sure?"

"Looks that way. They found his shoes and socks in his car. Evidently that's common. People take off their shoes before they jump for some reason. Took the easy way out, the bastard."

"You'll be home tomorrow, right?"

"Have to," he said. "Haven't had any clean clothes for days."

"Bring your dirty clothes here. I'll take care of them and other things that need tending to."

-26-

Shortly before noon, Sidney packed up his belongings, loaded them into the Buick rental car that had been delivered by Enterprise, checked out of the motel, and left Newport behind. He took Highway 20 east, the route that took him through Philomath, the town of Lamont Courter's miserable transgression. Philomath, a lumber town that had once hummed with a dozen mills, retained only a couple of operational mills from its heyday. Sidney drove slowly through its downtown and wondered where a boy on a bike had been riding on October 31, 1998, when Lamont Courter came out of the dark and ended his life. Sidney weighed the possible outcome of Courter's planned confession. How would his torturous years of guilt balance out against the life of a fourteen-year-old boy named Billy—who now would have been a twenty-year-old?

By four o'clock, he was standing at the door to Ellie's condo with a load of dirty clothes in his arms. She answered the door grinning widely, threw his clothes on the floor, and clamped him a breath-stopping hug before dragging him into the bedroom. He didn't resist. After the best body play they had enjoyed in months, Ellie made coffee and pulled out a cherry pie she had made especially for the occasion—an amazing act considering her limited culinary skills. They sat around the small round kitchen table in their robes and enjoyed looking at one another.

They had finished off the whole pie and were enjoying another cup of coffee when Sidney heard his cell phone ringing in the bedroom. He started for a moment but then remembered that John Marr was dead; there would be no more calls that made his stomach churn. By the time he dug the phone out of his pants pocket, the call had gone to voice mail. He carried the phone back into the kitchen and sat back down to finish his coffee.

"Who was it?" Ellie asked.

"Went to voice mail before I got there. Probably Nina or Ned." He retrieved the message; it wasn't Nina or Ned.

"Sidney, call me. It's all over the news." It was Janis. "I need to know that you're all right. Call me, please."

He put the phone down and drank the last swallow of coffee from his cup.

"Who was it? Ned?"

"No." He looked into her questioning eyes and wondered what to say.

"So who was it, then?"

He pulled his terry cloth robe around him and leaned back. For a long moment he studied Ellie's smiling face with its eager expression. "I need to tell you something," he said.

"What? Who was that, really?"

He reached over and took the cup she was holding out of her grasp, held her hand, and ran his thumb over the smoothness of the skin above her knuckles. And he told her about meeting Janis Hill, the classmate they both knew. When he had finished telling her about his time in Newport, she was quiet, and her eyes glistened. She smiled into his face.

"Are you hurt?" he asked softly.

"No, silly," she said. "This is so good for you is all."

"She's told me no at least twice. And this call," he looked at the phone on the table, "it's just her being worried about someone she knows. Not...well, not because she cares for me...you know, that way."

243

"Sidney, my darling, you still don't know how to hear what we say, do you? Didn't you tell me that she said something about three strikes?" He nodded. "She was married three times, right? There you go. She's afraid of the same thing you are."

"What's that?"

Ellie laughed and patted his hand. "Getting it wrong."

He stared into the eyes of the only person he'd ever totally trusted and wondered if she was right. When he picked up the phone she smiled. Janis answered immediately.

"It's me," he said.

"Sidney!" Her voice spiked. "My god, I heard about the car chase and then...the body in the Punch Bowl. And you were named as the driver of the car that had been chased. It's just awful."

"Yeah. But I'm all right. Safe now."

"Where are you?"

"Back in Portland. I'm at Ellie's right now."

Ellie frowned and shook her head.

"Oh." Janis hesitated. "Well, tell her hello from another Grant High General."

Sidney smiled at Ellie. "She says hello."

"Hello back," Ellie said. She stood, patted Sidney on the back, and left the kitchen.

"She says hi, too. So where are you, at work?"

"Yeah, I'm here but not worth much. All I can think about is what happened to you."

Sidney felt a sudden flicker of wonder but pushed aside any prospect that something might have changed with her. "Yes, well, thanks for that, but I'm okay. Really, I'm fine. It's over...finally."

"Yes, finally," she sighed. "I was so worried. It must have been terrifying." She hesitated. "And it happened right after you left here, didn't it?"

"Uh-huh. As soon as I pulled onto the highway, there he was, right behind me—ramming into my car."

"Oh, Sidney. It gives me the chills."

He paused as Ellie walked through the kitchen carrying his dirty clothes. She winked at him.

"It's over now. My nightmare. I've quit my job with Beeman's, too," he added.

"You quit?" Janis waited a moment then added, "Well, I can understand that, I suppose. Guess I won't be seeing you anytime soon, least ways not selling me geegaws, huh?"

"Probably not."

"Here I'll be stocking shelves and selling seashells, and you'll be off slaying new dragons. Nothing new ever happens at Courter's."

He thought of Lamont Courter about to face the unending nightmare of his past. "Never say never," he said. "Things can happen you couldn't even imagine."

"Meaning what?"

He laughed. "Just never say never." He heard the washing machine begin to agitate. "So anyway, I'll be looking for another job. Who knows, maybe I'll get down your way one day."

She was quiet. "Sidney?"

"Yeah, still here."

"I'm sorry for how I was to you that night. When you came by."

"Uh-huh."

"I don't know what I was thinking, you know?"

"You were being honest. Life has a way of setting our boundaries. You told me yours."

"Yes but...wait a sec." Her voice was muffled as she spoke to someone, her hand over the mouthpiece. "Sorry, Sidney, duty calls. Can I call you later?"

"Sure," he said quickly, "let's keep in touch." He said good-bye and disconnected.

He was holding the phone in his hand, staring off across the room, when Ellie came in and sat down across from him. She began to talk to him, gently and cautiously. He didn't respond, but he listened to her talk of their lives together. In the process, she told him who she knew him to be: of his strengths, weaknesses, talents, inhibitions, inabilities, self-doubts, dreams, and failures. He listened and at times smiled, frowned, or shrugged. Ellie was the only person who could dissect his life to his face and not have him get up and walk out.

"Of course, a part of me is jealous of what I can see this woman means to you. But I mostly want you to have a good life—even if it means losing our...what we have."

He laughed. "Not a problem," he said. "I doubt that I'll hear from her again. And maybe I don't want to."

"No," she said, "maybe you're afraid to take it any further for fear of being turned away."

They sat quietly holding hands at the table. When the laundry was done, Sidney carried a bundle of clean clothes out to his car and drove to his apartment, which greeted him with a stale silence and a blinking answering machine. He dumped his duffle bag on the bed, put away his Ellie-washed clothes, and went to see how many people had cared to call him in two weeks.

The number was four. Not many. The first voice was that of John Marr well before all hell had broken loose. Sidney shuddered at the sound of his voice, deleted it, and breathed a sigh of relief. He erased a telemarketing message for aluminum siding; apartment dwellers don't do siding. When the female voice from the third message came at him, he actually took a step back.

Helen Marr was literally screaming. "I know who you are, Mr. Sidney Lister! I remember the day you came by our home. And now you are accusing my dead husband of attacking you. How vile can you be? And the police are saying John committed suicide—claiming he jumped to his death. That could never be true. John was too strong and devoted to his family to do such a thing. But if he did it was because you somehow drove him to it. May your soul rot in hell!"

Sidney listened to Helen Marr's message twice more before erasing it and stood looking at the blinking light for a long time before hitting the button for the fourth call. The voice was of a reporter for the *Eugene Register-Guard* wanting to talk to him about John Marr. He left his phone number and urged him to call at his earliest convenience. Sidney decided that there would be no earliest convenience and erased the message.

———•———

He slept in the next morning. Didn't even know what day of the week it was and didn't care. Around ten o'clock he got up to take a shower but had to let the tap run until rust-colored water cleared from the water heater after it had sat idle for nearly two weeks. He dressed in clean clothes for the first time in days, found nothing but sour milk, three eggs, and half a loaf of bread that had molded, and went out for a late breakfast at Besaw's Café in northwest Portland before driving out St. Helens Road to meet with Ned and Nina at the Beeman's office. They fawned over him, purred their thanks for all he had done, and moaned for all he had endured.

"Horrible, just horrible," Ned said. They were all three seated in Jonesy's old office around the desk. The office had been purged of all things that had belonged to the dead man. Nina brought them each a cup of coffee; they sat sipping for a vacuous amount of time.

Ned suddenly held out an envelope. "Here. Your paycheck, plus a nice bonus," he said with a flair at the end. "And well deserved, right, Nina?"

"Oh yes, Sidney. My goodness, all you've been through. We appreciate what you've done for us. "And we've received at least half a dozen calls from our customers on the coast asking how you are after hearing about that awful business. You made quite an impression, it seems."

"Now about this business of you quitting, Sidney," Ned said leaning forward, on the desk. "Just forget that." He knifed the air with the edge of his left hand.

"Look, Ned," Sidney said, "I'm serious about that. I—"

"Look, I know your résumé." Ned's face reddened. "It's a bloody roadmap to nowhere. You've been everything but anything."

"Ned!" Nina slapped her hand on the desktop. "What on earth...you're insulting
Sidney."

"No, no, I'm not." Ned pointed a finger at Sidney. "He knows what I'm saying. Don't you, Sidney?"

Sidney was smiling. "You're wearing your brass balls this morning, Ned. Swinging for the fence?"

"Damn right I am." Ned's face softened. "What the hell, we need you, Sidney. You pulled us out of a jam, made a believer outa me for sure, now you want to walk away. Not going to happen. Leastways not until I lay out my offer to you." He raised his eyebrows at Sidney.

"I'm listening."

"Stegland Glassware," Ned said and raised his arms. "Hello!"

"The company that made Stegland, Ohio, famous?"

"The very same. And we're signing a deal to be their West Coast distributors."

Sidney laughed. "You're kidding me."

"You're laughing, but it's no joke." Ned sat back and inhaled. "Contract is in the mail, as they say. Helluva break for us, and— by god, Sidney—you're gonna be part of it."

Nina spoke up. "Sidney, we want you to be our sales manager. Hire a sales force and be head of business expansion. At a substantial increase in salary."

"Plus the use of a new Cadillac every year," Ned added beaming.

In the end, Sidney accepted their offer. He left the Beemans with their big plans, climbed into his old Camry, settled into the seat molded to his anatomy, and drove away wondering just how desperate Stegland Glassware was to sign on with Beeman's. What the hell, he might just share in a little success for once.

———•———

He slept in again the next morning, got up at nine, ate a bowl of Wheaties and, while lounging in his boxer shorts, had two cups of coffee and scanned the *Oregonian*. The coverage of John Mar's death was relegated to a small paragraph deep inside the paper: "Death of Eugene man judged suicide".

Sidney had just finished reading about the Oregon State Police's determination that Marr's death in Devil's Punch Bowl had been ruled a suicide, when the phone rang. Ironically it was Detective Miller from the Eugene Police Department. He wanted to discuss the John Marr case again; it was agonizingly repetitive. Sidney calmly answered Miller's questions again and again until the man finally seemed finished.

"So anything else you can think of, Mr. Lister?"

"Like what?"

"Just a routine question. Anything you may have forgotten to mention, something out of the ordinary?"

"No, nothing…oh, I did get a call from Mrs. Marr."

"That right. Mrs. Marr. What did she want?"

"She left a message on my answering machine. A rant more than a message."

"Really? What did she say? Upset?"

"Oh yeah." Sidney inhaled. "That she knew who I was, that I was vile accusing her husband of attacking me, and so on. Claimed that her husband wouldn't have committed suicide—he was too good, but that if he did I drove him to it. She wants me to rot in hell—and like that."

"Sounds like she's not your biggest fan."

Sidney didn't respond. Detective Miller asked a few more inconsequential questions and ended the call saying he'd get back to him if he needed anything more.

———•———

The very next day Lamont Courter hit the front pages. The story of a boy's unsolved death being revived after so many years with no answers and the emerging story of a man's guilt and remorse was riveting the public. The Benton County District Attorney held a press conference at the courthouse to announce that a break had come in the long-ago hit-and-run killing of a local boy. He expressed his outrage over a young life snuffed out by a cowardly act that had remained hidden for years. He promised that the culpable party would be held accountable. Of course, Lamont Courter's attorney had first advised his client to forget it, to not turn himself in, as there had been no witnesses and no connection to him in any way; that if he had to do something he could anonymously set up a scholarship fund in the deceased boy's name and move on. But Courter had made up his mind. He wanted—he needed—to acknowledge his deed and be punished.

The negotiations went on behind the scenes long before the media event at the courthouse. Courter's attorney had presented an option to the district attorney: solve a long-unsolved crime or have nothing. He presented the profile of his client: a man who was compassionate, a successful businessman, a philanthropist—a man who could no longer live with the tragic events of October 1998 and would come forward of his own volition to accept responsibility for his actions and bring closure to the family. The story played out on the front pages and on local television for several days until the court's ruling of the plea-bargained case was released. In the end, Lamont Courter's negotiated sentence was twelve months in the Shutter Creek Correctional Institution, a minimum-security prison on the Oregon coast in North Bend, three years of probation after serving his time, and an undisclosed financial settlement with the boy's parents.

Sidney followed the story and considered that Courter was probably at peace for the first time in many years. Whatever prison life he faced would likely be a respite from the self-made prison he had been in.

-27-

That same week, with the stony face of Lamont Courter staring out from the front page, Sidney hired a sales staff: three men and one woman. Ned Beeman had secured a new warehouse with suite of offices attached; the Promised Land lay just ahead. But even when Ned handed him the keys to a new Cadillac, and they toasted to brighter days in Jonesy's old office the day before the movers came, Sidney kept his smile shallow and tilted his glass just slightly. He'd been at such a juncture before—many times—and the new car smell was so reminiscent of tantalizing schemes that had come to nothing.

———•———

After a day-long session of facing applicants for the new sales force, Sidney let himself into his apartment, loosened his tie, and poured a bourbon with a little Seven-Up in it. He stepped out onto the balcony, took a big drink, it burned its way down, and he broke out laughing. It was April 1st—fitting. He had sat in his new high-backed chair and interviewed hopefuls. He had done that. He had questioned those people about their qualifications. He had watched as they searched for the best answers as to why they should be hired; as if the job they sought was worth humbling themselves.

The oldest prospect, a man with years of experience, calmly answered Sidney's questions even as his face reddened at the inanity of the interview; Sidney smiled and felt ridiculous. And he had done that in succession with each candidate he had hired: the woman nearing-forty with the cigarette voice, the natty dresser who kept looking at his watch, and the skinny young man who'd decided to give up selling cars—he had questioned them all as if he'd had a right to.

He drained his drink, chuckled some more, and went in to fix another one. In the end he had given each one his expectations and tried to swallow his self-satisfaction as if it were deserved. *What the hell,* he thought, *time to ride the pony and see how far it can run. Who knows, maybe this time things will work out.* He fried up a small T-bone steak, sautéed a handful of crimini mushrooms, steamed some broccoli, and poured a glass of affordable Chianti. The first bite of medium-rare beef was in his mouth when the doorbell rang.

She stood in the doorway looking like she'd been sent to the principal's office. They stared at one another for a long moment before he stood back and she stepped in. Sidney swallowed the meat he was chewing.

"I wondered what it would look like," she said, "where you live."

He looked around as if seeing his own space for the first time; suddenly it had all the charm of a doctor's office waiting room. "Interior décor is my real calling."

She laughed.

He looked back at her. "I must say this is a surprise."

Janis smiled. "I know. For me, too."

"I don't give donations at the door," he said, "no matter how worthy the cause."

"Really. I'd heard you were a soft touch. Must have been misinformed."

"Seems like." She looked wonderful. He couldn't take his eyes off her.

"What?" she said and raised a hand to her hair then touched

her face. "I have spinach stuck to my teeth or something?"

He smiled. "No. I was thinking how great you look."

"Ever the salesman," she said.

"So here you are in Portland." He hesitated before coaxing himself to ask, "What's the occasion?"

She looked around again. "Mind if I sit down?"

"Of course, sorry." He pointed and sort of lurched after her toward the small space the landlord called the living room. She sat on the couch; he remained standing. "Nice to see you," he said.

"You too."

"You want something to eat? I was just—"

"I'm sorry—I'm interrupting your meal."

"Never mind," he said. "That's what microwaves are for. You eaten?"

She waved him off.

"How about a glass of wine?"

"Sure, that would be nice."

He returned with another glass of the Chianti.

She took a sip, swallowed hard but didn't grimace, and said, "I suppose you've read all about Lamont Courter."

"Yeah," he said and sat across from her in his weathered recliner. "Quite something."

"That's an understatement." She paused then asked, "Did you know about him, about the hit-and-run? I mean, before it came out?"

He nodded. "For a while, not long."

"He really was a bastard."

"Maybe," he offered. "But he lived in his own private hell for all those years. Couldn't take it anymore."

"He got off pretty light," she said, frowning. "Don't you think?"

"I couldn't say. Haven't walked in the man's shoes."

"I suppose, but—"

"So," he interrupted, "why are you here?"

She inhaled and looked at her hands in her lap. "Seems like I asked you that very same question recently." He didn't respond. "I could say it's my twice-annual trek to refurbish my wardrobe, I'm in town to visit a friend, or I miss the big city. Let's see, what's left?" She played at ticking off options on her fingers. "Oh, I remember." She looked right at him. "You."

"Me?" He felt his eyes open wider and took another swallow of wine.

"Uh-huh." They sat quietly studying one another.

"Did I leave another piece of clothing behind?" Sidney finally said and laughed.

"Nothing like that." She smiled patiently and took in a breath. "That night in Newport? When you came by my place?"

"You mean just before John Marr and I played tag out on the highway?"

She closed her eyes and shuddered. "Yes. I was less than honest when you came to my door."

Sidney waited.

"I think I said something about not being in a relationship. Said there's no list...or something like that."

Sidney nodded but didn't say anything.

She lowered her eyelids for a moment. "Well, there has been someone in my life...for a while now."

"I see." He drank some more wine. "So what was that—what we did? One for good old Grant High?"

"I don't know...maybe. I guess it was more that than anything. For old time's sake, as pitiable as those days were for me."

"So you say."

"Well, they were." She looked at Sidney. "What was it you said about walking in someone else's shoes?"

"Sorry," he said. "But anyway, here you are, and you have someone." He regretted his flippant tone the moment it left his mouth.

"Sidney," she said softly. "Please."

254

His face turned rosy. "I'm sorry…again."

"His name is Ronald. Gill is his last name. He's a biologist at the OSU Marine Center. He's three years older than me. We met two years ago after a concert at the Newport Performing Arts Center. We began dating. It's been an easy relationship."

"Easy?" Sidney said.

Her smile was almost shy. "No rockets' red glare, no bombs bursting in air," she said. "Respectful. He's a nice man: steady, intelligent, and kind to me. I enjoy his company. We have a loving relationship."

"Sounds like the best you've ever had. I'm happy for you." Sidney took another swallow of wine and confirmed that it wasn't very good. "So why are you here?" he asked again. "Is there something wrong?"

She shook her head and set her glass down on the lamp stand beside the couch. "Maybe six months ago, Ronald nearly drowned. He was in the hospital for several days. I remember going into my coping mode and seeing to his welfare: visiting him, taking care of his house, mail, dog, and so on. I got him home and watched over him until he went back to work."

"He's okay now?" asked Sidney.

"Yes, he's fine." She gathered her thoughts for a moment. "But when you were being attacked, I had no coping mode. I got the shakes just thinking of what had happened to you. I had trouble sleeping for worrying. I was a wreck."

The room was still, the only sound being the muted throb of bass from music being played in the apartment directly below. They looked at one another, smiling but uncertain. Sidney reached for the bottle of wine and held it up; Janis shook her head. He settled back and studied her face and felt a thickness in his throat that he couldn't swallow away.

"I told him about you," she said. "Ronald. About you and me. About our past and meeting again after all these years."

"Must have wowed him. There's nothing like someone else's

stories about old classmates to get a guy's blood up. Was he fascinated?"

Janis finally reached for the glass of wine and took a shallow sip; her hand trembled. "No, but he understood…about how I felt. And that we wouldn't be seeing each other again—in that way."

"In that way," Sidney said. She nodded and smiled sadly.

After they had stared at one another through a long rumble from downstairs, she said, "So. What now?"

He hesitated. "I don't know." He saw the disappointment in her eyes and wanted to wipe it away but couldn't. "I…don't know. Do you?"

"Only if you do." When Sidney didn't reply, she waited for a moment then stood. "I'd better be going." She pulled at the coat she had not taken off and studied his face again. "It's a relief to see you—safe and unharmed. Be happy."

She crossed to the door, turned and smiled, stepped out, and pulled it closed with a soft click. For a moment Sidney was rooted to his chair before jumping up and crossing to the door, his heart pounding. He yanked it open; she was standing there facing him. He reached out and put a hand on her cheek.

"I'm a fool," he said. "Don't go."

She tipped her head against his hand. "Okay."

He pulled her in, closed the door, and they stood right there holding one another for a long time. He kissed her gently and helped her out of her coat. They embraced again; then he led her into the bedroom where they helped each other shed their clothes. Sidney shuddered when he saw her body again. She came to him on the bed and together their hands moved, each caressing the other, until they joined and felt the tremor that acknowledged what they both had known and wanted.

In the morning she was sleeping soundly when Sidney woke. It was only six o'clock. He slipped from beneath the covers and stood looking down at her. His smile came from somewhere inside where he knew that this was different. He studied her sleeping face, lips slightly parted, eyelids with smudges of eye shadow; the black and white checked comforter was pulled up to just below her chin. It was different. Different from having been with other women, even Ellie, different even from having gone to bed with Janis in her own bed, only ten days before. Maybe he hadn't ever been in love before: not with Ellie, not with the others so faceless now, and of course not with Janis, in absentia for twenty-nine years. He smiled and inhaled. All he knew was that he wanted to be with this woman in his bed for as long as she'd have him.

He was on his second cup of coffee and halfway through the newspaper when she walked into the kitchen in bare feet; his burgundy pajamas hung on her, but he thought she still looked spectacular. They smiled at each other until they had to laugh. She leaned over him and wrapped her arms around this shoulders.

"Good morning," she said. "What's your name again?"

"Mister Most Likely," he answered.

"And so you are." She leaned down to kiss him.

"Coffee?"

"You bet." Janis sat at the table, rolled the sleeves up on the baggy pajamas, and watched him pull a mug out of the cupboard, pour the coffee and carefully set it in front of her. Everything was different; every move each of them made was new and had to be observed and taken in. When he sat back down across from her, they stared at one another with smiling eyes; nothing had to be said. In the quiet of being together, she looked around the kitchen, examining his space, the things in it, the way he had arranged things on the counter, the colors of the dishcloth, and how he hung the kitchen towel from the refrigerator handle—absorbing all of it.

"So you actually told him? Ronald?"

She looked at him smiling. "About us?"

"Uh-huh."

"Well, I told him about *you*," she said. "I wasn't sure there'd be an *us*. Is there?"

He grinned. "Guess so."

"Guess so," she echoed. "We're in that silly mode, huh?"

"Oh yeah, very silly. So how did he take it—you breaking out the news about another guy?"

"He was good about it," she answered.

"Good about it? That says something."

"Uh-huh. We were more pals than lovers, it seems. Suppose I would have been the same if he'd come to me about another woman."

"Sort of like me and Ellie," he said. "Like when I told her about you."

"You told her about me? What?"

"What do you think?"

When she smiled, he got up and refilled her coffee from the Mr. Coffee pot. "So how are we going to do this with you in Newport and me up here? I'm staying with Beeman's."

"I know. Nina told me." She sipped from her cup and looked at him over the rim. "I let my lease lapse on the condo."

Sidney's eyebrows went up.

"I quit my job, too."

Sidney laughed. He felt a chill. "Janis."

"I know," she said. "Rolled the dice, didn't I?"

He laughed hard, and she joined in. They laughed and laughed.

"My god," he said at last. "Do you know how long it's been since either of us have done this?"

"Long time."

"I'm not housebroke anymore," he said, grinning. "How about you?"

"Used to my own ways for sure."

"How can we do this?" he asked.

"No idea. Guess it depends on how much we want it, you fig-ure?"

"I'm in. You?" she asked and held out her hand; he grasped it and savored the touch of her smooth skin and long, fine fingers.

They shook on it, laughing some more.

-28-

Three weeks after Janis had moved in, Sidney received another call from Detective Miller in Eugene. Janis and he had just finished eating and were clearing the table one evening when the phone rang. Sidney recognized the man's voice and felt a chill across his shoulders; he'd always wondered if he had ever been under suspicion for John Marr's death.

"Detective Miller, it's been a while," Sidney said, trying to sound light and easy. "What can I do for you?"

"Just thought I ought to call and let you know," Miller said. "It'll be in the news tomorrow. We've indicted Helen Marr for the murders of Virginia and Ralph Snyder," Miller answered.

"What! My god," Sidney blurted. "You're kidding."

"No, she did it all right. We went back to the fire and looked at it all over again. Didn't find much new, just a few indicators that maybe some kind of accelerant might have been used, but pretty slim, really. Funny thing, as a routine measure, we brought Helen Marr in for a wrap-up interview. She had her lawyer with her, and we'd only begun going over old ground when she broke down and confessed."

Sidney sat dumbfounded. Janis mouthed, "What's happened?" but Sidney waved her off. When Miller had told him everything, Sidney thanked him and listened for the disconnect click and the dial tone before putting the phone down. He led Janis to the couch and, with their knees touching, held her hands and told her about Helen Marr.

Having come from a dirt-poor background, Helen Marr became absorbed with being successful, wealthy, and socially notable. At some point she learned about her husband's sexual affair with the underage girl, Heather Cole, and that is when she took control of things. In no way did she ever intend to lose her status; she wouldn't allow it. She orchestrated John Marr's manipulation of the sexual abuse and subsequent pregnancy catastrophe, fully intending that they would pay off the parents.

But before that happened, the girl took her own life. The parents knew she was pregnant but never knew who the father was. John Marr stepped forward as Heather's compassionate wealthy softball coach and offered to cover all expenses of the girl's funeral. At Helen's insistence, John convinced the distraught parents to cremate the girl as a path to cleansing her memory in their minds. There was no autopsy at the parents' request; thus there would never be any possible test linking John Marr to the girl.

At that point, Helen Marr felt she had saved everything she coveted about her life and status, but John erred again by playing his sadistic game with Sidney and, eventually, by firing Ginny Snyder. The supposedly erased blot of Heather Cole surfaced again. Enraged, Helen took control: she sent her husband after Sidney with instructions to kill him while she made plans to eliminate the only remaining threat, that of Ginny Snyder and her husband. She planned carefully, studied about arson and deaths by fire, and with her husband out searching for Sidney, she went calling on the Snyders.

Once in their home, Helen Marr held them at gunpoint and first made Ginny Snyder tie up her husband; then Helen did the same to Ginny. Then she forced plastic bags over their heads and watched them suffocate. When both were dead, she removed the bags, dragged them into their bedroom, calmly dressed them in nightclothes, and wrestled them into their bed. She then went to her car and brought in an electric space heater she had purchased from a secondhand shop and put it in the bedroom where the bodies rested. She poured some kind of accelerant around the room and into the heater and plugged it into an outlet. Even if arson was suspected, she had expected the fire to obscure how the Snyders died, but never did she imagine the inferno that ensued, causing near total destruction of the house and the bodies.

"It was John's inability to kill me that ruined Helen's plans," Sidney said. "Can you believe it? Then when he committed suicide, she couldn't take it and caved in when the police brought her in for routine questioning."

Janis grabbed him and held him for a long time. When she sat back, she swiped at the tears streaming down her cheeks.

"And you did all that, Mister Most Likely, just to wow Electra Bly?" she laughed.

"Yes. It worked, right?"

"We'll see."

Epilogue

Once Sidney was settled in to his new role at Beeman's International, he took care of two matters that had been stored in his head under the heading *obligations*.

First he went to the Shutter Creek Correctional Institution to visit Lamont Courter. He didn't stay long. Courter had agreed to see him and seemed okay, relaxed, even refreshed. It wasn't like reconciliation between estranged brothers; it was just something Sidney had to do. As Sidney stood to leave, Courter made firm eye contact and nodded. That was it; he went back to working in the facility's laundry and counting off the days of his absolution.

When it came to finding a lost person, Sidney asked his closest law enforcement contact, Detective Everett Miller, to put him in touch with a colleague in the Portland Police Bureau. With the help of cops on the street, he located Sarah Thompson, the daughter of Crystal and John Thompson, owners of the Laughing Clam in Florence. She was working as a bartender and had been off the street from hooking for over six months. Not long, but a start. Sidney asked the slender young woman with her father's features for a bourbon and seven before he introduced himself. When he told her that he knew her parents, she stepped back and snarled, "Who are you?" A man behind the bar came up and asked what the hell Sidney was up to.

Sidney raised his hands to calm things and said to Sarah Thompson, "All I want you to know, Sarah, is that you are still loved and missed." He stepped off the stool and put his money down for the drink: "Go see them."

When he reached the doorway of the bar, he turned. Sarah Thompson was crying. He waited until she looked at him; he raised a hand. She wiped at her eyes with a bar towel; she didn't respond but didn't take her eyes off Sidney. *I guess it can't hurt her to know she's still loved,* he thought, and shoved out through the door.

————•————

On an August weekend in 2005, the Grant High School Class of 1975 celebrated its 30th reunion. The Friday night barbeque at the imposing Portland home of Randolph "Randy" Kennedy, former all-state football quarterback and successful real estate investor, was a festive gathering of those who had little else to prove and less time in which to prove it to themselves or their fellow classmates. At the mostly identical age of forty-eight, hair had been lost, skin had given up its bloom, careers were what they were or weren't, children had passed from sweet infants into turbulent teens and young adults, and many who showed up were not recognizable but for the name badges with their senior class photo on it. And yet the occasion confirmed that everyone had a place where they belonged and could not be turned away.

When Sidney Lister arrived at the event with his new wife, Janis Hill-Lister, accompanied by his ex-wife, the former Mary Ellen Conway, and the new man in her life, it caused a bit of a stir and a coming home that hadn't been possible before.

The following January, Sidney put the finishing touches to his journal about Jonesy. He called it *A Salesman's Eulogy.* Janis insisted that he do something with it, that it was good. In the end he had fifty copies printed up by a local copy shop and bound. He self-consciously showed it to the Beemans and his colleagues, more out of a tribute to Jonesy than anything else. The volume of a little over 100 pages soon began to be passed from person to person, mostly among other salespeople. Sidney was encouraged to publish more copies, but he never did. Some say photocopied versions of *A Salesman's Eulogy* have been seen as far away as China and Australia.

Adieu, Jonesy.

GEORGE BYRON WRIGHT is the author of four previous novels: *Baker City 1948, Tillamook 1952, Roseburg 1959,* and *Driving to Vernonia.* He lives with his wife Betsy in Portland, Oregon.

COLOPHON

The text of this book is set in Garamond Premier Pro, an Adobe Type Foundry OpenType version of the classic typeface newly rendered by Robert Slimbach. Titling and folios are set in ITC Serif Goth Standard. Principal tools were the programs of Adobe Creative Suite 3 on a Macintosh computer system.